WHEN WISHES COLLIDE

Barbara Freethy

WHEN WISHES COLLIDE

@ Copyright 2011 Barbara Freethy
All Rights Reserved

No part of this book may be used or reproduced in any manner whatsoever without written permission except in the case of brief quotations embodied in critical articles and reviews.

This is a work of fiction. Names, characters, places, and incidents are products of the author's imagination or are used fictitiously. Any resemblance to actual events, locales, organizations or persons, living or dead, is entirely coincidental.

For information contact:
barbara@barbarafreethy.com

Also available in the Wish Series

A Secret Wish

Just A Wish Away

When Wishes Collide

Prologue

July ...

  Adrianna took off her white long-sleeved chef's coat and tossed it into the laundry basket in the break room of Vincenzo's Restaurant. She then released her long, brown hair from a constricting tie, feeling an immediate release of tension, as the waves cascaded down her shoulders. It had been a long, exhausting night in the kitchen, but it was the kind of exhaustion she loved. Becoming a chef had been her dream since she was a little girl, and at twenty-eight she was beginning to make a name for herself.
  Lindsay Rogers entered the room and gave her a tired smile. The tall, willowy blonde was one of the sous chefs and also a good friend, which sometimes surprised Adrianna, because they were as different in personality as they were in looks. Lindsay was outgoing, funny, and while she liked her job, Lindsay wasn't particularly ambitious. Adrianna had a quieter sense of humor and was far more focused and driven. But then she hadn't had time for a lot of fun in her life. Survival had been her single focus for as long as she could remember. One day, she wanted to get to that place where she could relax, take a breath, look around and see what she'd been missing. But that day wasn't today.
  "That last party took forever to leave," Lindsay said, as

she removed her jacket. "Toast after toast until they were all drunk. Will had to call two cabs to get them out of here."

She smiled. "They were having a good time. That's what it's all about." Nothing made her happier than watching people enjoy her food and enjoy themselves.

"I guess." Lindsay rolled her head around on her shoulders.

"We're lucky business has been so good," Adrianna added. "The winter was very slow."

Throughout January and February, she'd been worried that the restaurant might have to close because the owner and executive chef, Giovanni Ricci, was having health problems. Fortunately, his nephew, Stephan, had stepped in and taken over, turning things around in just a few months. She missed Giovanni's tutelage in the kitchen, but because of his absence she'd also gained more responsibility. Her life always seemed to be a mix of good and bad.

"The customers are coming because of you," Lindsay said as she stepped up to the mirror to apply some lip gloss. "Your reputation is growing. Stephan is about a day away from making you executive chef."

"I'm not so sure about that. In sixty years, Vincenzo's has never had an executive chef who wasn't a Ricci."

"That's true, but while Stephan is a competent chef, he's better in the front of the house. He loves to market and greet customers. You're the one who makes the magic in the kitchen, and Stephan is smart enough to know that. You're pretty much doing the job anyway," Lindsay added, as she turned around. "And you know Will is talking you up to Stephan every chance he gets."

"He's been very supportive," she said. Will Grayson was the head bartender, and her boyfriend, although, it still felt a little strange to think of him in those terms. She and Will had been friends for four years until a coworker's wedding reception and a lot of champagne had taken them from friends to lovers.

"Speaking of Will -- he seems distracted lately," Lindsay said. "Is something going on with him?"

"Nothing that I know about. He was probably just stressed with all the big parties we had tonight."

"You're right. You need to take him home and make him feel better, as only you can," Lindsay said with a teasing smile. She moved away from the mirror, grabbed Will's jacket off the coat rack and tossed it to Adrianna.

As the jacket flew through the air, something fell out of one of the pockets onto the floor.

Lindsay and Adrianna both reached for it at the same time, but it was Lindsay who came up with the blue velvet box.

"Oh my God," Lindsay said, meeting Adrianna's gaze. "Will is going to propose to you."

Adrianna stared at the ring box in shock and wariness. "No. It's way too soon."

"You've been friends forever."

"But not boyfriend, girlfriend. That's new. Don't open it," she warned as Lindsay's fingers toyed with the lid.

"Why not? Don't you want to see the ring?"

"We don't know that it's an engagement ring. It could be something else."

"Only one way to find out."

"No." She shook her head and scrambled to her feet, worry and panic running through her. She wasn't ready for an engagement, for marriage, or even for a promise. She didn't want Will to give her a ring of any kind.

"If it's a bad ring, you'll have a chance to compose your reaction when he shows it to you," Lindsay said practically, as she stood up. "You don't want to have a look of disappointment on your face. I know you would try to be polite, but let's be real, a sucky ring is not the way to start out a marriage."

"I don't want to see it," she said quickly.

Lindsay frowned. "What is wrong with you?"

How could she explain to someone who was as easy and casual about love as Lindsay that for her love, marriage, and family was a huge dream but also a terrifying proposition? She'd locked her heart away a very long time ago, and while Will had been chipping away at her resolve to stay detached, he wasn't even close to breaking through. How could Will think otherwise?

"Please, put it away before he comes in here," she said shortly.

"Okay, okay, calm down." Lindsay slipped the ring box back in Will's jacket pocket and hung the jacket on the rack. "There -- it's out of sight. And we'll pretend we never saw it."

"Good," she said, blowing out a breath.

"Can I ask why you're so rattled? I thought you and Will were happy together." Her gaze narrowed thoughtfully. "Don't you want Will to propose? I thought you two were getting along really well."

"I haven't thought about it. It's all about work for me right now. And I thought it was for him, too."

"Oh, I don't think so, Adrianna. Will isn't as driven as you are, but then nobody is." Lindsay gave her a soft smile. "I'm going to go. I have a late date. It's Jack – as in Jack who gives me a heart attack because he's so hot."

"Lucky you," she said, thrilled that the conversation was no longer about her.

"Call me tomorrow. I want to know what happens with the ring."

As Lindsay left the break room, Adrianna stared at Will's jacket for a long moment. Maybe it wasn't what she thought. Perhaps the ring belonged to someone else. He might be holding on to it for one of his friends.

Despite her rationalization, there was still a gnawing feeling in the pit of her stomach. Will had always been the one after her, the one pushing for more. But he also knew her better than anyone else, so he had to know she wasn't ready.

With a sigh, she grabbed her own coat and bag and returned to the kitchen. The room was empty. Everyone had left, except for Will, who was staring at his phone with an odd expression on his face.

"Everything okay?" she asked.

He looked up and nodded, but his gaze was distant, as if he were thinking about something else.

"Are you sure?" she prodded.

"I need to talk to you, Adrianna."

"That doesn't sound good."

His eyes darkened. "It's not bad. It's just ... important."

Her stomach tightened. "Can we do it later? It's been a really long night. I'm exhausted, and I just want to go home and fall into bed."

His lips turned down into a frown. "I don't think this can wait until tomorrow. I've been putting it off, and I can't do it any longer."

"Well, it has to wait a few more minutes," she said, stalling for time. If he did ask her to marry him, what on earth would she say? *No* would hurt his feelings. But *yes* didn't work either. She wasn't ready to get married. She set her bag on the counter and picked up the box she'd left out. "I promised the kids pizza."

Disappointment and annoyance filled his eyes. "Adrianna, you told me three days ago you would call the police about those homeless kids."

"I will – tomorrow."

"You always say that. I understand that you had problems with the system when you were a kid, but it's there for a reason. Those children need more than leftover pizza."

He was right, but she was still debating her options. About a week ago, she'd found three kids digging through the trash, and she'd given them a hot meal. Since then they'd come by the restaurant almost every night around closing time. She didn't know if they were homeless or neglected, but she knew they needed help. She also knew that they weren't going to let her help them if they didn't trust her.

"I'll be back in a minute." She grabbed the pizza box and headed out the back door into the alley behind the restaurant. She was only a few feet away from the door when three kids emerged from the shadows.

The oldest, a boy, seemed to be about twelve. Then there was a girl around ten, and a younger child, who appeared to be about eight. She'd tried to get their names, but only the boy had been willing to tell her that his name was Ben. He'd assured her that they had somewhere to stay; they just needed food. He'd begged her not to call the police, and his words had hit a nerve. She'd once been a child of the street and sometimes a back alley was safer than a foster home.

But sometimes it wasn't.

She needed to think like an adult now.

"This can't go on," she told Ben, holding the pizza hostage until she got some answers. "You shouldn't be out alone this late. It's not safe or healthy. I want to help you, but you're going to have to tell me more about your situation."

"We just need a little extra food."

"Where are your parents?"

"They're coming back tomorrow. We'll be fine then," he said.

She didn't believe him. She glanced from him to the two girls. The older girl looked so sleepy she could barely keep her eyes open, but the younger one was alert, wariness in her bright blue eyes.

"Can we have the pizza?" Ben asked.

"Who's watching you until your parents come back?"

"My mom's friend," he said.

"And where does this friend think you are right now?"

"She works til late. We'll be home before she gets there."

"Why don't I take you home?" she suggested. "I'll just get my coat and bag."

"It's not far from here. We'll be fine. You don't have to worry."

"I want to help you, Ben."

"The food is enough," he said.

Before she could continue the argument, she heard a crash, followed by two loud pops.

It took a second for the sounds to register in her brain. *Gunshots!*

Her heart jumped into her throat. She'd grown up in neighborhoods where gunshots were not that uncommon, but this was North Beach, an upscale part of San Francisco. It didn't make sense.

She looked down the alley and saw two dark, hooded figures running down the street. A sudden terror swept through her. Had the shots come from inside the restaurant?

Oh, God!

Will was alone in the kitchen.

She ran through the back door, praying that the shots had come from somewhere else. The kitchen was empty.

"Will," she screamed.

No answer.

Running into the dining room, her worst fear came true. Will lay on the floor near the bar, blood pooling around his head.

"No!" she screamed, dropping to her knees.

His open eyes stared back at her, but there was no longer any life in them.

"You can't be dead," she said, shaking her head in denial. "You can't be. You have to wake up. This is just a bad dream. You're all right." She put her hands on his face.

His skin was still warm. She needed to do something, CPR, call 9-1-1, but even as she pressed her hands against his chest, she knew it wasn't going to matter.

Will was dead.

Sirens split the air, and then cops were coming in the door, pulling her away from Will, asking her questions, setting up crime scene tape, and all she could do was stare at the man who had been her best friend, her lover, and if she'd never left the restaurant, maybe her fiancé.

Chapter One

August ...

 Seven weeks had passed since the robbery at Vincenzo's had left Will dead and destroyed her life. Adrianna had run through all the stages of grief -- shock, denial, pain, guilt, anger, bewilderment, and depression. Now she was supposed to be able to move on with her life, but so far she hadn't been able to do anything but cower in her apartment, watch daytime talk shows, attempt to find some sort of interest in knitting and avoid her kitchen and anything that had to do with cooking. Cooking had once been her therapy, but every time she saw the gleaming steel of her appliances, she was reminded of Will, of Vincenzo's, of a life that had been so good but had gone so wrong.
 She'd hoped the police would find Will's killer or killers and that justice would bring closure, but that had yet to occur. There were no witnesses. Vincenzo's had had no security cameras operating. They'd planned to put in cameras during a future remodel. The only motivation for the robbery seemed to be money. The police believed that Will had surprised the thieves and possibly attempted to stop them, resulting in his getting shot.
 It was difficult to come to terms with a murder so random, so impulsive, so impersonal. But there didn't seem

to be any other explanation, not that any other explanation would have changed the results. Will was dead. She'd lost a friend, and the world had lost a really good person.

Adrianna drew in a quick breath as she stepped out of her apartment building into the sunshine. Being outside made her feel shaky and uncertain. She'd gotten used to the shadowy interior of her one bedroom apartment, and she rarely ventured out unless she absolutely had to.

Today, she absolutely had to ...

Stephan Ricci wanted to talk to her about her job, her future, and she couldn't put him off any longer. Stephan had reopened Vincenzo's three weeks after the shooting. He'd told her that he'd added new security measures and had made cosmetic improvements to the restaurant so that it wouldn't feel the same to either the staff or the customers. But she doubted a coat of paint and new furniture would erase her memories.

It was different for the others. They hadn't been there that night. It was easier for them to return to work. They hadn't witnessed the tragedy first hand. They hadn't ended up with Will's blood all over their clothes. She shuddered at that thought and wondered if she'd ever be able to remember Will without remembering him staring up at her with unseeing eyes.

Stop it, she told herself. Stop going back there.

As she walked down the sidewalk, she tried to think of something else. Her apartment building was only a few blocks from Vincenzo's, and ordinarily she enjoyed the walk to work. North Beach was known as San Francisco's Little Italy, and there were plenty of red-checked Italian cafés and old world delicatessens. There were also coffee houses that didn't just serve up lattes but also hosted poetry nights, folk singers and jazz musicians. There was plenty of nightlife in this part of town.

There was also lots of shopping. Vintage clothing stores sat next to art galleries, and upscale boutiques competed with cozy bookstores selling books about the history of the city, the tale of immigrants, the rush for gold, the first stories of the Barbary Coast. Adrianna loved feeling like she was connected to a rich and vibrant past. She didn't have family connections, but she was part of a city neighborhood that was very special.

The warm summer weather, the strolling tourists, the kids eating ice cream by the park, the clang of a nearby cable car reminded her of a life she'd been missing. She just needed to find a way to stop being afraid. Fear was something she'd grown up with, and she'd thought she'd put that feeling of uncertainty behind her, but one random act of violence had reminded her that she could never truly be safe or in control of her destiny. Life was about chance.

The irony was that the worst night of her life was being followed by the invitation to accept her dream job. Stephan wanted her to be the executive chef of Vincenzo's. She'd spent the last ten years working toward this exact goal. How could she say no? On the other hand, how could she go back into the restaurant, look at the floor, and not see Will's blood? How could she enter the kitchen and not hear Will tell her that he wanted to talk to her about something important? How could she go into the break room and not see his jacket or the blue velvet ring box?

She didn't know what had happened to the ring. Will's parents had driven down from Marin and taken charge of clearing out his personal belongings from both the restaurant and his apartment. They'd never mentioned the ring to her, but then they didn't seem to know anything about her relationship with Will. She'd tried to express her sorrow to Will's mother, but the woman had been cold and distant, and uninterested in her condolences.

When she had asked about the funeral, his mother had told her there wouldn't be one, that Will would be cremated and his ashes would be spread at sea. She'd known Will had not been close with his parents, but she'd never realized the extent of their estrangement. Not that it mattered anymore.

Squaring her shoulders, she forced herself to keep walking. She wasn't sure she could make it all the way inside the restaurant, but she was hoping to make it to the front door.

It was a beautiful Thursday afternoon, no fog on the horizon, just a few wispy clouds to mar the light blue sky. As she headed down the hill, she could see the Golden Gate Bridge and the colorful sails on the boats dotting the bay. Turning the corner, she walked toward a beautiful cobblestone square where four streets met.

Vincenzo's was on the far corner, across from St. Margaret's Church and the Fountain of Wishes, a popular North Beach destination. The fountain was owned by the church and had been built more than a hundred years earlier. It had survived the earthquake of 1906, and had been part of neighborhood lore for as long as anyone could remember. Throwing a coin in the water was supposed to bring luck and good fortune.

Over the years, numerous people had come forward sharing miracle stories of wishes that had been granted. She'd never been a big believer in wishes – maybe because none of her wishes had ever come true. Her prayers had also gone unanswered. She'd learned early on in life that she was on her own, that the only one she could depend on was herself.

For the most part, she'd been strong. But today, she felt weak, uncertain ... and she had to find a way to shake it off. Cooking was her livelihood. It was all she knew how to do. Her savings was running down fast. She needed to get over her fear of going back into a kitchen.

On impulse, she walked across the square, pausing by the fountain. She could really use some help from the universe right about now. She opened her purse and pulled a quarter out of her wallet. The practical side of herself told her that quarter could buy her seven minutes on a parking meter, which might be a better investment then throwing twenty-five cents away on a foolish wish.

While she was considering her options, her gaze caught on two girls on the other side of the fountain. Her pulse began to race. They looked like two of the kids she'd met up with in the alley behind the restaurant the night Will had been shot. Since then she had wondered many times if things would have been different if she hadn't taken the pizza out to the kids, if she hadn't stopped to question them, if she hadn't been avoiding what she thought might be a proposal. Would she have been able to save Will, or would she be dead, too?

The girls looked just as ragged as she remembered. She wondered what had happened to the boy who had been with them – Ben. And had they gone hungry without her leftover offerings?

She felt a wave of guilt that she hadn't thought more about their welfare.

She walked around the fountain. The youngest girl looked up, and her blue eyes widened in recognition. She said something to the other girl, who quickly glanced her way. Then they both turned and ran.

"Wait," she called, breaking into a jog as they sprinted across the square and darted through an alley.

It suddenly seemed imperative that she catch up to them. She needed to fix something, to save someone, because she hadn't been able to save Ben. Maybe she could help these children ... Five minutes later, she realized the girls were gone. They'd vanished down one of the many narrow alleys that ran through this part of town. Turning, she walked slowly back to the square.

The sunlight was streaming through the spray of water coming off the fountain, beckoning her forward. She still had the quarter clenched in her hand. She just needed a wish – the right wish – one that would really make a difference.

She was stalling again, anything to postpone going into Vincenzo's, but at least she was getting closer...

* * *

Another August, and he was no closer to finding his daughter. Wyatt Randall stared at the calendar on his computer. Two years had passed since he'd seen Stephanie, and he still had no idea where she was. Familiar frustration sent a wave of anger through his body. He was an inspector with the San Francisco Police Department. He located missing persons and solved crimes for a living. He was damn good at his job. He'd closed more cases than anyone else. But he couldn't close the one case that meant the most to him. And he was starting to think he might never find his daughter again.

He didn't want to give up, but time kept marching on. He picked up the photograph that he kept on his desk. Stephanie's blue eyes stared back at him. The picture had been taken on her sixth birthday. They'd gone to the beach, barbecued hot dogs and roasted marshmallows. For that day they'd been happy. It made him feel marginally better now to see the smile on her lips as she waved her marshmallow at the camera, the color in her sunburned cheeks, the traces of sand in her hair left over from when they'd made sand angels. What a great afternoon that had been. He'd never imagined it might be the last they would have together.

Stephanie had his eyes, the same direct, intense expression. Looking at her was like looking in a mirror, but she didn't have his dark hair, she was blonde like her mother.

Her mother ...

Fury ripped through him as he thought of his ex-wife. It was Jennifer who had stolen Stephanie from him, who had violated the custody agreement, who had turned his life into a living hell. Crazy, messed up Jennifer, who had somehow believed their daughter was better off with her. The only thing that had kept him from losing his mind completely was the knowledge that Jennifer loved Stephanie. He had to hope that she was being a good mother, that she'd found a way to shake the drugs and the bad friends, but he couldn't count on that being true. And he would never be able to relax until he had Stephanie back in his arms.

Most of his friends and family had given up. They tried to pretend otherwise, but he knew the truth. It had been two very long years of false leads, dead ends and crushing disappointment. Stephanie's disappearance had once triggered Amber alerts, search parties and news media coverage. For months they'd set a place for her at family dinners. His mother had bought presents for every occasion, stashing them in a closet for *some day*. But *some day* seemed to be getting further and further away. He set the photo down on his desk, silently promising his daughter that he would never give up, no matter how long it took.

Even as he made the promise, his gaze tripped over the stack of file folders on his desk. There were other missing kids, other victims, other people who needed his attention. As much as he wanted to devote himself full time to the search for his daughter, he also had to make a living. He'd spent the first year of Stephanie's disappearance crisscrossing the country, following endless clues that had ultimately gone nowhere. Eventually, he'd had to go back to work, if for no other purpose than to make enough money to keep a private investigator working on the case. Unfortunately, that investigator had also come up with nothing and had moved on to other clients. Two years of work and he was back at square one, as lost as he'd been that very first afternoon.

"Wyatt, I have something you should see," Josh Burton said, waving him over.

He got up from his desk to see what his friend and former partner had to say. He'd met Josh in the police academy eleven years earlier, and they'd worked their way up the ranks together. They'd once been partners, but during his six-month leave, Josh had partnered with someone else. Once Wyatt had come back, he'd been assigned a new partner. He was always happy to collaborate though. He'd done some of his best work with Josh.

"I was reviewing the security footage we picked up from cameras in the area around Vincenzo's restaurant," Josh said.

He nodded. They'd all spent some time working on the robbery/homicide at the popular North Beach restaurant. "What did you find?"

"Take a look." Josh hit a button on his computer and the grainy video of the outside of a liquor store appeared. Three kids walked out of the store, pausing on the sidewalk to open a box of candy. There was a boy and two girls, all of whom appeared to be under the age of twelve. A moment later, the smallest girl turned her face toward the camera. In a split second, a pair of familiar blue eyes met his. His breath caught in his throat, and his heart began to race. Then she looked away, and the kids ran out of range of the camera.

"Play it again," he ordered, adrenaline racing through his veins.

Josh did as requested, pausing on the frame of the little girl. "She looks a little like Stephanie, don't you think?"

A knot was growing in his throat as he stared at the computer screen. "More than a little."

"She's older, and her hair is darker."

"It's been two years since we saw her, and who knows what Jen did to her hair."

"But why would Jennifer bring Stephanie back to San Francisco? She has to know you're still looking for her.

And you have a lot of support and resources here. It's not logical."

"Jen was never known for her logic."

"It's more likely she'd be in Los Angeles where she grew up, where her parents still live. Someone has to be funneling her money, and they're the most likely suspects."

Jen's parents had definitely been on their daughter's side, but then they'd spoiled Jen rotten. She was their only child and they believed she was perfect in every way. The problems in their daughter's marriage had all been his fault.

"Tom has been following Jen's parents for months," he said, referring to the private investigator. "He's never been able to connect them to Jennifer. He's never been able to find a money trail. I don't know who's helping her live, but it doesn't appear to be Greg and Wendy Miller."

"Well, I still think it's doubtful Jen is here in the city. To be honest, I debated whether I should even show you this video. There have been so many false sightings. We've seen Stephanie in a lot of little girls who turned out not to be her. I hate to see you chase another bad lead."

Everything Josh said was true. It didn't make sense that Jennifer and Stephanie would be in the city, and the girl whose image had been captured by the security camera wasn't an exact match to his daughter, but there was something about her eyes that made his gut clench. He had to follow up, even if this lead turned out to be as bad as the others.

"Don't ever debate showing me something that might be important," he said sharply. "You don't need to worry about me. Stephanie is the only one who matters. Can you print out a screen shot for me? I'll take the picture by the liquor store and see if the clerk knows anything about these kids."

"Already done," Josh said, handing him a photo. "I'd go with you, but I have a witness to question."

"It's fine," he muttered. "I don't have anything pressing

at the moment."

"Josh sent him a warning glance. "Don't let the captain hear you say that. You're already on his last nerve."

He was well aware of that fact. In the beginning, the captain had been generous about giving him time off and looking the other way when he used department resources to look for Stephanie, but their caseload had increased in recent months, and the captain had warned him that if he continued to take time off, he might need to resign. It seemed unthinkable that he could lose his daughter and his job, but right now Stephanie was his main concern.

"Fortunately, we just wrapped the Delgado case," he said. "And I have a lot of overtime on the books."

"Are you going to Summer's engagement party tomorrow night?" Josh asked, leaning back in his chair. "I wish I could go, but I have to work."

"We'll see," he said vaguely. "There's going to be a big crowd. My sister won't miss me."

"She will definitely miss you, along with the rest of the family. Taking an hour out for yourself and your family doesn't make you any less of a dedicated father," Josh said pointedly.

He'd heard the same argument from his mother, his father, his brother and his sister. Two years was a long time to run head-down at a dead sprint toward a finish line that kept moving farther away. But he didn't know how else to live. Every time he found himself thinking about something else or he caught himself smiling or laughing, he felt guilty. He couldn't have a life without his child.

"Just think about it," Josh said.

"I will. I want Summer to be happy, and Ron seems like a good guy, but who knows? I certainly never imagined Jennifer would turn into a monster."

"Neither did I," Josh said, regret in his eyes. "She was so sweet at your wedding. She looked up at you with adoration, like you were the only man in the world. I wanted what you had."

"Well, thank God you didn't get it," he replied. "Getting married was the biggest mistake of my life, and no doubt Jen feels the same way. Once the dream wedding was over, our lives turned into a nightmare."

"Her expectations were too high," Josh said. "After a moonlit wedding with a horse and carriage and a thousand perfect roses, reality was bound to suck a little."

"No kidding. That's why I told my sister when she announced her engagement that she should elope or go down to City Hall and skip the big wedding. It's not supposed to be about a day; it's supposed to be about a lifetime. But Summer wants the dream, too. You'd think she'd learn from my example." He paused. "I'll check in with you later – hopefully with some good news."

Chapter Two

As Wyatt drove across town to the liquor store, his gaze automatically scanned the streets for Jennifer and Stephanie. It had become a habit, especially when he drove through the Tenderloin, a run-down area of the city. A magnet for addicts and drug dealers, the Tenderloin had drawn Jennifer like a moth to a flame.

It had seemed unthinkable at first that his well-bred wife who had been raised in an expensive home, and educated in private school, would even consider venturing to such a bad neighborhood on her own. But maybe he should have seen it coming, because Jen had always needed to cling to someone, to be taken care of, to escape from any reality that wasn't quite to her liking, and she'd found the perfect way out with an array of painkillers that became her best friends in the world. It had become clear that every thing and every person in her life would take a back seat to her high, and that included Stephanie.

His daughter was both the reason he'd tried to stay married and the reason why he'd finally filed for divorce. A bitter, angry battle filled with hateful lies had ensued, but by the end, he'd won sole custody of Stephanie. He'd wanted to keep Jennifer in Stephanie's life though. He'd thought it was important for his daughter to have her mother around, which was why he'd given Jennifer generous visitation rights, especially after she'd agreed to go to rehab.

He'd thought she'd recover, that she'd regain the part of herself that he'd fallen in love with. But his decision to keep her around had come back to haunt him. It was on one of those visits that Jennifer had taken Stephanie and gone on the run. Two years later, they were still missing. How Jennifer had managed to disappear so completely still baffled him.

He parked his car at the end of the block and walked down the street. The liquor store was empty when he walked inside, the afternoon lull, he suspected. The clerk was a middle-aged man, who appeared to be more interested in the Giants game playing on the small screen behind the counter than what was going on in the store. He didn't bother to get up from his stool until Wyatt flashed his badge. Then he hopped to his feet.

"What can I do for you?" the clerk asked.

"I'm looking for these kids," he said, pushing the photo across the counter, "in particular, the smallest girl. Have you seen them?"

"I don't know."

"This picture is from your security camera. They bought candy here."

The clerk shrugged. "There's an elementary and a middle school two blocks away. Kids come in here all the time for candy. There was a dozen or more of them in here half an hour ago. I might have seen them. I don't remember. Kids look the same to me." He handed the picture back to Wyatt. "Maybe you should check with the school."

He'd checked all the schools in the city several times in the past two years, but it was obviously time to check again. "I'll do that." He pulled out his wallet and took out a photo of Stephanie. "What about this girl?" The picture had been taken when Stephanie was six years old and just starting first grade. "She's a few years older now, so she might look a little different."

"Sorry," the clerk said. "She doesn't ring a bell."

"Are you sure?"

"Like I said, I don't pay much attention to the kids."

Wyatt blew out a breath of frustration. Eleven years as a cop had made him very aware of the fact that most people preferred not to look too closely at things going on around them, which made his job more difficult. "If you see any of the kids again, I want you to call me right away," he said, handing over his card.

"All right," the clerk promised.

"Thanks."

He headed out the door, pausing on the sidewalk to regroup. Pulling out the picture of the three kids, he studied it again. There was no evidence of fear in their faces, but there was intensity. They were sharing one box of candy, and the boy seemed to be disciplined in the division of the pieces, which spoke to the idea that these kids didn't have much money. Their clothes also looked worn, as if they had come from a second-hand store. Focusing his gaze on the youngest child, he felt angry with himself for not being able to definitively say that she was his daughter. If only the image was sharper. He felt like he was looking through a cloudy lens.

Other questions ran through his mind. If Stephanie was one of the kids, who were the other children, and why was she with them? And if she was out on her own, away from her mother, why hadn't she tried to contact him, or ask someone for help? She was eight, but he'd taught her how to dial 9-1-1 when she was five.

The obvious answer was that either Stephanie didn't think she was in trouble, or she didn't believe he would want to help her. God knew what lies Jen had told his daughter about him.

Putting the photo back in his pocket, he spent the next hour canvassing the neighborhood. He talked to store merchants and the staff at the nearest elementary and middle school. Some people thought they had seen the kids, but no one could say for sure. By four-thirty, he realized his new lead was fizzling out fast – just like all the others.

Heading back toward his car, he entered McClellan Square. In the center of the square was a large fountain that had been built by the nearby church, St. Margaret's. It was a popular spot for tossing coins and making wishes, but it wasn't crowded today. Only one other person stood on the far side of the fountain, a pretty brunette dressed in skinny white jeans, and a bright blue top under a darker blue sweater. Her long, curly, dark brown hair, drifted halfway down her back, and her gaze was intensely focused on the coin in her hand. She was putting some pretty serious thought into whatever wish she was about to make.

He didn't believe there was any magic in the fountain, or in the world for that matter. He'd once been a man of faith, but that faith had been tested to the limit, and he wasn't sure he would ever get it back.

He moved closer, staring down at the rippling water, at the sparkling coins on the bottom. So many wishes begging for answers. What if he added one more?

A wind whipped the cool spray of the fountain into his face. He blinked the water out of his eyes and reached into his pocket for a coin. What the hell? He had nothing to lose.

Before he could act, his phone rang. Pulling it out, he saw his mother's name flash across the screen. He was tempted to let the call go to voice mail, but not answering his mother's calls usually only made her more determined to get a hold of him.

"Mom," he said shortly. "What's up?"

"Your sister's engagement party, as if you didn't know. I've been calling you for two days, Wyatt. I want to make sure you're coming. I know that these family events are difficult for you, but Summer really wants you to be there.

You're her big brother."

"It's just an engagement party. There's still the wedding."

"Yes, but this is the only time we'll have both families present. Ron's brother is being deployed next week. That's why we're doing a party now and the wedding next month. But you know that. I've been telling you for weeks."

"Yeah, I got it," he said with a sigh. "I'll try to come, but I have a new lead on Stephanie."

"You do?" she asked in surprise. "What is it?"

"A little girl was caught on tape by a security camera in the North Beach area. I'm checking it out right now."

"In North Beach? So close to where you work? That would be amazing."

The disbelief in his mother's tone echoed the cynical voice inside his head, but he couldn't let doubt stop him from following any possible clue. "It's a neighborhood Jennifer knows well," he said. "She could have come back. She might still have a friend in the city willing to help her out. There's no way she could have stayed gone for this long without help."

"That's true. I was actually thinking about that the other day when I got the RVSP's for the engagement party. Mandy Meyers is coming to the party," his mother added, referring to one of Jennifer's high school friends. "She's dating Ron's best man, and we can't hold her responsible for what Jennifer did. Just because they went to school together doesn't mean that Mandy had anything to do with Jennifer's disappearance."

"She was quick to take Jennifer's side," he reminded his mother.

"Well, she didn't have all the facts at the time. She's apologized since then. But you do have the perfect opportunity to talk to her again if you come tomorrow night."

"You're very shrewd and persuasive," he said.

His mother laughed. "Well, I really want you to come. We love you, Wyatt. And we may not always say the right thing or know what to do, but we're always here for you."

"I know that, and I appreciate your support. I have to go now, but I'll try to come by the party."

"Do better than try."

"Good-bye, Mom."

He slipped his phone back in his pocket. As he did so, his fingers slid over the smooth surface of a coin, reminding him that he hadn't yet made a wish. He pulled out a dime, not much of an offering. He dug around for a quarter but he had nothing else. Well, a dime would have to work.

He noticed that the woman on the other side of the fountain was still rolling a coin between two fingers as she stared into the spray. Maybe she was also debating the value of throwing money into a pool of water and hoping that a wish would come true. Not that there weren't plenty of suckers in town, judging by the number of coins covering the floor of the pool.

And he was joining those suckers today, because he was desperate and running out of options. "*Help me find my child,*" he muttered.

Then he tossed the coin toward the wild spray of water coming out of the fountain, shocked when it clinked in mid air with another coin. One of the coins fell into the pool, the other flipped out toward the pavement.

What were the odds of that happening?

His gaze clashed with the woman on the other side of the fountain. She looked shocked.

Had his wish gone astray?

Or had hers?

* * *

Adrianna couldn't believe her coin had been knocked out of the fountain. She needed her wish to get her past her fear. Without it, she might never be able to get herself through the door of Vincenzo's. She moved quickly around the fountain, as did the man whose coin had collided with hers.

"Did you see where it went?" she asked. Her gaze swept the pavement, but there was no sign of her quarter.

"I thought it landed around here," he replied, looking down at the ground.

"I can't believe that happened," she said. "I didn't even see you throw your coin. I really need to find it."

"How do you know it was your coin that didn't make it into the water? It could have been mine. In fact, it probably was mine. Because I have just that kind of luck," he said cynically.

His frustration resonated with her. She had just that kind of luck, too.

As he searched for the errant coin, she took a closer look at him. His appearance suggested someone who had had a very long day. His dark tie hung loosely around the neck of his white-collared shirt, and his sleeves were rolled up to his forearms. His dark brown hair was wavy and windblown, and his blue eyes were weary and a little angry. The faded scar by his left eyebrow matched his rugged look. Not a man to mess with, she thought. But judging by his demeanor, someone had done just that.

As she stared at him, she realized there was something familiar about his gaze. She also realized he was staring back at her.

She had to fight the impulse to draw her sweater across her breasts or tuck her hair behind her ear. She hadn't put on make-up in seven weeks. In fact, most days she didn't make it out of her yoga pants, even though she hadn't gone to a yoga class in months. Fortunately, today she'd garnished enough energy to pull on some decent clothes.

Not that it mattered what this guy thought about her. He was nobody. Still, his steady gaze unnerved her. It had been a long time since she'd really looked at someone or had someone look at her. She'd been living in a gray, foggy world of bewilderment and confusion. Somehow this man's steel gaze cut right through the curtain that had dropped down the night Will was killed. She wasn't sure she liked that. She didn't want anyone to really see her. Then she might have to answer questions that she didn't want to answer.

Rattled, she cleared her throat and returned her attention to the ground. "I don't know for sure that it was my coin, but I figure it's a fifty-fifty chance," she said. "I threw a quarter. What about you?" she asked, kicking some leaves around in the hopes of seeing something shiny on the ground.

"A dime."

"That's it?" She gave him a quick look. "Big spender, huh?"

"It was all I had," he said a little tersely. "And not representative of the importance of my wish."

"I wasn't judging."

"Weren't you?"

"Okay, maybe I was. Sorry. I'm not having a great day. In fact, I'm not having a great month. I was hoping my wish might change that. Not that I really believe in wishes, but I was feeling a little desperate." And now she was rambling.

"I know the feeling," he said.

Again, she felt an intangible connection, as if something inside her recognized something in him. "Have we met before?"

"I don't think so."

"It's weird. I feel like I know you from somewhere." A piece of shiny metal a few feet away made her pause, and with relief she retrieved her coin. "Here it is, and it's a quarter," she said with resignation. "Mine. Probably a sign I shouldn't be relying on a wish."

"You can wish again. You have a second chance."

"I doubt it works that way."

"It probably doesn't work at all – if that makes you feel better," he said dryly.

"If you don't believe, why did you throw the coin?"

"I was feeling a little desperate, too," he said, repeating her words.

Their gazes locked once again. She felt a shiver run down her spine, and this time she did pull her sweater more closely about her. She was suddenly aware of the lengthening shadows, the fog sweeping in from the ocean, the aroma of garlic coming from Vincenzo's where they were no doubt prepping for dinner service.

"What time is it?" she asked.

He checked his watch. "Four-forty-five."

She was forty-five minutes late. "Well, I've been stalling a long time."

"Stalling? Is that why you were staring at your coin for so long?"

"I have something I don't want to do. I need to do it, but I don't want to. And I don't know why I just told you that. Except that perhaps our conversation is becoming part of my stall." She gave him an embarrassed smile. "I'm really good at procrastination."

"But apparently very self aware."

"I suppose."

"What do you have to do?"

"Face my fear," she said, surprising herself with the answer. She didn't know why she was telling him something so personal, so embarrassing. They'd only just met, but for some reason when his blue eyes focused on hers, she felt like talking.

"Which is what?" he asked.

She hesitated. "You're going to think I'm nuts."

"Try me."

"I need to walk through that door over there," she said, tipping her head in the direction of the restaurant.

"Vincenzo's?" he echoed, following her gaze. "Oh, I get it. Your fear has to do with the recent robbery, right?"

She wasn't surprised he'd heard about it. The robbery and Will's death had been all over the news. The violence of the crime had shocked the neighborhood. "Yes, I was there that night. I worked in the kitchen."

Recognition flashed in his eyes. "You're the chef, Adrianna ..." He snapped his fingers as if he was trying to remember her name.

"Cavello," she finished, surprised he knew her name and also a little concerned. The shooters had never been caught, and while she hadn't seen anything, she didn't want to be tied to the crime in any sort of public way. "How did you know my name?"

He pulled out a badge. "I'm an inspector with the SFPD."

Of course he was. She was really off her game not to have pegged him for a cop. There had been a time in her life when she could have spotted a police officer from a mile away.

"Were you there that night?" she asked. "Maybe that's why you look familiar to me."

"No, I was out of town when it happened. One of the other inspectors, Josh Burton, is working the case."

She nodded. "I spoke to him, but I haven't heard anything in weeks. Has there been any progress on the case?"

He shook his head. "Not yet, unfortunately. So you knew the man who was killed?"

"Yes, he was a very good friend," she said shortly, feeling a little guilty for labeling Will as a friend and not a boyfriend. But what did it matter to anyone else? "What is your name?" she asked, wanting to divert the conversation away from Will.

"Wyatt Randall."

"What did you wish for?"

"Help in finding my daughter."

His answer surprised her. She didn't know what she'd been expecting, but it hadn't been something so intense, so dark. "How long has she been missing?"

"Two years this month."

She put a hand to her mouth. "Oh, my God, I'm so sorry. And I'm really glad your coin made it into the fountain. Your wish was far more important than mine. How old is she?"

"She's eight now. Her name is Stephanie." He pulled out his wallet and handed her a photograph of a little girl with blonde hair and blue eyes. The edges of the picture were well worn, as if he'd shown this photo a million times.

A knot formed in her throat as she stared at the little girl. She looked familiar, too.

"What?" he asked abruptly. "Have you seen her?"

"I – I don't know," she said slowly. The little girl resembled one of the kids she'd met behind Vincenzo's, one of the girls she'd seen a short while ago, but she was younger, and her hair was blonde. The girl she'd seen had brown hair.

"She's older now," he added. "Two years older."

"I've seen a couple of kids running around this area, and the youngest one sort of resembles your daughter in the eyes, but nothing else is the same. Her hair is much darker."

He straightened and pulled another piece of paper out of his pocket. "Are these the kids?"

She stared at a blurry print of three kids outside a liquor store. "Yes," she said, uneasiness rolling through her stomach. "That's them. Why do you have that picture?"

"Where did you see them?" he asked, ignoring her

question.

"I first saw them a few months ago in the alley behind Vincenzo's. They asked me for some leftovers, and I gave them pizza. They looked hungry."

"And you didn't think to call the police?"

"They weren't causing trouble, just asking for food. I did try to question them, but the boy said they were fine. He referred to the girls as his sisters."

Wyatt's mouth drew into a tight line. "Do you think he was telling the truth?"

"They looked like they could be siblings."

"What else can you tell me about them? Did this girl say anything?" he asked, pointing to the youngest child.

She shook her head. "No, only the boy spoke. He said his name was Ben. I didn't get a last name." She paused. "I saw the two girls a little while ago right around here. I called out to them, but they ran down that street when they saw me." She pointed across the square. "They went that way."

His gaze moved across the square. "How long ago was that?"

"Probably almost an hour ago."

He shifted his feet, as if he were about to take off.

"I tried to follow them, but they disappeared," she added.

"Why do you think they ran away from you?"

"I don't know. I was a little surprised. But then again maybe it's understandable. The last time I saw them was the night of the robbery."

His face paled. "They were there?"

She nodded. "Yes, in the alley. I was talking to them when I heard the gunshots."

"I don't recall reading anything in the report about children being in the alley."

She flinched at his sharp tone. "I thought I mentioned it," she said, not really sure what she'd said. Everything about that night was a blur.

"What else can you tell me?" he demanded.

She thought hard, seeing the need in his eyes, and wanting to help. "Ben said the people who watched over them would be home that weekend."

"Is that exactly how he said it? He didn't refer to the people as parents?"

"He wasn't specific. I assumed they were parents."

"Anything else? Did he tell you where they lived, where they went to school? Did they wear a school uniform – carry a backpack, a skateboard, a stuffed animal? Did they have any scars, anything that would stand out about them?"

His questions came so fast she could barely keep up. "I'm sorry. I want to help, but they weren't carrying anything and their clothes didn't stand out in any way. All I can say is that they looked like kids who were used to taking care of themselves and each other. That's why I was surprised today when I saw the girls without their brother. I thought of them as a trio."

"If he even was their brother," he said, doubt in his voice.

"All I know is what they told me."

He pulled out his card and handed it to her. "I want you to call me if you see the kids again, any time, day or night. And if you can get them to stay with you or talk to you, that would be even better."

"All right." She took the card out of his hand. "Can I ask how your daughter disappeared?"

Anger filled his gaze. "My ex-wife took her."

"Her mother?" she asked, shocked again. She'd been thinking it was a stranger, but this was far more personal.

"Yeah, her mother," he said bitterly. He gave her a hard look. "You should have called the police when you saw that those kids were in trouble." Without another word, he took off, moving quickly across the square, disappearing down the same street the girls had taken earlier.

She let out a breath as he left, feeling shaken by the encounter. Wyatt Randall had made her feel guilty for doing nothing, but how was she to know that one of the kids wandering around the alley behind the restaurant had been kidnapped? The little girl hadn't asked for help.

As she thought about his story, she couldn't help wondering why a woman would take her daughter away from her father? Wyatt Randall seemed like a good guy, but was he? She'd met bad cops before, men who hid behind their badges, whose public face did not match their private life.

Had she just put three little kids in danger by telling him as much as she had? Or had she put a desperate father one step closer to finding his daughter?

Chapter Three

Adrianna's fingers curled around the quarter in her hand. Glancing back toward the fountain, she thought about wishing again, but her previous wish seemed insignificant now. She thought about wishing for Wyatt to find his daughter, but she was unsure. She didn't understand the concept of parental abduction. In her experience, most parents fought more over who had to take care of the children, than who didn't.

"Adrianna?"

She looked up at the sound of her friend's familiar voice. Lindsay waved as she headed out the door of Vincenzo's and walked quickly across the street, joining her by the fountain.

"What are you doing out here?" Lindsay asked. She wore a chef's coat over black jeans, and her hair was pulled back in a knot. "Stephan told me you were supposed to come in almost an hour ago," she added. "He said he called you twice, and you didn't answer. He adores you, but he's pretty pissed."

"I didn't hear my phone," she muttered.

"Because you probably have it on silent," Lindsay said knowingly. "So what's the deal? Are you going to talk to Stephan or not?"

"I'm still thinking."

"You're this close. Why not just take the last step?"

"Again, I'm thinking." Her gaze moved to the cigarette in Lindsay's hand. "Are you smoking again? I thought you quit."

"I did quit – three times. It's been a stressful month," Lindsay replied, a guilty expression on her face. "The kitchen is chaos. We need you to come back to work."

"It's not that I don't want to," she said with heartfelt sincerity.

"But you're still afraid to go inside?" Lindsay's gaze filled with compassion.

She nodded, feeling like a fool. She'd always prided herself on being tough and resilient. She'd had to be that way to survive her childhood. So why couldn't she just walk through a damn door?

"It looks different now," Lindsay said, pulling out her lighter. "The dining room has been painted. The seats have been reupholstered. You won't recognize the place. It's had a makeover."

"What about the kitchen?"

"Well, not much has changed there," she admitted. "But is it really the kitchen that bothers you?"

"It's everything." She frowned as Lindsay started to light. "You are not seriously going to smoke that."

Lindsay sighed. "Fine." She put the lighter away. "Now you do something for me. Come inside."

"It sounds so easy. I know I'm being a coward."

"You were traumatized. Everyone understands that. You found Will, and it wasn't like he was a stranger. You were together. You were in love. He was going to ask you to marry him. It's tragic what happened."

She swallowed back a knot of emotion. "We don't know for sure that he was going to propose."

"Well, we know he loved you. And finding him the way you did had to be horrific. I wish I hadn't left early that night. I wish I had been with you."

"Do you? It might have been you who ended up on the floor, Lindsay. It might have been me, if I hadn't gone out the back to talk to those kids. Or we could all have escaped if Will and I had just left right away. Did you know that the front door wasn't locked? They didn't even have to break in. They just walked in."

"I do know that, and I feel guilty about it, but none of us knew what was going to happen, Adrianna. This is normally a very safe area."

"Logically I accept that, but emotionally I'm still a mess."

"That's why you need to talk to someone."

She shook her head. "I'll work it out."

"A mental health professional could help."

"I don't do shrinks," she said flatly.

"Okay, all right," Lindsay said. "I recognize that stubborn look on your face. So what do you want to do today? You don't have to decide for tomorrow or next week or next year. You just have to figure out the next five minutes."

"That doesn't sound so hard." She lifted her chin. "All right. Let's go inside."

As they walked across the square, Adrianna's resolve was weakened by a wave of panic. By the time they reached the front door, her heart was beating too fast, and she felt dizzy and nauseous, exactly the way she'd felt when she'd seen Will lying on the floor, blood pooling around his head, running through his blond hair.

She stopped abruptly. "I don't think I can do it."

Lindsay put a hand on her shoulder. "Will would want you to move on with your life. He knew that running Vincenzo's was your dream. He wouldn't want you to let his death stop you from having the career you're meant to have."

Lindsay's words rang true, but still …

"Maybe my career is not meant to be in this restaurant," she said. "I could work somewhere else."

"And that would be different? Tell me if I'm wrong, but have you been able to go into any restaurant in the last two months?"

"No, I haven't," she admitted.

"The first step is always the hardest."

"That's what I tell you when you pull a cigarette out, and you ignore me."

"Don't do what I do, do what I say." Lindsay opened the door. "After you."

Adrianna peered inside for a moment, her gaze only reaching as far as the podium where the hostess stood.

There was no carpet at the entry any more, just hardwood floor, and the paint on the walls was a dusky peach color. The hustle and bustle of the restaurant rang a familiar bell in her head. For a second, she felt a pang of longing that didn't quite banish the fear, but reminded her that this restaurant had once been her second home.

She took another step, crossing the threshold, feeling so stressed she thought she might have a heart attack. Her panic increased when she heard the door close behind her, but somehow she managed to keep breathing. The hostess was new, a young, tall blonde, who gave her a curious look, but didn't say anything after she glanced at Lindsay.

Adrianna swallowed hard as she moved a few steps forward. She tried to look anywhere but at the floor.

"Adrianna!" Stephan's booming voice rang across the room.

She focused her gaze on him, grateful for the distraction. Stephan was a short, robust Italian with black hair and dark eyes, a charming personality and a charismatic smile. He loved people and people loved him. He greeted her with a hearty, tight hug that was filled with genuine affection. Vincenzo's was a family restaurant, and the staff was considered part of the family.

"You are very late, but I'm glad you came," he said. "Shall we go into the kitchen?"

She shook her head. "Not today."

He gave her a speculative look and then said, "We'll talk in the office."

"Yes." The office would be safe. There were no bad memories in there.

Stephan ushered her around the bar and down the hall.

She felt better when she entered the office and took a seat in the chair in front of Stephan's desk. The clean, organized atmosphere was calming. Stephan was an excellent businessman and neat to a fault. While he had a warm, gregarious personality, there was no question about his high standards when it came to the restaurant. She'd become a better chef working under his management.

"What do you think of the remodel?" he asked.

"It looks good."

"The dining room is now in excellent shape, but I cannot say the same for the kitchen. We need you, Adrianna. The customers miss your specials. There isn't a day that goes by that someone doesn't ask for you. I want you to be our executive chef. That will mean a raise and better hours. In fact, you can tell me when you want to work. If you need to start part-time, we'll do that."

He was being incredibly generous, and she wanted to say yes to everything, but she had to be honest with him. "It sounds great, but I don't know if I'm ready. I have nightmares. I keep reliving that moment when I heard the shots, when I raced through the kitchen …"

Stephan sat back in his chair, pressing his hands together. "I can't imagine how difficult that was for you." He paused. "We all loved Will, but you two had a special relationship. He was your biggest supporter. He used to tell me I was a fool to wait to name you as my executive chef."

His words only twisted the knife in her heart.

"I'm not sure I can even remember how to cook," she

said.

"It will come back to you, Adrianna. It's in your blood. You breathe food. It's who you are. It's what you live for."

He was right. Without cooking, without her career, she had no idea who she was. Which was exactly why she'd been floundering the last two months.

"I don't want anyone else running our kitchen," he continued. "If that means waiting a few days or a week, then that's what we'll do. But I can't wait forever, Adrianna. I hope you understand that."

"I do. You've been generous to wait this long. I really appreciate it."

A knock came at the door, and Stephan said, "Come in."

One of the servers appeared with a large bag. "Hello, Chef," she said to Adrianna.

Adrianna felt a surge of pride at the address. She had worked so hard to become a chef, was she really going to let fear rule her life?

"Your order," the server said to Stephan, setting a bag down on the desk. Then she left the room.

"What's all this?" she said to Stephan, suddenly suspicious.

"It's your take-out order. The spaghetti isn't as good as when you were making it. Try it, and tell me what's missing."

"Lindsay knows the sauces as well as I do."

"I want your opinion. I put some other entrees in there as well. Just give them a taste, and call me, all right?"

She saw the challenge in his eyes and gave a helpless smile. "You're very sneaky."

"I'll do whatever it takes to remind you of why we need you." He stood up and came around the desk, handing her the bag as she got to her feet. "Call me."

"All right," she replied.

"I'll walk you out."

Stephan didn't say anything more, but she was grateful for his presence as she re-entered the dining room. Again, she managed to keep her gaze focused straight ahead. When they reached the door, Stephan gave her a kiss on each cheek.

As she stepped out of the restaurant, she felt a wave of relief that did not bode well for her returning to the kitchen, but she would leave that for another day. She'd gotten through the door. That was the first step, and for the moment, it was enough.

* * *

"These kids were in the alley behind Vincenzo's the night of the robbery." Wyatt tossed the print from the security camera down on Josh's desk the minute he returned to the station.

Josh glanced up at him in surprise. "How do you know that?"

"Because I ran into the chef from Vincenzo's, Adrianna Cavello. She told me she went into the alley to give some kids pizza. That's why she wasn't in the restaurant during the robbery. And she identified these children as being the ones she spoke to."

"Hold on. She didn't say she saw anyone in the alley when I interviewed her," Josh replied with a frown. "And where did you talk to her?"

"By the fountain near Vincenzo's. I showed her the photo, and she identified the kids. She also said that the youngest girl bore a resemblance to Stephanie." He paced around the desk, adrenaline surging through his veins.

Ever since he'd talked to Adrianna, he'd felt renewed energy. He'd spent an hour searching the streets around the fountain, and while he'd come up empty, he still felt more hope than he had in a long time. "This is the break I've been looking for, Josh. We find the kids, and I think we find

Stephanie."

Josh didn't appear convinced.

"What?" Wyatt demanded. "You've got something to say – say it."

"You don't know the youngest girl is Stephanie. The photo is blurry. And why would she be running around San Francisco late at night with two other kids? It doesn't make sense, Wyatt."

"It may not make sense, but it's all I have. I want to get this photo out to every officer in the department. Even if Stephanie isn't one of the children, these kids may be witnesses to the robbery and homicide at Vincenzo's."

"All right. Hang on a second." Josh flipped through a file on his desk. He ran his finger down the page. "Here it is. When I interviewed Adrianna, she said she was in the alley by the garbage bin when the shots rang out. She didn't mention anyone else. I assumed she was taking out the trash." He shook his head, annoyance in his eyes. "I should have asked more questions, Wyatt. She was so traumatized when I first interviewed her, I couldn't get much out of her. The second time we spoke, she was still fuzzy on the details. But I should have pressed harder."

"She should have volunteered the information," he said with a frown, wondering why Adrianna hadn't included the children in her statement. Had she been trying to protect them? But she hadn't been concerned enough about their welfare to call for help when they first showed up at the restaurant.

The click of heels lifted his gaze from Josh to the sparkling, irritated green eyes of his partner, Pamela Baker.

"Where the hell have you been?" she asked. "You told me you'd be back an hour ago."

"I have a lead on Stephanie," he said.

She immediately softened. "Seriously? What is it? Can I help?"

"Josh will fill you in. I need to make some calls. I'm

sorry I bailed on you today."

She waved away his apology. "It's fine. I was just annoyed you left me to do all the paperwork on the Delgado case. I didn't realize something more important had come up. You should have told me."

"I wanted to check things out first." While Josh was filling Pamela in, he headed back to his desk. His first call was to a friend at Human Services. Adrianna might not have thought to call for help when she talked to the kids, but maybe someone else had.

Chapter Four

Adrianna stared at the foil containers of food sitting on her kitchen counter. The aroma made her mouth water and also triggered a lot of memories, some beautiful, some painful.

As a child, she'd grown up hungry. She'd gotten used to an ache in her stomach that never quite went away. Food had always been a focus for her – how to get it, how to pay for it, how to stretch noodles into a full meal, how to make sure she had something for the next day. Like the three children who had come to her in the alley behind Vincenzo's, she had also had to scrounge for food at the back door of restaurants or supermarkets.

Wyatt Randall had wanted to know why she hadn't called the police. Will and Lindsay had asked her the same question. But she'd felt a connection to those kids, and when Ben had pleaded with her not to say anything, she'd heard her younger self making that same plea.

But she should have been thinking like an adult instead of like a scared twelve-year-old girl. She should have contacted someone to take the children in. Or at the very least, she should have asked more questions. Should have, could have ... guilt was getting her nowhere.

Opening the first container of spaghetti, she pulled a

fork from the drawer and twirled the long strands of pasta around it. Her first taste was good, but not great, she thought with a frown, wondering what was missing. She took several more bites. The flavors were close but not quite there. Turning to the mushroom pizza next, she had the same feeling, and also with the lasagna and the cannelloni. The flavors were hinted at, but they weren't bold, or magical.

Setting down her fork, she stared at the containers. She wanted to fix the dishes, to add seasoning, to heat and stir, and love them into magnificence. But that would require her to cook. She could do it here. She didn't have to go into Vincenzo's. She could deconstruct the ingredients and figure out what was missing.

Jumping to her feet, she started pulling out pots and pans and ingredients. For the first time in a long time she actually felt like cooking again.

Two hours later, her kitchen smelled like garlic, onions, oregano and other delicious herbs. Pots and pans were stacked high in the sink, and she'd cleaned out her pantry and refrigerator in search of ingredients, but it had all been worth it. She'd teased the dishes into brilliance, and she was happy with her efforts.

In fact, it was the first time in a long time she didn't feel, sad, angry or guilty.

Cooking had always been her therapy. Which was exactly why she should go back to work.

The restaurant needed her and she needed the restaurant.

The doorbell rang sharply and abruptly, startling her out of her thoughts. Like most apartments in San Francisco, visitors had to be buzzed in. A quick glance at the clock on the wall said it was nine-thirty. Lindsay would still be at work, and she really didn't have any other friends who would just drop by without calling.

She pushed the Intercom and said, "Yes?"

"It's Wyatt Randall. I need to speak to you."

Her heart skipped a beat. *Wyatt Randall*? What the hell was he doing here? "Why do you want to talk to me?" she asked.

"I have a few more questions about the kids you saw the night of the robbery."

"I told you everything I know."

"Can you let me in? I won't take up much of your time."

She hesitated. He was a police officer. He should be trustworthy, but she was scared of shadows these days, and letting a strange man into her apartment didn't seem like a smart move. She also suspected she would not like the questions he wanted to ask.

The buzzer rang again, reminding her that he was waiting, and not patiently.

"All right," she said, buzzing him into the building. Then she moved through the living room to the front door.

Her one bedroom apartment was small and cluttered, a mix of colors, styles and furniture she'd picked up from a furniture consignment store. It wasn't much by anyone's standards, but it was home, and it was all hers. Will had suggested they move in together, pool their income and get a bigger place, but she'd put him off. While it had sounded like a lovely idea, she hadn't been ready to give up the first place she'd ever called home. Nor had she been interested in sharing her home with Will. That probably should have told them both something about the depth of their relationship, but it wasn't a subject they'd spent much time discussing.

A knock came at her door, and she quickly opened it, relieved to have a distraction from thinking about Will and the home they would never share.

Wyatt strode through the door, not waiting for an invitation. A man of action, she thought – the kind of man who could turn a woman's life upside down. Not that he was here because he was interested in her, she reminded herself. He was a man on a mission, and she'd somehow become part of that mission.

"What do you want?" she asked.

"Why didn't you tell anyone about the kids being in the alley at the time of the robbery? Inspector Burton and I reviewed your statement, and you made no mention of the children."

She'd realized her omission after her first interview with the inspector, but she hadn't come forward, because the information wasn't relevant. The kids had had nothing to do with the robbery and they couldn't have seen any more than she did. She hadn't wanted to put them in the middle of a situation that didn't concern them.

Guilt must have shown on her face, because Wyatt's gaze narrowed. "What's going on, Adrianna? Why did you lie?"

"I forgot about them at first, but they weren't witnesses to anything. They were outside the whole time. I didn't think it was relevant."

"You saw two figures running down the street from your vantage point in the alley. They could have seen them, too."

"The people were far away, and they had on hoods."

"Where did the kids go when the shots rang out?"

"I don't know. I ran inside. I think they ran the opposite direction."

"You think, but you don't know."

"No," she admitted.

"Why are you trying to keep the kids away from the police?" he asked.

"I'm not doing that."

"I think you are, and I want to know why."

She saw the resolute gleam in his eyes and knew she was going to have to give him a better answer. "I used to be one of those kids. I spent some time on the streets. I know what it's like to have a social worker put you in a foster home or a group home that sucks. I know what it's like to be scared and hungry and not trust anyone. I saw kids ripped apart from their siblings." She paused. "I didn't turn those kids in, because they asked me not to, and because I knew that there could be worse places to stay than the street."

"They're children. Just because you might have had a bad experience –"

"Two bad experiences," she said, cutting him off. "But we're not talking about me. I want to be very clear about something. If I thought the kids could help the investigation, I would have mentioned them. My – my boyfriend died that night. I want justice for Will. He didn't deserve what happened to him. I wasn't trying to hide anything, but those kids were not part of what happened. And by the time I remembered they were there, I didn't think there was anything to gain by talking about them. So is that it?"

"Not even close," he said, putting his hands on his hips, an aggressive stance that made it clear he had no intention of leaving until he was ready. "I need to know everything about those kids. One of them might be my daughter."

"I've told you everything."

"You seem to have a habit of remembering things later," he said pointedly.

"You haven't known me long enough to know about my habits."

"Then let's get better acquainted."

"Yes, let's," she said sharply. "You want answers from me? Well, I have a few questions for you. Why would a mother take her child away from the child's father? She must have had a damn good reason."

His face whitened, sharp points of anger lighting up his blue eyes. "She had no reason. She was a drug addict. A spoiled, selfish woman, who thought only of herself." He paused. "That's why the judge gave me full custody of Stephanie. That's right, Adrianna. My ex-wife violated a court order. She kidnapped my daughter. She took her away without even a change of clothes. She even left her favorite stuffed bear behind, the one that Stephanie couldn't sleep without. But that wouldn't have occurred to Jennifer, because she was only thinking about herself."

Silence followed his harsh words. Wyatt ran a hand through his hair. "What else do you want to know?" he demanded.

"I – I don't know," she said, not sure where to go next. "Look, I don't want to get in the middle of this."

"You're already there. You want out, you're going to have to help me."

She felt torn, not sure what to believe. She needed time to think, but from the determined expression on Wyatt's face, it was clear she would not get that time now. "I don't know how to help you," she said. "I really don't know anything about the kids, and your personal situation seems to be very complicated."

"It's not at all complicated. I just explained it to you."

"Your side," she said pointedly.

"There is no other side. You want more answers, ask me more questions."

"I'm in the middle of something," she said, waving a hand toward her kitchen. "Maybe we could do this another time."

"I thought you didn't cook anymore," he said, his gaze shifting toward the stack of dishes in her sink.

"I'm testing some recipes for Vincenzo's."

"So you made it through the door?"

"Yes, I made it into the office. I wasn't quite ready for the kitchen." She paused for a long moment, as they looked into each other's eyes. There was something about his compelling gaze that wouldn't let her glance away. "I don't know what you want from me," she murmured.

He didn't answer immediately. Finally, he said, "I don't know either, but ever since our coins clashed, I feel like you're … important."

"In what way?" she asked, startled by his comment. As much as she wanted to say he was crazy, she couldn't deny that she felt the same intangible connection, as if this man had been brought into her life for a reason.

"That's what we have to find out." He walked over to her kitchen counter. "This looks good. Maybe I should help you test the recipes."

"You want me to feed you now?" she asked in surprise.

He gave her a brief smile. "Why not? You said you wanted to get to know me. That's going to take some time."

"I said I don't know you. I didn't say I wanted to change that," she corrected. "You could tell me anything you wanted. That wouldn't make it true."

"You're very cynical."

"I've met a lot of liars."

"Liars that were cops?" he asked.

She sighed. "Yeah, liars that were cops."

"Another reason you didn't call the police." He crossed his arms in front of his chest. "I'm not a liar, Adrianna. And while I might be a police officer, I'm first and foremost a father desperate to find his daughter. You're my only link."

"To a little girl who may not be your child," she reminded him.

"That's what I need to find out."

She debated for a long moment. "I have to clean up. You can have some food, if you want. I'll try to answer your questions, and then we're done. All right?"

Without waiting for an answer, she walked around the counter and pulled a plate out of the cupboard. She hadn't put everything away yet, so she had a variety of dishes for him to sample.

While she was getting the food, she saw him get to his

feet and amble around the apartment, checking out her photographs on top of the side table. She didn't have anything to hide, but still she felt a little uneasy under his scrutiny.

"Is this Will?" he asked a moment later, holding up a photo.

The picture had been taken the previous Christmas. They'd gone skiing in Lake Tahoe. Actually, Will had skied; she'd sipped hot chocolate in the lodge and sat by the fire.

"That's him," she said shortly.

"Was he a good skier?"

"Yes, he was excellent. His parents had a house in Tahoe. He spent every winter vacation on the slopes."

"What about you?" he asked, setting down the picture.

"I've never been on skis or a snowboard. I don't really like the idea of flying down a steep mountain."

"It's fun. You should try it."

She wasn't at all surprised he would think so. He looked like a man who enjoyed the outdoors and pushing his limits.

"Who's this?" he asked, picking up another photo.

"That's Lindsay," she replied, taking a quick look. "She's a sous chef at Vincenzo's and one of my good friends. We celebrated her birthday with a sail around the Bay. One of the waiters at Vincenzo's took us out in his father's boat."

"You don't have any photos from your past. No awkward moment captured in braces or braids," he commented.

"Never wore braces or braids," she said.

"No pictures of parents or grandparents."

"I never had any," she said.

"Never?" he asked with a raised eyebrow.

"I have one picture of my mother. It's in my bedroom. It's the only one in existence."

"That sounds like the beginning of a story."

"A very short one," she said. "Your food is ready."

He crossed the room and sat down at her counter. His gaze moved to the plate of food she set in front of him. "Wow, that looks amazing."

"It's a sampler. You'll be my guinea pig."

"I'm up for the challenge." He picked up a fork and took his first bite of the cannelloni.

She watched him chew, wondering why she was so interested in his opinion. She knew she was good. She didn't need his validation. Still ...

"Excellent," he finally said. "Incredible," he added after the next mouthful. "I think I'm going to run out of adjectives very quickly."

"Just eat," she said, feeling foolish pride at his compliment. Cooking had always been the one thing at which she'd excelled. She might not have gotten herself back in the restaurant kitchen, but at least she hadn't lost her touch.

While Wyatt ate, she loaded the dishwasher, happy to have something to do to keep herself busy. Wyatt took up a lot of room in her small kitchen, not just with his physical presence, but also with his personality. He wasn't a man who could be ignored, and that made her a little nervous. She felt like she needed to be on her toes around him.

It was a very different feeling than when Will had been in her kitchen. Will had been comfortable and easy, fun. He'd never rattled her. Never created an odd catch in the pit of her stomach, the way this man did.

But Wyatt wasn't here because he was attracted to her, and she hadn't let him stay because she was interested in him, she reminded herself. He was just here for his daughter.

"Who taught you how to cook?" Wyatt asked, interrupting her thoughts.

"I taught myself. I had a little more help later on."

"You said you spent time on the streets. What happened to your parents?"

"My mom got cancer when I was about six. She was sick for a long time. I started cooking for her," she said, drying her hands on a towel as she turned around. She leaned against the counter. "She couldn't eat much when she was going for chemo, so I learned how to make soup. It was all that she could keep down. I remember feeling so good when she could eat the whole bowl. Most food just made her nauseous."

"It sounds like a big responsibility for a little girl," he said, compassion in his eyes.

"I guess it was. I didn't know any differently. She was a great mom, but we were all alone, and we didn't have any money. That situation got worse the sicker she became. She couldn't work anymore, and she didn't have any insurance."

"What about your father?"

"He wasn't around. He took off when I was three. I don't remember him." She paused. "From soup, I graduated to breakfast food." She felt a pang in her heart at the memory. "My mom loved pancakes for dinner, and so did I. So we ate breakfast at night. It was fun. Sometimes we ate by candlelight."

"Because the electricity was turned off?"

"Yes. I didn't know that at the time. Mom made it sound like an adventure. She created a world of make-believe and wrapped me up in it as best she could. But then she got worse. And one day a policeman came with a social worker, and they took me away from her." She had to bite down on her lip to keep back the pain of that memory. "The cop grabbed my arm so hard he left a bruise. He had to drag me out of the house. I didn't want to leave her. They said she was going to the hospital, but I never knew if that happened. The next day the social worker told me she died, and I never got to see her again."

Wyatt shoved back his chair and stood up. He walked

over to her, putting a kind hand on her shoulder. "I'm sorry."

His touch warmed and comforted her in a way that surprised her. In fact, the whole conversation surprised her. She rarely told anyone about her past.

"It was a long time ago."

"No wonder you don't like cops. But you have to know somewhere in your head that those adults were worried about you."

"That wasn't the bad experience I was talking about." She stepped out from under his touch, feeling like she needed to move away before she started to like it too much. She'd been living in a cold, gray, emotionless world since Will had died, and she wasn't quite ready to jump back into life.

"So you went into foster care after your mother died?" Wyatt continued.

"Yes. The next couple of years were bad. I ended up in some rough homes, ran away a couple of times. Everything changed one night when I went scrounging for food at a diner called Joe's."

"I know that place. It's run by that cranky old woman who keeps a baseball bat behind the counter."

"Josephine Cooper," she said with a smile. "The restaurant was named after her husband, Joe. She is a mean bitch when she wants to be. But she gave me a job bussing tables when I was fifteen, and she let me stay with her when I didn't have anywhere else to go. She saved my life."

"You don't get the kind of food I just tasted at Joe's," he said dryly.

"Well, I learned a few more things after I left there."

He let out a sigh. "I think I understand why you didn't tell anyone about the kids."

"I knew where they were coming from. I wanted to help them the way Josephine helped me. I was trying to gain their trust, but I feel badly now that I didn't go back to the restaurant after the robbery. I didn't think about their welfare, and I should have. I was too caught up in my own trauma."

"You can make up for it by helping me now."

She grabbed his empty plate off the counter and placed it in the sink. "I still need to know more about you."

"Ask away."

"Why did you get sole custody?"

"Because Jennifer was arrested for drug possession and DUI. She had my daughter in the car with her at the time."

She gave him a long, thoughtful look. "You're a cop. You didn't know your wife was using drugs?"

"Not at first. She started with prescription drugs after a knee injury. I never imagined she'd get addicted to painkillers, that she would put everything aside in her determination to get high. When I finally realized the truth, I tried to get her help. I forced her into rehab. But after the DUI, I had to file for divorce. She'd risked my daughter's life."

He appeared to be speaking from the heart, but the cold ruthless note in his voice when he spoke about his ex-wife reminded her that there were two sides to every story, and she was only hearing one.

"I should never have let Jen see Stephanie without me being present, but she seemed like she was getting better, like she was the old Jen again. She was just playing me. She took Stephanie to the park. I had the nanny go with her, but Jen ditched her, and I haven't seen my daughter since."

"Two years is a long time," she murmured.

"A hell of a long time," he agreed. "But I'll fight forever to get her back. She needs me, and I need her."

She was touched by his determination and his devotion. She wondered how her life would have been different if she'd had a father who'd wanted her that badly – or at all.

"Tell me about the kids, Adrianna," he said, taking his

seat again.

She sat down on the stool next to him. "They came by the restaurant twice before the robbery. Both times were on the weekend, a Friday or Saturday night. Ben assured me that they had a place to stay and that things were going to get better."

"He's the only one who spoke to you?"

She nodded. "The middle girl always seemed kind of sleepy and like a tag-along. The youngest was alert, wary, looking around." She paused. "I remember thinking that her eyes were so blue and the others were so brown."

"Blue like mine."

"Like a lot of people," she said. "I can't swear that the girl was the same girl I saw in the photograph of your daughter."

"But you can't swear she wasn't the same girl."

"No. So what now?"

"I've distributed photos of the kids throughout the department, and I'm checking with Human Services to see how many boys named Ben are in the system. I've contacted the schools, and I'll probably go back and canvass the neighborhood around Vincenzo's tomorrow. I'd like you to come with me."

"Why?" she asked, surprised by the request.

"Because the kids know you. If they see you, they might seek you out."

"They ran away from me earlier today," she reminded him.

"Maybe they won't the next time."

"It seems like a long shot."

"It's all I've got, so I'm going to take it."

"You're very determined. I'm a little confused as to why you haven't found your daughter before now. Your ex-wife must have had a pretty good plan to disappear so completely. She's hiding from a cop with a ton of resources at his disposal."

He frowned. "I hear the doubt in your voice again."

"I'm just trying to figure things out."

"My ex-wife came from money. Her parents swear they don't know where she is. I've had a private investigator on them for over a year, and I haven't been able to prove they're lying. But they could have helped her before she left, set up an account somewhere, gotten her a place to live, fake identity."

"Why would they help her if she's a danger to your daughter – to their granddaughter?"

"They don't see her that way. They see the little princess they raised, and Jen is a very good liar. She knows how to manipulate them."

"You have an answer for everything."

"Because you're asking questions I've thought about a million times in the last two years." He got to his feet. "I'm going to be at the fountain tomorrow, a little before three. You saw the kids about that time today, right?"

"I think it was a little after three."

"Which would imply that they might go to school somewhere. Anyway, I'd like you to meet me. You said you wanted to help them. This is your chance." He walked to the door, then paused. "When you do your Internet search after I leave, you'll find out that Jennifer accused me of domestic violence and child abuse during the custody hearing. She also made those accusations in the press, hoping to sway the court with public opinion."

Her stomach turned over.

"They were lies," he continued. "And the judge agreed that there was no evidence to back up her claims."

"Why are you telling me?" she asked, as she got up and walked across the room to the front door.

"Because you're going to find out anyway, and I don't want you to think I have anything to hide. I never hurt either one of them. You can ask Inspector Burton. He was the best man at my wedding. He's Stephanie's godfather."

"You guys protect each other," she said quietly.

"We also protect the innocent, and sometimes we even put away the guilty."

"Sometimes," she muttered.

"We do the best we can." He met her gaze. "Meet me tomorrow, Adrianna. You grew up without a father. You had to live on the streets. I know you don't want that for any other child. If my daughter is out there somewhere, hungry and neglected, I need to find her as quickly as possible."

"I'll think about it," she said and then shut the door behind him.

Chapter Five

Wyatt woke up with a jolt early Friday morning, rattled by the image of Adrianna in his head. She'd haunted his dreams, with her long, curly dark hair, her soft, sweet lips and big, expressive brown eyes. Those eyes had told him a lot, probably more than she'd wanted him to know. She'd been hurt, not once, but several times, hurt by people who were supposed to take care of her. He didn't know her whole story, but he knew one important thing. She didn't trust anyone – especially him.

Adrianna wasn't the first person to doubt him. Jen's friends had looked at him with the same suspicions, as if he had a secret life, an evil side. But as Jen had found out it was easier to spread lies than to make them true. The judge had seen through her stories. So had the social worker assigned to their case. None of that mattered in the end, because a court order had just driven Jennifer to take matters into her own hands.

Over the years, he'd wondered how far in advance she'd made her plan to leave, and who had helped her, because as Adrianna had reminded him the night before, Jennifer had done a damn good job of keeping his daughter away from him.

Stumbling out of bed, he got into the shower. The

pounding spray of water reminded him of the fountain where he'd met Adrianna, the moment when their coins had collided. If that hadn't happened, they never would have spoken to each other. He might never have showed her the picture. She might never have told anyone about seeing the kids.

A tingle ran down his spine at the thought of how easily they could have missed speaking to each other. His self-protective instincts warned him not to get too far ahead of himself. He still only had a seed of a clue that could turn out to be nothing, but it was more than he had had yesterday.

He hoped Adrianna would show up at the fountain later in the day. She was the link to the kids, and while it was a long shot, he felt sure he had a better chance finding them with her cooperation. But after researching him on the Internet, would she come? Would she believe his story or the lies that had been spread about him? It didn't help his case that he was a cop. She was still holding a grudge against the officer who had prevented her from saying good-bye to her dying mother, and who could blame her for that? But maybe she would put her past aside and help him. It was probably a long-shot, but he was going to gamble on her.

After getting dressed and grabbing a quick breakfast, he headed into work. He spent most of the morning working on some ongoing cases and then with Pamela's promise to cover for him, he headed out to McClellan Square.

There were tourists by the fountain, taking pictures, tossing coins, making wishes. He watched the crowd, searching for any child of the right age, but there were none in sight. The nearby schools would let out soon, and then the square would probably be swarming with kids, hopefully the three he was looking for would be among them.

It was difficult to wrap his mind around the thought that he might see Stephanie today. He'd wondered a million times what kind of reunion they would have. In his fantasy, Stephanie ran to him, throwing her arms around him, telling him how much she loved him and how much she had missed him. But would reality be the same? Who knew what lies Jennifer had told Stephanie? She could have told Steph that he'd hit her, that he'd abandoned them, that he didn't want her or that he was dead. He felt real physical pain when he considered the possibility that his daughter might think that he didn't love her or that he didn't want her.

But he couldn't dwell on that possibility now. First he had to get her back. Then he would have all the time in the world to prove how much he loved her.

Two young girls turned the far corner, and he felt a tingle run down his spine as they approached the fountain.

Were these the girls?

His heart beat faster. He didn't want to scare them, so he moved slowly and quietly, until he was just behind them. One of them swung around, giving him a fearful look. The other followed, and his heart sank. He didn't recognize either one of them.

The girls went running across the square to a woman pushing a stroller. She gave him a suspicious look and then they all headed down the street. He'd gotten those looks before. He'd spent a lot of time at places where children gathered, and he couldn't blame the moms and dads for their protective instincts. He was glad they were watching out for their children. Fortunately, his badge usually got him off the hook and once he explained why he was there, everyone offered to help out. Unfortunately, nothing had ever come of those spontaneous offers.

He felt a brief moment of defeat, but he pushed it away. He had all afternoon and the weekend, too. For the next seventy-two hours he wouldn't have to juggle his job and his search. Hopefully, by Monday he'd have Stephanie back in his arms where she belonged.

As he turned around, his optimism increased when he saw Adrianna walking towards him.

She looked like summer in her flip-flops, jeans and tank top, her hair was pulled back in a thick pony tail. His heart skipped a beat, surprising him with the one emotion he hadn't felt in a very long time – attraction.

Wrong time, wrong place, he quickly reminded himself. The last thing he needed was the distraction of a woman. His relationships for the past two years had consisted of a few one-night stands with women who hadn't expected a follow up call. He had no mental or emotional energy for anything more complicated than casual sex.

He needed to stop looking at Adrianna as a woman and think of her more like a partner, he told himself. She was just assisting him in his investigation. But his resolve did nothing to slow the rapid beat of his heart. It had been a long time since he'd let desire into his life, and it shook him that he felt anything now. He would just have to ignore the feeling. It wasn't like she wanted anything from him. She had her own baggage to deal with.

Adrianna stopped a few feet away, wariness in her eyes.

"I wasn't sure you'd come," he said, clearing his throat, shoving his hands into his pockets.

"I wasn't sure I *should* come," she replied.

"You did your research."

"Yes," she admitted. "And I found everything you told me I would find. The press were really interested in your story."

"Because I work for the city and I'm a police officer. I faced enormous scrutiny, but I checked out."

"That's what I discovered."

"And you came." He felt ridiculously pleased about that fact.

"I found some good things about you, too. You ran into a burning building and rescued an old woman before the firemen could get there."

"I was the first on the scene."

"But you weren't on duty. You were just walking by."

"I don't have to be on the clock to do my job."

She gave him a long, thoughtful look. "I want to believe you're one of the good guys, but maybe you ran into that building because you like being a hero."

"Wouldn't that make me a good guy?" he asked.

"Possibly," she conceded.

"You're tough."

"I've had to be. Taking people at face value can sometimes be dangerous."

"Some day I want to hear your story."

"Well, that won't be today." She glanced around. "Have you seen any familiar faces?"

"Not yet."

"It seems like it would be a little too easy to have the girls just show up here."

"Nothing so far has been easy, maybe I'm due," he said with a sigh.

"You could make another wish," Adrianna suggested.

"I'll stick with my original one. What about you? Did you ever throw your coin in?"

"Not yet. I think I'll save it until I know what I want to wish for."

"So your wish has changed?"

"Not entirely, but I did make it inside the restaurant yesterday, so that was a good first step. And I cooked last night. Second step."

"What's next?" he asked, keeping a close eye on the people coming in and out of the square.

"Still figuring that out," she replied.

"You're too good in the kitchen to quit being a chef."

"Thanks for the compliment," she said, a pleased note

in her voice. "I am good, and I don't want to quit. I'm just scared."

He turned to face her. "Of what? That it will happen again? Because the odds are against that."

"I think I'm more afraid of reliving that night. Even though I've relived it a million times in my dreams."

"The fear might be worse than the reality," he suggested. "You've built it up in your mind."

"You could be right. You're probably used to seeing people who have been killed," she said, her voice a little unsteady as she hit the last word.

"I've seen a few," he said. "But it's worse when you know the person. It was just the two of you in the restaurant, right?"

She nodded. "Yes, Lindsay had just left. I came out of the break room. Will was in the kitchen. He wanted to talk to me, but I told him it would have to wait because I had promised the kids pizza. And I knew they'd be in the alley." She paused. "Will had asked me to turn the kids in, too. He was a little annoyed that I was being so stubborn about it. I never imagined that would be the last conversation we would ever have."

"What was he like?"

She seemed surprised by the question. "Why do you want to know?"

"Just curious."

"Well, he was fun. He was friendly. He always had a big grin on his face, and he was the life of any party he attended. Girls loved him, guys loved him ... He was a good time." She paused for a moment. "We met at another restaurant called *The Gardens*. It was all vegetarian food, and while I love vegetables, I was eager to work on a broader menu. Will worked the bar there, and he decided to follow me to Vincenzo's. What if he'd never done that? What if we'd never met? He'd be alive now."

He heard the recrimination in her voice and knew that

no amount of persuasion would change her mind. He'd gone down that same guilty path – hell, he was still there most days.

"Anyway," Adrianna continued. "We were friends for a long time, and then one day we were more. It was just right."

There was suddenly doubt in her voice, and he wondered why. "Was it?" he questioned.

She bristled at his question. "Of course it was. What could be better than falling in love with your best friend?"

He shrugged. "I guess nothing."

"Was it love at first sight with your ex-wife?"

"I don't remember. I was twenty-one years old. We met in college. Life was one big series of parties, finals and hookups. Reality was way in the distance. Love was a romantic fairytale, and somehow I got caught up in it. We got married after graduation. Ten years later, here I am – in my own private hell."

"You were very young to get married."

"Obviously too young."

"Maybe if your wife hadn't gotten addicted to drugs, things would have been different."

"I don't do *maybe* anymore," he said firmly. "I've spent too many months thinking *maybe if I'd done something differently, I wouldn't be in this position.* But there aren't any do-overs. It is what it is. And frankly, I don't want to talk about Jennifer right now."

"I don't want to talk about Will either."

For the next twenty minutes they didn't talk. They watched opposite sides of the square as groups of children walking home from school passed by them. Unfortunately, none of those kids were the ones they were looking for.

"Are we just going to stand here all afternoon?" Adrianna asked.

He let out a sigh. Stake-outs had never been his favorite thing to do -- too much waiting, not enough action.

"I have another idea. Why don't you show me the alley where you first saw the kids?"

She immediately shook her head, a dismayed expression appearing on her face. "I never agreed to that. I don't want to go near Vincenzo's."

"You went in yesterday."

"I know, but the alley ..."

"Is where you saw the kids," he finished. "Nothing bad happened there. It might help for me to see what else is around there, and it might help you, too. It's one step closer to getting you back into the kitchen."

"You could go on your own."

"I could, but if the kids are around there, they'd be more likely to show themselves to you."

A debate went on in her eyes. Finally, she gave him a short, quick nod.

"All right. Come on, before I change my mind."

* * *

As Adrianna led Wyatt into the alley behind Vincenzo's, she felt a familiar surge of panic. Wyatt was wrong when he'd told her nothing bad had happened in the alley. That's where she'd been standing when her whole life had been shattered. But as her steps faltered, Wyatt's hand centered on the small of her back, and his reassuring, solid strength behind her kept her walking. She paused when the back door of the restaurant came into sight. It was closed, and she felt immense relief that she would not catch a glimpse of the busy kitchen.

"This is it. Nothing really to see," she added, sweeping her hand around. Several other restaurants and stores backed up to the alley. There was a van parked down the street, but no one in sight. With several smelly dumpsters, it wasn't a popular place to hang out.

Wyatt's gaze moved down the alley. "What direction

did the kids come from?"

She had to think for a moment. "From there," she said, pointing her finger toward the back doorway of a clothing shop. They just sort of materialized out of the shadows. I think they might have hidden behind one of the dumpsters until I came out the back door."

"Did anyone else at the restaurant see them or talk to them?"

She licked her lips. "Will saw them the first time they came around, but I was the only one who spoke to them, and the only one who saw them that night. I'm not sure if anyone else in the kitchen had contact with them on nights that I didn't work. No one mentioned it, but that doesn't mean it didn't happen. They're not the first homeless people to come knocking on the back door."

"I thought you said they weren't homeless."

"That's what Ben said," she corrected. "I wasn't sure."

She saw the annoyance on his face, but thankfully he didn't put his irritation into words. She was tired of defending herself. Maybe she hadn't made the right decision, but she'd done what she'd thought was best at the time.

Wyatt started walking down the alley, and after a moment, she followed. He seemed to be making note of which door led to which business, pausing occasionally to check the stairs of a fire escape. There were some residences on the upper floors of the buildings as evidence by the curtains blowing in some of the open windows.

"Maybe they live in one of the apartments," she suggested.

"It's possible," he said. "You really didn't see them come out of any particular doorway?"

"I wish I could give you a different answer than I don't know."

"So do I," he muttered.

When they reached the corner, Wyatt looked in both

directions, his gaze settling on a run-down motel a block away.

"The *Fantasy Inn*," he murmured, casting her a quick glance. "Doesn't look much like a fantasy to me."

No, but it looked like a lot of places she'd lived in.

"Let's check it out," he suggested. "Maybe someone there has seen the kids."

She followed him down the street to the motel, and when they entered the building, she felt like she had stepped back in time. The small lobby boasted nothing more than a chair, a half-empty snack machine, and an old coffee maker surrounded by paper cups.

The last time she'd been in a motel like this had been with her mom, just a few weeks before she'd died. Every day she'd collect loose change from the streets in order to buy a candy bar out of the machine. Every night she'd split the candy with her mom. That sweet was their midnight treat, her mom used to say, never questioning how she'd come up with the candy or the money. There were a lot of things her mom hadn't wanted to question. Even as a little girl, Adrianna had known better than to share too much.

Shaking the memories out of her head, she watched Wyatt approach the counter. The clerk looked like a hundred other desk clerks she'd seen in her childhood, a middle-aged, balding, overweight man, who didn't look too closely at anyone or anything. The kind of guy who wouldn't get involved if someone was being hurt right in front of him.

Wyatt flashed his badge, which made the guy stand up a little straighter, and then Wyatt showed him the photograph of the kids leaving the liquor store. "Have you seen these children?" he asked.

The clerk nodded. "That's Ben. Nice kid. Comes in to get candy, doesn't talk too much. I've seen the girls in the parking lot."

"Who are they with? What room are they in?"

"They were with a woman. But she left about a week ago."

"Do you have a name?"

"We don't take names here. Everyone pays cash."

"Look, I've got some kids in trouble. Help me out here."

The clerk hesitated. "The woman said her name was Delilah, but I'm a hundred percent sure that wasn't her real name. She was here off and on for about four months." He paused. "And then there was another woman, a real looker, great legs," he said, blowing out a long whistle. "She came by a few times. Always had a big, sweet smile when she asked to use the phone."

Wyatt frowned, and Adrianna could see his patience wearing thin.

"Did you get her name?"

"Carly."

"What did she look like?"

"Dark hair, brown eyes, I think, long, long legs, the kind that could wrap –"

"Yeah, I get the picture," Wyatt said grimly. "When did you last see her?"

"A couple of weeks ago."

"Did they leave anything behind?"

"Housekeeping takes whatever is left."

"If they come back, call me," Wyatt said, handing him his card.

"I don't want any trouble."

"Then don't forget to call me, or you'll have all kinds of trouble," he warned.

Wyatt's ruthless tone made the clerk back up a step. "Got it."

"Good." Wyatt strode briskly out of the lobby.

Adrianna followed, happy to be back in the sunshine. She hadn't imagined that helping Wyatt would take her back to places that reminded her of her own past.

Wyatt walked down the path in front of the motel and around the corner where two machines offering ice and drinks were located. The motel was shaped like a U with the parking lot in the middle. There were three cars in the lot and an old man sitting in a folding chair in front of his room. When he saw them staring, he got up and went inside, as if he was afraid they were going to ask him questions.

"I feel like knocking on some doors," Wyatt said.

"I doubt many will answer," she said. "But you can try."

He shot her a quick look. "I've got nothing to lose."

She shrugged. "It's your call."

As she'd predicted, only one person answered his knock, an older, confused woman who seemed to think they were going to give her a ride to the drug store. It took a lot of explanation to convince her otherwise. In the end, she finally just went back inside.

"Okay, now you can say, *I told you so*," Wyatt said as they circled back to the front of the building.

"Can I say I'm impressed instead?"

"Impressed by my failure?"

"No, by your determination. You're relentless."

"The stakes are high," he said.

She nodded. "Did one of the women the clerk described sound like your ex-wife?"

"The long legs could have been hers, but who knows?"

"What did Jennifer do? Did she have a job?"

"At one time, she wanted to design clothes. But after we married, she got pregnant, and that seemed to be the end of that. One time, when we were arguing, she told me that I'd stopped her from having her dreams, because I'd wanted a kid."

"So she didn't want to get pregnant?"

"Oh, she wanted a baby. That was part of the fairytale, until she actually had a baby and realized the fairytale literally stunk. She used to say she didn't have time to work because she was taking care of a baby, but her parents got her a nanny, and she spent more time having lunch with her friends than pushing a stroller to the park." He let out a sigh. "This was a waste of time."

"It was a good place to check. It's more than likely that the kids are staying in a place like this and that it's close to Vincenzo's. Maybe they'll come back here."

"I hate to say I hope so, because this place is a dump."

"Yeah, it is," she said. "But for a lot of people it's home."

His gaze met hers and he gave her a questioning look.

"I used to live in a place called the Oceanview Lodge," she said, answering his unspoken question. "It didn't have a view of the ocean. Our room overlooked the dumpsters behind the strip clubs. The clerk was just like the guy inside. He didn't care who was staying there as long as they paid cash, and I doubted if he could have described anyone who came through the door. He made a point of not looking. I was actually happy about that at the time. It was the ones that looked at me that made me nervous."

"What a shitty life you had," he said, shaking his head. "I don't understand why someone wasn't looking out for you."

She was taken aback by his passion, by the anger in his eyes. "My mom was sick."

"What about the rest of your family? Someone should have tracked your father down. And weren't there any grandparents, any aunts, any cousins?"

"They did look for my father, but I didn't have any information for them to go on. He wasn't listed on the birth certificate. I only knew what my mom had told me, and I was twelve. I was in shock after her death. At first, I didn't care if they found him. He would have been a stranger to me, too, but then when I ended up in really bad spots, I used to dream that he'd come looking for me and turn out to be this great guy. That didn't happen. And as for the rest ... I had a grandfather, but he was in a nursing home, and my grandmother was dead. So it was just me. It took me a long time to accept that fact. It was actually easier when I let go of the hope."

"I'm sorry."

"It wasn't your fault."

"No, but you just made me realize how lucky I was to grow up with a family."

"You were lucky. My mom was my family, and I don't want you to think badly of her. She did the best she could under terrible circumstances. Anyway, when I was about fifteen, I ran into Josephine, and she took me in, made me realize I could fight for something better or I could give up, but it was my choice. It was the first time I felt I had any control over anything."

"And you chose to fight."

She nodded. "Yes, and I thought I was doing really well. I had a good job, friends, a boyfriend, and then my life went spinning out of control once again."

"Sounds like you're going to have to make the same choice -- give up or fight."

She took a breath and slowly exhaled. "I'm tired, Wyatt. I've been fighting a long time."

"You just need to regroup."

"I need -- something."

He glanced down at his watch, and she suddenly realized the sun was going down.

"I didn't realize it was so late," he muttered.

"You have somewhere to be?"

"Actually, I do. Some place I don't want to be."

"Ah, so you're using me to stall. No wonder you're so interested in my life all of a sudden," she said with a smile. "I was doing the same thing yesterday by the fountain."

He smiled back. "Guilty."

"What do you have to do?"

"Have dinner with my family."

"Well, that doesn't sound so hard."

"It wouldn't be normally, but the last two years …"

"Oh, so the problem is -- they ask a lot of questions or they don't ask any."

"How are you so perceptive?"

She shrugged. "Am I right?"

"Yes, it's awkward as hell when I'm around. You should come with me."

She was shocked by the invitation. "I don't think so. I'm not in the mood for a family dinner. In fact, I'm not good with families. I never know what to do or say. Talk about awkward. I can't tell if people are teasing or angry with each other. I don't get the whole bickering thing. It's like a foreign language to me. Will took me to his parents' house once, and I swear I was so uncomfortable I was actually sweating, beads dripping down my face."

"Why was it so bad?"

"Because his parents scared the crap out of me. And they had all this silverware on the table. I'm a chef, and even I don't know why someone would need four different sized forks for a meal made up of salad, steak and dessert."

"Well, my family is big on paper plates and plastic silverware, so you don't have to worry."

"Why would you want me to come?" she asked.

"Well, I'm thinking dinner is the perk to the favor I'm going to ask of you."

She gave him a suspicious look. "I'm here. I'm already doing you a favor."

"This is something else. I've been thinking, and the kids came by the restaurant on the weekend nights at closing time. It's Friday night."

"You want to stake out the alley at Vincenzo's tonight?"

"Yes. They saw you by the fountain. They might think you're back at work."

"So I'm the bait?"

"You're the link to the kids. I need you to bring them out of the shadows."

"If your daughter saw you, don't you think she'd run to you?" she asked. "Why would you need me?"

Wyatt gave her a pained look. "Because I'm not really sure what Stephanie would do if she saw me. I don't know what Jen told her about me."

"But she lived with you. She knows you."

"We had some loud fights," he said. "Jen was a screamer. She loved to shout. Stephanie was in her room, but I don't know what she heard, what she thought. Even when Jen started the fight, she'd be in tears by the end. Did Stephanie think I was the one who made her mother cry?"

Adrianna hesitated. Just when she thought she was starting to trust Wyatt, he said something that made her pause. Was he the good guy he said he was?

"I don't know, Wyatt."

"Because I've given you doubts again," he said flatly. "You need to trust me, which is why you need to meet my family."

"They would only support you."

"Not if I was doing something wrong. They'd be the first to call me out. Come with me to dinner, Adrianna."

"I'm not dressed," she said half-heartedly. Actually, the idea of spending another night alone in her apartment was very unappealing. However, the idea of meeting a bunch of strangers was equally unexciting.

"We'll stop by your apartment, and you can change."

"It's your family, Wyatt. I'm sure they don't want a stranger there."

"I need you, Adrianna."

He was only speaking about needing her help, but for some reason his words touched off a cord deep within her. His bright blue gaze burned her with its intensity. Even if she wanted out, she doubted he'd let her go. That thought shook her a little, because she had the strange feeling she didn't want him to let her go.

That was crazy. They were practically strangers, and she couldn't be interested in anyone. It was too soon. It was the wrong time. It was a ridiculous thought.

She intended to say no, but *yes* came out instead.

"You won't be sorry," he said.

"I hope not."

Chapter Six

"So are you one of those women who says she'll be ready in ten minutes, and it's like an hour and a half?" Wyatt asked as she ran into her bedroom to change.

"When I say ten, that usually means five. I'm habitually on time. But give me an actual ten."

"No problem," Wyatt said as he paced around Adrianna's living room. He was having second thoughts about inviting her to dinner. Her presence would no doubt generate more questions he didn't want to answer. On the other hand, she would be a distraction. He didn't want to ruin his sister's night, and when he was around, everyone toned things down -- their conversation, their laughter, and their smiles. They did it out of respect, but he was tired of being pitied. He didn't need them to stop living their lives. He just needed to start living his again.

He had a feeling that Adrianna was his lucky charm. He didn't know why, but every instinct told him that he needed her to get his Stephanie back. It made no sense. It wasn't logical, but still he felt sure that meeting her by the fountain was some sort of omen. Their coins had collided. She'd seen the kids – and one of those kids might be his child. He was going to keep her close – until she shoved him away.

She didn't completely trust him. Hopefully, this trip to his parents' house would change her mind. If there was one thing his parents did well, it was to charm the people around them. Especially his father. He had always had a way with the ladies.

Wyatt smiled at the thought. Not that his mother let his dad get away with too much flirting. She knew just exactly how much space to give him before she reeled him back in. Their relationship worked. Next year they'd be married thirty-seven years. They'd done it right.

He glanced again at the picture of Will and Adrianna at the ski resort. Will had light blond hair and fair skin. He was tall and lean and had a lazy arm around Adrianna's shoulders. They were opposites in appearance, but they looked good together, comfortable and relaxed. He had yet to see that stress-free smile on Adrianna's face, but that wasn't surprising. She'd lost someone she loved in a violent crime. It would take some time to get past that.

He moved over to the side table, his gaze catching on a magazine that was half open. The article named the winners of the James Beard Foundation award for Rising Chefs and there was Adrianna's face. "Hey, you won an award," he said loudly. "It says you're a rising star."

He read through the announcement, gaining more respect for her by the moment. He'd known she was good when he'd tasted her food. But now he knew just how good. She'd certainly come a long way from her troubled childhood.

"Okay, I did it in nine minutes," she said, returning to the room in a short, sleeveless floral dress that showed off her curves.

Her face was pink with color, her eyes bright, and her beautiful hair fell in shiny waves along her bare shoulders and arms. His gut clenched. And for a moment he couldn't find his breath.

"What's wrong?" she asked worriedly. "Should I wear

pants? Something fancier or more casual? I told you I wasn't good at family gatherings."

"You look fine," he said finally cutting off her nervous ramble. "You look – pretty."

"Oh, well, thanks. This is probably the first time I've put on make-up in a couple of months."

He cleared his throat. "It sounds like you need a night out."

"Yeah, I think I do," she said.

He held up the magazine. "Can I brag about this to my family?"

A flood of pink spread across her cheeks followed by an embarrassed smile. "You don't want to do that. No one outside the cooking world cares about that award."

"You're too modest."

"I'd just rather let my food speak for itself."

"It speaks quite well -- in my brief experience."

"Thank you again. We could skip your family dinner, and I could cook for you," she offered.

"While that would be a lot less stressful for both of us, this is something I need to do."

"But I don't need to do it."

"You'll like them. Trust me."

"I guess that's what this evening is all about," she said.

* * *

"Where are we going?" Adrianna asked Wyatt as they drove across the Bay Bridge. "Your parents don't live in the city?"

"No, they live in the Berkeley Hills. It's not far."

She was actually happy that they had a bit of a drive ahead. She was feeling a little too nervous, and she needed to calm down. It didn't matter what Wyatt's family thought about her. She wasn't trying out for them. They weren't involved in a romantic way, although, they were definitely involved in something. She just wasn't quite sure what it was. Ever since they'd met, she'd felt a pull in his direction, and he seemed to feel the same thing.

That damn fountain, she thought. Maybe it had more power than they realized.

Wyatt reached out and put his hand over hers. She suddenly realized she was tapping her fingers against her leg.

"Nervous habit," she said, meeting his gaze.

"My family is really not that bad."

"I'm sure they're not. I'm just not good at this."

"Were Will's parents that judgmental? I can't imagine what they wouldn't like about you."

"They didn't like that I was poor, that I had no family. They thought I was dragging Will down, that I had convinced Will that he should be a bartender instead of a lawyer. But in truth, I had little influence on Will. He was a free spirit. He had quite a few different jobs, and bartending was just one of them. He liked serving drinks, chatting it up with people. He was the king of the bar, and I was the queen of the kitchen."

"Sounds like you were a good match."

"Yeah," she said a little heavily, not really wanting to get into a discussion about Will.

"I'm surprised his parents couldn't see that."

"To be fair, we only spent the one evening with them. I saw them briefly after he died, and they acted like I was a stranger. I don't think he ever talked to them about our relationship." She paused. "But when I said I was bad at meeting families, I was actually talking about when I was younger, when I had the chance to be adopted after my mother died. I met with two families on two different occasions, who were thinking they might take me in, but after meeting me, they said I wouldn't fit in. Apparently, I didn't make a good impression."

"Their loss."

She appreciated the compliment. "Thanks."

"But you're not trying out for anyone tonight. Believe me, the focus will not be on you."

"That's good." She took a moment and then said, "Did your parents like your wife?"

"In the beginning, yes. My mom lost a little patience with Jennifer after Stephanie was born, but she still tried to give her the benefit of the doubt. She used to tell me that she thought Jen had postpartum depression and that I should make sure to pay special attention to her, see if she needed help."

"Did she have that?"

"I think the depression started when she got pregnant. She didn't like anything about having a baby, the pregnancy, the delivery, the nursing. She didn't want to hold Stephanie after she was born. She saw her doctor, and I think she got some antidepressants, which we didn't know at the time were a very bad idea. It wasn't until Steph was about a year and a half that Jen felt comfortable being with the baby on her own. I had to take over a lot of the care in the early days, the diapers, getting up at night, bottle feedings." He looked over his shoulder, then changed lanes. "But the real turning point was when Jen got into a car accident a couple of years later. She hurt her knee, and she had a lot of pain. That's when the painkillers came into play. Long after her injury healed, she seemed to need them. After that, it was a spiral that just didn't end. Whatever was going on in her life was too much. Every problem had to be medicated. There came a point where I barely recognized her; she was so different from the woman I'd married."

As Wyatt spoke about his ex-wife, his tone seemed to vary between anger, guilt, and bitterness. But however it had ended, it seemed clear that Wyatt had loved his wife at one point in time.

"It's strange how love can go so wrong," she

murmured.

"Has there been anyone else in your life besides Will?"

"No one serious. I was too busy surviving to do the usual teenage stuff, and when I got older, it was still about making my way in the world. I couldn't let myself be distracted. I was too serious for most boys. I was too serious for Will, but he kept telling me he knew I had a fun side, and he was determined to find it."

Wyatt gave her a small smile. "Did he find it?"

"Well, it was more like he helped *me* find it. I'll always be grateful to him for that."

"He sounds like a wonderful person."

She let out a sigh. "Let's not talk about Will."

"Sorry."

As they crossed the bridge between the city and the East Bay, she gazed out the window at the big ships in the Oakland harbor, and the smaller boats returning home from a day's fishing or a sail under the two bridges that connected San Francisco to the rest of the world. It felt good to be away from her apartment, from the restaurant, from all the familiar streets. She'd been feeling claustrophobic, and now she felt like she could breathe again. "It's a nice night," she said. "No fog yet."

"My parents have a great view of the city from their house. I'll have to show it to you."

"I'd like that. Growing up the way I did, I was always wishing for a view, something to remind me that there was a better life out there somewhere. That's why I wanted to live on the top floor. Unfortunately, my apartment building is only three stories high."

"You could go for a skyscraper."

"Maybe when I win the lottery."

"Or when you take that job at Vincenzo's?"

"Don't remind me that I'm in danger of throwing away everything I worked so hard to get."

"You shouldn't throw it away. Don't let what happened

at the restaurant take away everything you've achieved. You've lost too much already."

"I don't want to let that happen," she said. "I just don't know how to stop it."

"You have to fight fear, and from what I know about you, I'm sure at some point that will happen. You just need a little time."

"So tell me about your family," she said, changing the subject. "What are your parents like?"

"My parents are ... what's the right word ... adventurers."

"Really?" she asked, turning in her seat. "That sounds exciting."

"They're aging hippies," he said. "They met in Haight Ashbury in the late sixties. My father wore his hair in a ponytail and played in a band, and my mother was a tattoo artist."

"No way," she said in surprise. "And they had you?"

"What does that mean?" he asked, raising an eyebrow.

"Well, you're a cop, and you seem kind of buttoned up."

"That's because you've seen me on the job. I can let loose."

"Okay, if you say so," she said doubtfully.

"It's true." He paused. "Anyway, my parents grew up on Bob Dylan, flower power, and peace signs. They lived in a commune for a few years before they got married and grew organic produce. My mother even had a cow for a while, and to this day she is very proud of her milking skills."

"She sounds amazing."

"She's a character. So is my dad. After his band split up, he became a carpenter. He learned how to build cabinets, and little did he know that his business would become quite lucrative. He went from being a poor hippie to a successful businessman, although he still doesn't like to admit that. My mom eventually left her farming days behind and became a nurse/midwife."

"Again, she sounds amazing. They both do."

"It gets better," he continued.

"How is that possible?"

He shot her a dry smile. "They volunteer to help at every big catastrophe in the world. They went to New Orleans after Katrina, to Haiti after the earthquake, and right now they're planning a trip to Africa. They're big believers in we're all one family, one community, one planet. I spent a lot of summers building houses in Mexico."

"Now, I'm impressed by you, too."

"If that gets me one step closer to gaining your trust, I'll take it."

"So you have perfect parents."

"No, they're not perfect. They're nosy. They like to meddle. They're disorganized and always late, especially my mother. She likes to say that life is too short to wear a watch, whatever that means. Oh, and they hug way too much. You can't stop them, so don't even try. Just surrender. It goes quicker that way."

She smiled, touched by his words. "I can hear the love in your voice."

"They've been good to me."

"Tell me about your siblings. Are they just as wonderful?"

"My oldest brother, Connor, is a curator in a museum. I had no idea he could turn his love of dinosaurs into an actual profession, but somehow he did it. My little sister, Summer, is a dancer. And when she isn't on stage, she teaches ballet to first graders."

"And then there's you," she said. "The cop."

"Odd man out, not a creative bone in my body," he said.

"What did your hippie parents think of you becoming a

police officer?"

"My father was horrified. Like you, he doesn't have fond memories of the police force. He got arrested at several protests, and he doesn't like authority figures."

"But you did it anyway."

"It's what I wanted to do. And my parents always have been big believers in following your heart. So even though my heart took me to a job they don't particularly like, they still support me."

He had the kind of family she'd always dreamed about, loving, supporting, kind, and generous. "You're lucky," she said. As soon as the words left her mouth, she realized her mistake. "I mean, you're lucky that you have good parents and that you grew up in a loving home. Obviously, your current situation is not so great."

"Not even close to great. But that's going to change."

Wyatt fell silent as they exited the bridge and merged into the traffic heading north into Berkeley. They got off the freeway and drove up a very crowded University Avenue. While the nearby college was only in summer session, there were throngs of young people strolling the streets.

Leaving the city behind, they made their way up the narrow and winding hills behind the university, eventually stopping at the end of a long drive, behind four other cars. Beyond the drive, she could see a huge Mediterranean style house with peach-colored stucco and a red tile roof. There was a large front patio, a garden full of colorful flowers and several tiers of decks working their way around the house. On one of those decks was a large group of people, who appeared to be dressed up, and as Wyatt turned off the car engine, Adrianna could hear music playing.

"I thought we were just having dinner with your family," she said.

"We are having dinner."

"This is a party," she said pointedly.

He nodded. "It's my sister's engagement party."

"Are you serious?" She couldn't believe he was taking her to such an important family event. "Why didn't you tell me?"

"I didn't think you'd come if you knew."

"I absolutely wouldn't have come. I don't belong here."

"You wanted to know more about me. Everyone who knows me is here."

"I don't think I need to know that much."

He grinned. "It's too late now. Come on, the sooner we go in, the sooner we can leave."

"Soon won't be soon enough," she grumbled as she got out of the car.

Chapter Seven

Wyatt could feel Adrianna's tension as they headed up the driveway. She might not be happy to be with him, but he liked having her at his side. Family events were always awkward for him these days. No one knew what to say, so they either said too little or too much, just as Adrianna had guessed earlier. Usually, he tried to avoid the family occasions, but this was one event too important to skip. Hopefully, the dinner would serve two purposes. He'd make his dutiful appearance and he'd wipe away any lingering doubts Adrianna might have about helping him.

"Your parents must be rich," Adrianna said.

"I told you my dad accidentally made some money."

"Well, I'd like to *accidentally* make this much money," she said dryly. As they passed a waiter holding a tray of champagne glasses, Adrianna added, "Do you have a housekeeper?"

"Well, *I* don't live here, but my parents do have help. Although, my mother refers to Gloria as her good friend and not her housekeeper. She doesn't like class distinctions."

"But Gloria still cleans the toilets?"

"She does," he said with a nod. "But my parents also gave her extra money to pay for her daughter's college tuition. So it seems to all work out."

"Wyatt." His mother's excited voice broke out over the chatter of the guests on the deck. She ran down the front steps to greet him, her floor-length sundress flowing out behind her. She had dark brown hair that showed no trace of gray today, and her eyes were the same color blue as his. She wrapped her arms around him and squeezed tight. She smelled like peaches, an ingredient in her favorite shampoo. For some reason, the smell made him feel safe, as if home would solve all his problems. But this wasn't his home, he reminded himself. His home was with his daughter.

"I'm so glad you're here," she said, stepping back to give him a long look. Then she turned her gaze on Adrianna. "And you brought someone."

There was surprise in her eyes and no wonder. He'd made it clear to her that he had no intention of dating anyone until he had Stephanie back. He suddenly realized the number of questions he was going to have to field regarding Adrianna's presence.

"This is Adrianna Cavello," he said. "My mother, Daria Randall."

"It's nice to meet you," Adrianna said, extending her hand.

"And you, dear," his mother replied. "And we hug around here." She gave Adrianna's stiff body, a quick squeeze. "I hope you don't mind."

"I already warned her," Wyatt said.

"I feel like I'm intruding," Adrianna said as his mother released her. "Wyatt did not tell me this was an engagement party."

"Wyatt has always been full of surprises, but you're not intruding at all. We always have room for one more," Daria replied.

"Her favorite motto," he said to Adriana.

"It's true," Daria said, giving them both a big smile.

Then her lips turned down into a frown. "You look skinny, Wyatt. Are you eating?"

"Better now that I met Adrianna. She's a chef."

As expected, his mother turned to Adrianna with a whole host of questions. As they were talking, he looked around the crowd. His brother Connor was standing with his father and two other men. Connor gave him a wave, but he didn't move. He'd catch up with him later.

"Wyatt!" His sister squealed and came running across the deck, giving him a great big hug. Summer had light brown hair and the green eyes that matched their father. Today, there was a glowing smile on her face, and who could blame her? She'd put off her wedding for over a year because of Stephanie's disappearance. Finally, she'd given in and set a date, something she'd expressed some guilt about. But while he couldn't go on with his life, she needed to go on with hers, and he completely understood her decision.

"Thank you for coming," she said.

"You're welcome. You look happy," he added.

"I'm so happy," she said, her smile widening. "I have my whole family here, and so does Ron. It's perfect."

"I'm glad. This is my sister, Summer," he said, introducing her to Adrianna.

"Congratulations," Adrianna said.

"Thank you. I'm so glad you could come. Do you mind if I steal Wyatt for a minute. I promise it won't take too long."

"Uh ..." Adrianna sent him a pleading look, but he could hardly deny his sister at her engagement party.

"I'll take care of Adrianna," his mother said quickly, putting her arm around Adrianna's waist. "We'll get better acquainted. This will be fun."

"Yes, fun," Adrianna echoed somewhat weakly. "Hurry back."

"I will." He felt a little guilty for leaving Adrianna so

soon, but his sister was dragging him up the stairs and into the house.

They ended up in Summer's old bedroom. The room still bore the remnants of her youth, the posters of teen stars, the dance trophies and the enormous pile of stuffed animals on the bed. The furry brown bear in front made his gut clench. Summer had given Stephanie the same bear when she was born, and his daughter had loved that bear as if he were her best friend. But she hadn't taken the bear with her. Brown Bear, as Stephanie called him, had been laying on her bed, waiting for her to come home.

"Wyatt," Summer said, drawing his attention back to her.

"Sorry, what?"

"I know tonight is hard for you. I really appreciate you being here."

"I want you to be happy, Summer."

"I want *you* to be happy."

"I'm working on that."

"Mom said you had a lead. Is there any news?"

"Not yet. What did you want to talk to me about?"

She walked over and closed the door to her room. "I'm nervous, Wyatt. I love Ron. I've known him for four years, and I've wanted to marry him since our first date, but the closer the time comes to actually saying, *I do*, the more worried I become."

"Why?" he asked.

"Because of you and Jen. You were in love, too. You had a fairytale wedding. You left in a carriage with two white horses. It was beautiful."

"That was Jen's idea -- Jen and her mother," he added with an edge of bitterness. If Jen's mother hadn't spoiled her rotten, maybe she wouldn't have been so used to getting her own way in everything.

"It was such a perfect day," Summer continued. "And your first year was good, too, and then everything changed.

What if that happens to Ron and me? What if we wake up one day and we hate each other? I don't want to go through that kind of pain. I'm afraid."

"That won't happen."

"You didn't think it would happen to you."

He couldn't argue with that logic. "No, I didn't think it would go down that way," he admitted. "But love is a risk. No one knows what will happen. You put your heart on the line and hope no one breaks it. I don't think you have anything to worry about."

"Ron *is* wonderful. He treats me well, and he gets me."

"Then marry him. And stop thinking about my disaster of a marriage. You've got a great example right in front of you."

"Mom and Dad are still crazy about each other," she agreed.

"Still crazy in every way," he said with a grin.

"That's true." Her eyes clouded with tears. "I wanted Stephanie to be my flower girl, Wyatt. I had a dress all picked out for her. I couldn't ask anyone else to do it. And it's killing me that she's not going to be there. I love that kid. And part of me thinks it's wrong for me to have this wedding. I should wait."

He drew in a breath. "I appreciate the sentiment, but you've waited long enough. And there's still a chance I'll have her back before the wedding. We have a month."

She put her hand on his arm. "I really hope so. I'm sorry if I shouldn't have mentione Stephanie. I never know if I should talk about her or not."

"You can always talk about her. I wish she could be here, too."

"I didn't think it would take this long to get her back. I thought Jen would change her mind, or if she didn't, that you'd find them."

"That's still going to happen. We should get you back to the party." He held open the door for her.

As she walked through it, she said, "So who's the woman you brought with you?"

"She's a ... friend," he said. The word wasn't quite right. There was a connection between them that was more personal, more tense, but he couldn't explain that to his sister.

"She's beautiful with all that hair. Like a woman in an Italian painting."

When he didn't reply, Summer gave him a pointed look. "Don't tell me you haven't noticed."

"I've noticed."

"It's nice to see you with someone."

"Don't make any assumptions. She's just a friend," he repeated.

"Sometimes that's a good way to start," Summer said, a sparkle in her eye.

He knew he wasn't going to talk her out of anything, so he simply shrugged.

"You better go find Adrianna before Mom tells her all your dark secrets," Summer added as they walked down the stairs. "Or Mom starts showing her pictures from your childhood."

He nodded, then stopped abruptly as he saw Mandy enter the house.

Summer followed his gaze. "I'm sorry if she brings back bad memories, but she's dating Ron's best man. I had to invite her. And she's apologize to the family a number of times for not believing you right away."

"It's not a problem. I'd like to talk to her again."

"Really? Can it wait?"

"Don't worry. I'm not going to get into a fight with her."

"You know, it's fine if that happens. Whatever it takes to bring our girl home is okay with me."

"Thanks." As his sister walked away, he jogged down the stairs, catching up with Mandy in the living room. A short, busty redhead, Mandy had always been one of his favorites among Jen's friends. But their friendship had changed when Mandy had taken Jen's side.

Mandy stiffened when she saw him, but she held her ground. "Hello, Wyatt."

"Mandy," he said. "We could exchange polite conversation, but all I really want to ask you is if you've heard from Jen."

"You know I haven't," she said. "If she'd gotten in contact with me, I would have told you. I know now the things she said about you were lies. I'm sorry I ever doubted you. I didn't realize that Jen could be so devious or manipulative. And I never imagined that she could stay hidden so long."

"She has to have had help," he said.

"Her parents swear they don't know where she is. They're still friends with my folks. It came up again last Christmas."

Her answer jived with his investigation, so he let it go. "Right now I'm more interested in locating another woman about Jen's age. She has two kids, a boy about eleven or twelve and a girl about nine. The boy's name is Ben. Does that ring any bells?"

"I'm sorry, it doesn't," she said slowly. "Do you have some new information?"

He wouldn't tell her if he did, because he still didn't trust her. "I'm just following some leads."

"Maybe it's a new friend. Most people gave up on Jen after you won custody and she disappeared. No one wanted to get involved with her."

"It's possible that it's someone new," he said. "But what about someone further back in the past – maybe from high school?"

"That was a long time ago, Wyatt. I went away to college in another state. I didn't keep up with everyone."

"Just think, Mandy. It's important."

Mandy stared back at him for a long minute. "The only person I can think of is Rebecca Mooney. She has a boy and a girl and lives in San Francisco somewhere, but I don't think she and Jen have been friends in years."

"That name wasn't on anyone's list of Jen's friends." He'd been in contact with every person he'd ever heard Jen mention.

"I don't know if they've seen each other since high school. But she has a boy and a girl. I don't know the boy's name."

"Okay, I'll follow up on it."

"Do you really think Jen is in San Francisco?"

"I have a feeling she might have come back, or maybe she's been here all along."

"But she would have to know that you'd still be looking for her. It's hard to believe she'd risk getting caught now."

"Sometimes people start to believe they've gotten away with the perfect crime. That's usually when they mess up. If you hear anything, even if you don't think it's relevant —"

"I'll let you know," she said.

"Thanks." As he turned, he saw Adrianna in the hallway, surrounded by his mother, sister and an assortment of cousins. They all seemed to be talking at once and Adrianna looked a little like she was drowning. Time for a rescue.

* * *

"Did Wyatt tell you that he broke the national record in swimming when he was in college?" Daria asked.

"No, he didn't," Adrianna said, her mind now spinning with facts about Wyatt. She hadn't had to ask any questions. His mother and the rest of his family had been more than happy to share what appeared to be an endless supply of stories.

"He's so modest," Daria said.

"That doesn't sound like my big brother," Summer put in. "And if we're sharing personal records, you should know that Wyatt also set the record for the most beer drunk in a five-minute period."

"Oh, sh-sh," Daria said, shaking a finger at her daughter. "That was ages ago."

Summer laughed. "It still counts."

"Now tell us how you and Wyatt met," Daria suggested.

"Yes, tell us," Summer echoed.

"Well, we were both throwing coins in the Fountain of Wishes at McClellan Square and somehow they collided in mid air. Wyatt's coin knocked mine to the ground, and I went searching for it."

"And you found Wyatt instead," Daria said with a smile. "What a charming story."

"What's a charming story?" Wyatt asked as he joined the group.

"How you and Adrianna met."

"Oh, that," he said. "That was a fluke."

"Or maybe not," Summer said. "You were both making a wish."

"It wasn't to meet each other," he said sharply.

While Adrianna agreed with him, for some reason his quick denial irritated her a little bit -- also, his reference to their meeting being a fluke. Earlier, he'd implied that their meeting might be fate bringing him closer to his daughter. Now, she was being relegated to a chance flip of a coin?

"You can really be stupid," Summer told Wyatt, making a face at him. "I'm going to go find my smart husband-to-be."

Daria and Wyatt's cousin also excused themselves, leaving Wyatt and Adrianna alone in the hall.

"What did I say?" he asked Adrianna, confusion in his eyes.

"Nothing. Your family doesn't realize we're just friend. They want there to be something more."

He stared back at her. "Adrianna."

When he didn't keep going, she found her nerves tightening. "I'm hungry," she said, breaking the growing tension. "I think you promised me food."

He looked relieved by the change in subject. "I did. The buffet is in the dining room."

"Care to show me the way?"

"No problem. How about a drink first?" he asked. "It looks like you lost your champagne."

"I drank it in between stories about you. According to your family, you're a brilliant student, a talented athlete, a gifted musician –"

"Whoa, they did not say musician."

"You didn't play the clarinet in the 7th grade?"

"I did, but only at my mother's insistence. She wanted to see her boy in an orchestra. When we had the recitals, I didn't actually play. I just pretended."

"And she didn't know?"

He laughed. "I honestly don't know how she couldn't know. She heard me practice. I was terrible. Did she think I suddenly turned into a musician when I put on the shirt and tie and sat in the orchestra?"

"She's very proud of you. They all are."

Wyatt handed her a glass of punch. "This is spiked."

"Thank goodness," she said, taking a sip of the mango flavored rum punch. "I met your brother. He told me you'd received some medal for being injured on the job."

"It was stupid. I did nothing to deserve it."

She gave him a thoughtful look. "Are you really modest? Or just trying to put your best foot forward with me?"

"It really was nothing," he said. "I got shot in the shoulder. It was a graze. I've been hurt worse playing shortstop."

"I heard about your baseball career, too," she said.

He groaned. "I wasn't gone that long."

"Your mother talks really fast." She paused, taking another sip of punch. "What did Summer want to talk to you about?"

"She was having a panic attack about getting married."

"Really? Does she have reason to be worried? Have you met the groom?"

"He seems like a good guy. She was more concerned about following in my footsteps. I told her she'd never followed me in anything else, why start now?"

"That was nice of you, very big brotherly. I always wanted a big brother, someone to look out for me. She's lucky to have you and Connor."

"Most of the time she thinks I'm a pain in the ass. Connor -- she likes a little better. Ready for some food?"

"Did your mother make all this?" she asked, as they approached the buffet table. It appeared that most people were already eating, so there was no longer a line.

"She had it catered by some of Gloria's friends. You'll note the abundance of Mexican food."

"I love enchilada's," she said, grabbing a plate. "Actually, I love all food."

"What's the strangest thing you've ever eaten?" he asked, as she put some enchiladas on a plate.

"Probably sea urchin."

"Really? You ate sea urchin? Doesn't that have spikes?"

"It does, and it was part of a culinary class I took. It was on the menu one day. I didn't care for it, but I did learn how to cook it."

He shook his head. "And I thought I was being adventurous trying snails."

"Are you kidding? That's nothing. Snails taste just like chicken."

"I tried to tell myself that," he said with a laugh.

She grinned back at him. It was nice to see him in a lighter mood. He might have been dreading this visit home, but it was clear that being around his family was good for him. "I don't think I can fit anything else on my plate," she said.

He gazed down at her full plate and nodded. "I agree. Shall we find somewhere to eat?"

"I think there are some tables outside."

"I know a better place. Come with me."

A few minutes later, Wyatt led her into what appeared to be his old bedroom. She set her plate down on the desk and looked around. "So this is where the glory days began," she said, waving her hand toward the wide array of trophies.

"Right here," he said, sitting down on the double bed. "I would have thrown all the hardware out years ago, but my mother insists on keeping it. She says she paid for all my uniforms and batting lessons, and swimsuits, and the trophies are partly hers. I think she just likes to come here and pretend I'm still twelve instead of thirty-two."

"I think it's sweet."

"I think you should eat before your food gets cold."

She pulled out the desk chair and sat down. As she ate, she glanced at the books on the shelf in front of her. "You liked mysteries, didn't you?"

"I did until my life turned into one."

"Speaking of which ..." She turned sideways in her chair so she could see him. "I saw you having a rather intense conversation with a woman. What was that about?"

"That was Mandy, one of Jen's high school friends. I asked her if she knew anyone in the group who might have a boy named Ben and a girl about Steph's age."

"I assume she said no, or we'd already be on our way back to San Francisco."

"It's a long shot, but she gave me a name to check out – Rebecca Mooney."

"You have a name, and we're still here. You're showing amazing restraint."

"I searched the Internet on my phone before I came to get you."

She nodded, not at all surprised. "And …"

"And I texted Josh. He's at work tonight."

"So you have your bases covered."

"I knew I couldn't cut out on Summer that fast. She is my sister after all. And I really have no idea if Rebecca Mooney is anyone important." He paused, tilting his head. "So what do you think of me now? Have I convinced you that I'm a good guy?"

"Your parents certainly love you, but they're prejudiced." She paused for a moment, knowing that his serious eyes demanded a more serious answer. "I think I knew you were a good guy when our coins hit each other, and you tried to help me find my quarter."

"Really? So we could have skipped this dinner?"

She laughed. "I don't think *you* could have skipped it. They're really happy you came. They're probably less excited that we're hiding up here."

"You know that I'm not hiding you, right?"

"Oh, I know that. You're the one who's hiding. It's hard for you to be the center of attention. You're used to being the protector, the one looking out for everyone else. You don't know how to handle being the one who's in trouble."

"You're very perceptive, Adrianna."

"I'm used to studying people. I was a spectator of life for a very long time."

"I hope that doesn't continue. You don't want to miss out on the actual living part."

"I'm trying to get back there. I don't think you need to worry about your family. They'll be there to support you no matter what. And they understand that you can only give them what you can give right now. You're doing the best you can. No one can ask for more. So, do you still swim?"

He cleared his throat at the abrupt switch in subjects. "I usually hit the six a.m. workout at the local pool. What about you?"

"Never was a swimmer. My mom was too sick to teach me, and there weren't really any pools around. I can flap my arms around so I don't drown, but I don't get too far."

"I could teach you."

"Like you have time to do that."

"Well, not right now."

"I am impressed that you get a workout in so early in the morning. I'm not an early riser, but then I usually work late at the restaurant – or I used to," she amended.

"You will again. And my dedication to swimming is borne out of the desire not to succumb to the enormous stress I'm under. Swimming laps brings a sense of calm into my life. I need it to stay sane."

"Two years is a long time," she murmured, wondering again how he could hold it together for so long. "How do you not give up?"

He pulled Stephanie's picture out of his wallet and held it up. "I look at this face every day."

Her heart tore a little at the pain in his eyes. "I can't wait to meet her."

"I can't wait for you to meet her."

They exchanged a long, poignant look.

"One thing I don't understand," she said. "From everything you told me about Jennifer, it doesn't seem like she wanted to be a mother. Why did she take Stephanie? Why didn't she just take her freedom and go? It seems like that's what she wanted all along."

"I've asked myself that a million times. It had to be payback. Revenge. Most parental abductions have nothing to do with the child and everything to do with the spouse."

"She hated you that much?"

"She thought I was the one who got her arrested. I actually didn't know that she was driving under the influence at the time. But I was the one who forced her into rehab. I became her enemy."

"But all this time she's had to be a mother to your daughter. Did she decide after losing Stephanie that she wanted her after all?"

He considered her words for a moment. "That could be part of it. She always wanted things she couldn't have. What gets me through the night is the hope that she did discover a maternal instinct, that she loves Stephanie, and that she's taking care of her. I can't think about it any other way."

"Well, she took Stephanie and left everyone else in her life behind, that has to be love."

"Twisted love," he said bitterly. He put his empty plate aside. "Are you finished? Let's get out of this room. It's depressing."

"I think it's cute," she said. "I always wanted my own room. I didn't get one until I was twenty-three years old."

"Not even when you were living with your mom?"

"Nope. We shared a room. We were broke all the time, Wyatt. And once she died, I had to carry everything I had with me. If I put it down, it would be gone. So I hung on tight to the few tings I could keep."

"You have a nice apartment now."

"It's small, but it's home, and I love it."

He smiled. "You pulled yourself up by the bootstraps."

"Never wore boots. I don't find them at all comfortable."

"You know what I mean. You're impressive. But I have something else that's impressive to show you."

"Lead the way."

Chapter Eight

Wyatt took Adrianna down the hall and up a set of narrow, twisting stairs. He pushed open the door at the top and helped her out onto a flat portion of the roof. She'd told him that as a child she'd felt very small surrounded by skyscrapers and steep hills. He wanted to give her a different perspective on the city.

As she stepped out, she drew in a quick breath of startled surprise. "Oh, wow," she said, moving across the deck to stand at the rail. "What an incredible view."

It was an amazing view. From their spot high up in the Berkeley hills, they could not only see the city of Berkeley but the lights of San Francisco and two spectacular bridges, the Bay Bridge and the Golden Gate. It was a clear night, plenty of stars in the sky, and an almost full moon.

"The city is so pretty from here," Adriana murmured.

He moved next to her, his shoulder brushing hers. "I thought you might like to see it from up high."

"It's a much better view than the one I get from apartment."

"This is my favorite spot in the house. Whenever I was frustrated or pissed off or just wanting to grow up already, I used to come out here. The city called to me. I knew one day it would be my home."

"I like San Francisco," she said. "But it was more my home by default than anything else. I focused on working my way up in the city, never considering that I might go somewhere else."

"Why should you? The city has everything."

"It does," she said with a little sigh.

He gave her a shoulder a nudge. "What are you thinking?"

She turned to face him. "That I wish I'd had somebody to show me this view when I was a little girl. I imagined it, but I was so overwhelmed by my small place in the world, that I couldn't quite see the big picture. I just had to focus on what was right in front of me."

"That's not a bad way to go," he said. "Sometimes you can get distracted by all the choices."

She nodded. "Thanks for bringing me up here."

As he gazed into her eyes, he was struck by how pretty she looked in the moonlight, her hair clouding around her face, the sparkle in her expressive brown eyes, her soft, sweet lips. His gaze dropped to her mouth, and he heard her quick intake of breath. When he raised his eyes to hers, he saw the gleam and uncertainty of desire.

This time, he was the one who had to search for breath. His chest felt tight. His heart started pounding against his chest, and he felt an irresistible pull that sent his arms around her waist and his mouth down on hers.

She tasted like chili and hot peppers, or maybe that was just the heat running through his body. His demanding kiss parted her lips, and he slipped his tongue inside her mouth, so he could taste more of her. The sweet moist cavern of her mouth made him think of all the other places on her body that he wanted to taste, to touch. He'd been holding desire back, but now it was flooding past his defenses, and he couldn't stop the need that ran through him.

A need she must have felt, too, because she was kissing him back, running her hands around his back, her fingers seeking the skin beneath his shirt. He wanted to strip off his shirt and hers, too. He wanted to drag his mouth down the side of her jaw, to the curve of her neck, the valley of her breasts. He wanted to lay her down on the hard cold stone of the deck and warm her from the inside out.

"Stop, wait," Adrianna said, pulling back. "I – I don't think this is a good idea."

He couldn't think at all.

She slipped out of his arms, smoothing down her clothes, putting a hand to her hair, fingers to her lips. And all he could do was stare at her.

Reason came back slowly.

She turned away from him and looked out at the view.

He drew in a breath, and then another. Finally, he said. "I'm sorry."

"I don't want an apology," she said, casting him a quick look.

"What do you want?"

"Nothing. I just … we can't do this. It's not the right time."

He shoved his hands into his pockets. "I know. I wasn't thinking."

"Neither was I."

A moment or two passed in cooling silence.

"We should go back inside," Adrianna said.

He caught her arm as she moved past him. "Adrianna –"

"Don't say anything. It was just a moment. I got caught up in the view, and I think the punch had something to do with it."

She could blame the view and the punch, but he knew that his reasons for kissing her had nothing to do with those factors. He was attracted to her, and he liked her – probably too much. And for a short time, he'd let himself forget that the only reason they were together was to find Stephanie.

"Are you still going to help me tonight?" he asked sharply.

Her gaze met his. "Yes. I'll go to Vincenzo's. I'll wait in the alley with you. And we'll see what happens."

* * *

Adrianna's pulse was still racing when she left the roof and went downstairs, acutely aware of Wyatt following close behind her. She must have been out of her mind to kiss him, and not just a brief, innocent kiss, but a carnal lover type kiss. She drew in a shaky breath.

What the hell had she been thinking?

He wasn't the right man. This wasn't the right place or the right time.

Part of her wanted to run home and hide in her apartment the way she'd been doing the past two months, but she'd made him a promise, and she always kept her promises. Plus, she wouldn't want him to think that a kiss could send her back into hiding. A really, really good kiss.

What the hell had he been thinking?

But figuring out Wyatt's motivation was a little too much for her, so instead she concentrated on saying goodbye to his friends and family. It took them almost thirty minutes to get out of the house. By the time they got into the car, she'd been invited to Summer's wedding the next month. All efforts to say anything but yes were rebuffed, so she'd eventually given up, figuring she could always bow out later.

Wyatt didn't say anything until they had been in the car for fifteen minutes and were about to get on the Bay Bridge. Once they passed the toll booth, he seemed to relax.

"That wasn't so bad," he muttered.

"Are you talking to me or to yourself?" she asked.

"Maybe both of us."

She didn't know how to respond to that cryptic comment and was relieved when they passed across Treasure Island, and he pointed to the lights of the stadium up ahead.

"Looks like there's a Giants game tonight," he said.

"Are you a fan?"

"Oh, yeah. My dad tried to get me into the Oakland A's, but I was always a Giants fan. What about you?"

"I've been to a few games," she said, happy to be talking about baseball. She'd been afraid he would bring up their kiss again, and she really didn't want to go there. "My friend, Lindsay, had a crush on one of the players once, so we spent some time at the park and in the parking lot, hoping to catch a glimpse of the guy walking to his car," she added. "It was really stupid. I felt like a groupie."

"You don't seem like someone who would be impressed by a ballplayer."

"They can be kind of hot," she said.

"Did your friend ever meet her crush?"

"Not at the park, but he came into Vincenzo's one night with a couple of his friends. He was a jerk. Lindsay got over her love fast, and we had a celebration when he got traded to San Diego." She paused as he took the first exit off the bridge. "It's only nine-thirty. I think we should wait until at least eleven before we go to Vincenzo's. The kids wouldn't show up until the evening rush was over."

"All right. Do you mind if we stop by my place? I want to grab a coat. It's not too far from here."

"Sure, I guess. Maybe I should change, too."

"We'll hit my place first, then yours."

* * *

Wyatt's place was a two-bedroom townhouse not far

from the ballpark. As she lingered in the living room, Wyatt disappeared down the hall. She took the opportunity to look around a little.

His apartment was more spacious and less cluttered than hers. The furniture was all brown leather and dark wood. She saw no feminine touch in the decorations. She wondered if he'd thrown out all of Jennifer's things. Moving into the kitchen, she noted the empty counters and the very clean appliances. She doubted Wyatt put his stove and oven through much of a workout. She opened the pantry door and found six boxes of cereal and not much else.

"No, I don't cook," he said, walking into the room.

She quickly closed the cabinet. "Sorry, I was snooping."

"I figured."

"You like cereal."

"You've discovered my deep, dark secret. It's fast, easy, and it's allegedly loaded with vitamins."

"Don't forget the sugar."

He shrugged. "I work that off in the pool."

His words drew her gaze to his broad chest, his long, lean legs, and made her foolishly wonder just what he'd look like in a bathing suit – or nothing. Her cheeks burning, she turned back to the pantry. "You should get some other staples, rice, noodles, things you can whip into something else."

"That would require cooking."

"You might enjoy it," she said, turning back around.

"I'll cook again when Stephanie comes home," he said. "I'll make all her favorites, spaghetti and meatballs, mac and cheese, barbecued chicken – whatever she wants."

"So you do know how to cook, you just don't want to."

"It's not fun doing it for one."

"I understand. I enjoy cooking at the restaurant more than just for myself, or at least I did," she amended.

"You will again," he said confidently.

"How can you be so sure?"

"Because I'm getting to know you, and I don't think you're a quitter. You've just had a setback."

"Well, I hope so." She paused. "Can I see Stephanie's room?"

He started with surprise, his eyes hesitant.

"Unless ..." she began.

"No, it's fine. It's just that no one has been in there for awhile." He led her down the hall, pausing in front of a closed door. "I haven't changed anything since she left."

"I figured."

He opened the door, and she stepped inside.

Where the rest of the apartment was sparse and very male, this room was all girl -- pink walls, and a pink and white rug that matched the white furniture and bright pink bedding. There were books and toys and a massive number of stuffed animals on the unmade bed.

He hadn't even made the bed.

She'd heard the pain of loss in his voice, but now she could see it. Wyatt hadn't even been able to pull the sheets up on the bed. It wasn't that he hadn't changed anything; he hadn't touched anything either. Or maybe he had ... The pillow was slightly flattened.

He must have followed her gaze, because he said, "I used to lay down on the bed and think about her. I haven't done that in a long time."

"How long?"

"I don't know -- maybe a year. I closed the door after the first anniversary. It got too hard to walk down the hall every night, to remember all the times I read to her. She'd fall in love with a story and have to hear it every day for weeks on end, until we had it memorized. And she loved that bear," he said, pointing to the brown bear on the bed. "She called him Brown Bear."

"Very creative," she said dryly.

He grinned. "I know. We tried to get a bunch of other names to stick, but he was always just Brown Bear. She couldn't go to bed without him. She'd rub his shiny nose as she was drifting off to sleep. Jennifer knew that she adored the bear, but she didn't care. She took her without taking her favorite toy. I bet Stephanie cried for weeks." His lips tightened. "Jen should have at least taken the bear with her. Would that have been too much to ask?"

"Maybe she got her another one."

"You can't just replace something or someone you love."

She knew he wasn't talking about the bear anymore. She put a hand on his arm, feeling his tense muscles, wanting to ease his anguish. "I'm so sorry, Wyatt. I can't even imagine what you've gone through. Being in here it makes it so much more real. She's all around you, the things she liked, the pictures she drew, the clothes she wore…"

"That's why I had to stop coming in. It was too real." He drew in a ragged breath. "I didn't change things in here, because when Stephanie comes back, I don't want her to think that I moved on without her." He paused. "But the reality is that Steph probably won't even like the room when she comes back. She'll be so much older. Who knows if she'll still want pink everything?"

"So you'll paint and change the furniture. That's easy."

"Yeah, I'll do that. But what if she doesn't want to be here at all?"

Now she saw real fear in his eyes. He wasn't just scared that he wouldn't find his daughter, he was terrified that when he did find her, she wouldn't want him anymore."

"She'll want to come home," she said.

"Her home has been somewhere else for two years. I think about all the holidays she's lived through, the birthdays she's had, the things she learned, the places she's been. Jennifer could have married someone else. Steph could have a stepfather, or worse she could just be exposed to a random number of men –"

"Stop," she said, holding up a hand as his rant gained steam. "You'll drive yourself crazy thinking about every possible scenario."

"Too late. I've already thought of them all. Can you honestly say I'm wrong to worry?"

"No, you're not wrong, but it's not doing you any good. One thing I learned from my childhood is that you have what you have. And you have to live with it. Thinking about the past or the future is pointless. The only thing that matters is the moment you're living in. Surviving, enjoying, loving, whatever emotion you're feeling, that's all you get. That's it."

He stared back at her. "That sounds easy, but you're not a parent. You don't know what it's like to lose your child. I could handle whatever happened to me, but I was supposed to protect her, Adrianna. That was my job."

And she could see that was where the real sense of failure came in. Wyatt was a cop, a born protector, but he couldn't be there for the one person he loved the most. "You will get her back, Wyatt. And then you'll deal with what happened and what comes next. She's a little girl. She's going to need you for a long time."

He blew out a rough breath. "Sometimes, the waiting gets to me. The calendar is not my friend, the days ticking away. I want to stop time on one hand, and then on the other I want to speed ahead to the moment when I get my daughter back."

She gave him a compassionate smile. "For what it's worth, Wyatt, I'm in. I'll help you in any way I can."

"That means a lot to me. I can't tell you how many people have already given up."

"Well, I have fresh energy and new eyes. Speaking of which, do you have any pictures of Jennifer? It might help me to know what she looks like, too."

Wyatt stared back at her. "Yeah, I have some pictures."

Showing her photos of his ex-wife appeared to be the last thing he wanted to do, but he led her out of Stephanie's room and into the living room. He pulled open a drawer in the entertainment center. "There you go, have at it." And then he disappeared down the hall again.

She knelt down on the floor and saw a pile of framed photos that had obviously been on display at one time. The first one was a picture of a pretty blonde woman sitting next to a two-year-old. Jennifer and Stephanie, she surmised. It was the kind of photo you'd get from one of the photography places in the mall. Neither Jennifer nor Stephanie looked too excited about the event, but they were a pretty pair with their golden blonde hair and somewhat matching outfits.

The next photo took her further back in time to Wyatt and Stephanie's wedding. Jennifer looked much happier. She wore a spectacularly pretty wedding dress with a very long train. The picture had been taken at what appeared to be the reception. There was a mansion in the background as well as a horse and carriage decorated with white flowers.

"Wow," she murmured, rocking back on her heels.

Her amazement grew at the next photo, which featured Wyatt in his tuxedo, holding his bride in his arms. They looked good together, happy. In fact, Jennifer was gazing up at Wyatt with adoration in her eyes, as if he were the only man in the world for her.

For that moment, their love seemed to burn bright.

Putting the photo aside, she moved quickly through the others. Jennifer's happiness seemed to dim with each subsequent year, as if she were slowly fading away.

"Are you done?" Wyatt asked abruptly, stopping a few feet away from her, a hard look in his blue eyes.

"You had a fairytale wedding."

"That turned into a nightmare."

"I'm surprised you went for such an over-the-top

reception."

"I had no choice. I was just the groom. Jennifer and her mother planned everything out. Her parents are loaded, so money wasn't an object. And she was their only daughter -- their princess. They wanted her to have everything. According to Jen, all women want a fantasy wedding."

"I don't," she said.

He gave her a doubtful look. "Why not? I would think having had such a shitty childhood that you would want to celebrate with a big bash."

"I just think it's crazy to spend so much money on a single party. I'm more interested in building a life with someone, having a house, a yard for kids to play in, all that stuff. It's not a wedding that's important; it's a marriage."

"I completely agree."

She put the framed photos back in the drawer. "I'm surprised you kept these."

"I broke a bunch the first week. Cut my hand up pretty good on one of them. I had to go to the hospital for stitches. When I came back, my mom and sister had taken all the pictures of Jennifer down and cleaned up the broken glass. I didn't know they were in the drawer for a few months."

"Well, Stephanie is in some of the pictures. You wouldn't want to lose those."

"That's what I figured. Have you seen enough?"

"Yes, I'm ready to go."

* * *

After stopping at her apartment so she could change into jeans and a sweater, Adrianna suggested they walk to the restaurant. Parking was difficult in North Beach, especially at a Saturday night, and Wyatt had been lucky enough to find a free spot on her block.

When they arrived at Vincenzo's a little after eleven, Adrianna started to regret her decision to come to the alley.

She'd been distracted by Wyatt's problems, but returning to the scene of her trauma was still rough. As she walked behind the restaurant, she felt her earlier panic return. It was dark now, and all the ominous shadows took her back to the night two months ago.

Wyatt's arm came around her shoulders as if he'd read her mind.

"You can do it," he said. "It's just an alley. There's nothing going on out here. There's no one around."

"I know. I just keep hearing those shots in my head. I don't think I'll ever forget the sound or the moment when I realized that they had come from inside the restaurant. When I ran inside, I knew what I would find, but I was still shocked –"

"Sh-sh," he said, pausing in their walk to look at her. "Stay in the present. Follow the advice you gave me earlier. Don't think about what happened that night. Just what we're doing here now."

She wanted to follow his advice, but her head was starting to spin.

"Focus on me," he added, putting his hands on her shoulders.

Their gazes locked, as he kneaded her tight muscles.

"You're wound up tight," he said.

She couldn't speak. She wanted to relax, but she didn't know how to make that happen. Fear had a hold of her. For almost two months she'd hidden out in her apartment, afraid to feel the pain she'd felt that night.

"It's too much," she muttered.

"You're okay," he said. "Just keep looking at me."

She felt like she was drowning in his dark blue gaze, and somewhere in that moment her fear changed to something else. Her heart beat faster and her palms were sweaty, but she wasn't thinking about the robbery; she was thinking about the man who was standing so close to her and how her breasts were pressed against his chest. She was thinking about the kiss they'd shared earlier on the roof of his parents' house and how very much she wanted to do it again. She could kiss him and everything else would fade from her mind.

Tingles ran down her spine as his fingers tightened on her shoulders, the sharp, hungry gleam in his eyes telling her that he felt the very same need.

One of them needed to call a halt, but this time she couldn't find the words.

His hand moved through her hair, cupping the back of her head, tilting her face towards his. It seemed like things were happening in slow motion. The kiss before had started out hard and fast. It had surprised her. This time she had a million opportunities to move away, but she couldn't break the spell between them. And when his mouth touched hers, a spark of heat ran through her.

She closed her eyes, sinking into the kiss, letting herself do nothing but feel. Her senses were alive with something wonderful. She didn't feel sad or angry or guilty, she just felt good – remarkably, incredibly good.

And then the back door of the restaurant opened, and light from the kitchen lit up the shadows.

She jumped back at the sound of her name.

Lindsay came through the door, letting it clang shut behind her.

"Adrianna, what are you doing out here?" Lindsay asked.

"Uh," She had to think for a moment. She was still reeling from Wyatt's kiss, but she certainly couldn't tell Lindsay that. Her gaze caught on the cigarette in Lindsay's hand, and she jumped on it like a drowning woman who suddenly sees a life jacket. "You're smoking again? You said yesterday you were going to quit."

"I'm still trying, and jeez how do you happen to show up every time I want to take a smoke?" Lindsay paused, giving Wyatt a long look. "Who's the dude?"

"This is Wyatt Randall. He's a cop," she said, not sure why she'd added the tag, except that she suddenly felt like she needed a reason to be with him.

"You're working on Will's murder?" Lindsay asked.

"Among other things," Wyatt said tersely.

"What other things?" Lindsay asked, not one to be sidetracked when she sniffed a story.

"He's looking for his daughter," Adrianna answered. "We think she might be one of the kids who used to come by here looking for food. That's why we're here. We're hoping they might come back. You haven't seen them, have you?"

"No. I haven't seen them in weeks," Lindsay said, her eyes still very curious. "Maybe someone else has. Have you asked around?"

"No, I should," she said, knowing that would entail going into the kitchen.

"I'll do it," Wyatt said abruptly. "I want to show the staff the photo."

When Wyatt disappeared inside the restaurant, Lindsay turned on her with eager eyes. "Well, you are full of surprises. Tell me more about you and the hot cop."

"There's nothing to tell. I'm helping him look for his daughter," she said, hoping the warmth in her face was not revealing her lie.

"He had his arms around you."

"It's not what you think. He was just calming me down. I had a little panic attack when I got here."

Lindsay gave her a speculative look. "I can believe that, but still there's something else going on here. I know you, Adrianna. You do not get close to people very easily. It took five years for Will to talk you into bed."

"I'm not in bed with Wyatt," she said.

"That red on your cheeks suggest you've thought about it."

"I barely know him," she said, certain now that telling

Lindsay about their kiss would be a big mistake.

"Like I said, you don't usually let people get that close to you so fast. When we go to bars, you practically wear a sign that says don't approach me."

"I'm not that bad. Anyway, getting back to Wyatt... His ex-wife kidnapped his daughter a couple of years ago, and there's a possibility his little girl is running around with the kids I saw."

"That's crazy. His ex-wife is a kidnapper?" She shook her head. "Will always said you should have called the police about those kids."

"Don't remind me. I already feel guilty."

"Sorry. I know you were just trying to help them because of the way you grew up."

"I made a mistake. I'm trying to do better now."

"At least you have something else to think about besides what happened here." Lindsay paused. "Stephan said he sent some food home with you last night."

"Yes, and it wasn't very good. What's going on in the kitchen?"

Lindsay made a face. "Roberto is in charge. He changes all my sauces. He thinks everything needs more garlic."

"I can't believe Stephan is letting Roberto take over. You should be running things."

"He knows my limits," Lindsay said honestly. "I'm good at sauces but not at managing everyone else and getting the plates out on time. We need you, Adrianna. And I think you might need the restaurant, too. It's a good sign that you're this close to the kitchen door. Want to step inside?"

"I do want to," she said. "For the first time since it happened, I really do want to come back." She didn't know exactly when she'd made that decision but now that she'd said it aloud, she felt even better about it.

"Good," Lindsay said with an approving smile. "You

want to try now?"

"No."

"Adrianna!"

"I'm working up to it."

"All right. I won't push." Lindsay turned and then glanced back at her. "If there was something going on with you and the hot cop, it would be okay. You know that, don't you?"

"It's way too soon for me to be thinking about getting involved with anyone."

"So don't get involved. Just have some fun."

"Wyatt is not looking for fun right now."

"Then pick someone else."

"I don't need a man. I'm fine on my own."

Lindsay laughed. "You're *so* not fine. You're young, Adrianna. There are going to be other men in your life. Will would not expect you to stay single forever."

"We're not talking about forever."

"You never wanted to talk about *forever* with Will either," Lindsay said, her expression filled with speculation. "I've thought a lot about that last night when we found the ring. You were shocked. You did not want Will to propose to you."

"I wasn't ready."

"I could see that. It occurred to me later that you might never have been ready. Maybe Will wasn't the one. If you were really in love with him, you would have wanted to see that ring. You wouldn't have been so scared."

"I don't know why I reacted the way I did. Will was such a good guy, the perfect guy," she said. "I shouldn't have had any doubts."

Lindsay gave her a commiserating smile. "Those men are the hardest ones to break up with. You feel like an idiot, because a million other girls would want them, so you ask yourself, why don't I? Love isn't logical or practical or even smart sometimes. It just is. You can't help who you love …

or who you don't. And you need to stop beating yourself over the head with guilt." She blew out a breath. "I've been wanting to say that for a while, but I didn't think you were ready to hear it."

"You're right – I wasn't ready before to hear that."

"You're getting better. You're coming back to life. I can see it in your eyes. I'm glad."

"Me, too."

Lindsay paused as the back door opened. "I better get back to work. I'll call you tomorrow."

"Okay."

Wyatt held the door opened for Lindsay, who gave him a long look on her way back into the restaurant. Then he joined her by the dumpster, his gaze showing more frustration. "No one inside recognized the kids, although you might have better luck. I got a lot of wary looks when I showed my badge."

"I'm sure they would have said something."

He stared back at her. "About what happened before –"

"Let's not talk about it."

"A few hours ago, I told myself I was not going to kiss you again."

"I told myself the same thing."

He stared at her, his expression hard and unreadable. "I don't know why –"

"I really don't think we should talk about this now," she said, cutting him off. "We need to focus on why we're here. And I was thinking that maybe Josephine, the owner of Joe's Bar, could help us. She is very connected to the homeless population. We could go see her tomorrow. I'm sure you've already checked all the shelters."

"A hundred times, and they all have the photo from the security camera. But I'll talk to whoever you think would be helpful." He let out a sigh and ran a hand through his hair. "I feel like a hamster on a wheel. I go around and around, and I never get anywhere. I've done all of this a thousand times since Steph disappeared. I feel like I've showed her picture to almost everyone in this city and another thousand or so around L.A. where Jennifer's parents live. I was convinced for a long time that she'd taken Stephanie there. There are a lot more places to hide, cities within big counties, many different police departments."

She couldn't imagine how it felt to be two years into the search. For her, it was new, there were lots of possibilities to try, but for him, everything had been done not, once or twice but dozens of times.

"Do you ever take a break?" she asked.

"Not very often," he replied.

"How do you not go crazy?"

He sighed. "I try to concentrate on the positive outcome. But I'm human. I get tired. I think about other things once in a while. I've spent entire afternoons watching a ballgame. I've had dinner with friends."

"And probably felt guilty the whole time," she said.

"Yes," he admitted. "But like you said, two years is a long time. I almost lost my job the first year because I took so much time off, and I was so distracted I made mistakes. Eventually, I realized that I needed to work, not only to make money, but because I needed to do something for someone else. I needed to help another family find their answers."

"I'm sure you helped a lot."

For a few minutes there was nothing but quiet between them. Then a door opened further down the alley, and they both tensed. But it was just someone taking out the garbage from another restaurant down the street.

In the distance, she could hear music coming from one of the clubs, and occasionally they heard laughter or loud voices from the nearby street, but there were no children roaming about.

Some time around midnight, Lindsay brought them

two paper cups filled with coffee and a bag of cookies. She didn't say anything, but her pointed gaze told Adrianna there would be questions to answer in the morning.

    By one a.m., Adrianna's legs were aching and the chill in her body had turned to cold. But she no longer felt that strange about being in the alley. Her fear had dissipated. The shadows no longer seemed as scary. Maybe the same would happen if she went into the restaurant, if she faced the memories, instead of continuing to run away from them.

    "Let's go," Wyatt said abruptly.

    "You don't want to wait until two?" she asked in surprise.

    "You're freezing."

    "I can hang in a while longer."

    "Are you sure?"

    "Yes." Her gaze caught on a small moving shadow in the distance, one she'd seen before. "I think I see someone," she murmured. She stepped out into the light. "Ben, is that you?"

Chapter Nine

The shadow shifted, came closer. Adrianna moved down the alley. "I have some food," she said, holding up the bag of cookies that neither she nor Wyatt had touched.

A moment later, Ben stepped out of the shadows. She couldn't believe her eyes. It was really him. Their gamble had paid off.

"Who's he?" Ben asked, keeping some distance between them.

"He's a friend," she said. "I was worried about you Ben. I haven't seen you in a while."

"Did you say you have some food?"

"Cookies," she said, holding out the bag. "If you want more, I can go in the restaurant and get you something else." She couldn't believe those words had actually come out of her mouth, but there they were.

"Where are the other kids?" Wyatt interrupted.

Ben stiffened. "I don't know what you're talking about."

She knew Wyatt was impatient to find the girls, but they would get further if they didn't scare Ben away.

"I saw the girls you were with by the fountain in the square yesterday," she said. "They're not with you tonight?"

"No."

"What are their names?" Wyatt asked.

"I don't know," Ben said, edging away.

Adrianna had a feeling he was a breath away from taking off.

"Was one of them named Stephanie?" Wyatt demanded.

"Why do you care?"

"Because she's my daughter."

Surprised flashed in Ben's eyes. "You're lying. She doesn't have a dad."

"She does. And I've been looking for her for a long time."

"He's telling the truth, Ben," Adrianna added. "If you know where the girls are, you have to tell us. We just want to help."

"I said I don't know where they are."

"When and where did you see them last?" Wyatt asked.

His harsh tone made Ben bolt, and Wyatt was after him in a split second. Ben didn't get more than ten yards before Wyatt grabbed him and spun him around and up against the wall.

Wyatt was in full cop mode, and she doubted he even saw that Ben was a twelve-year-old boy. He was just someone who was stonewalling him.

"I asked you a question," Wyatt said. "Start talking."

She could see the fear in Ben's eyes, and for a split second, she flashed back on herself as a kid and another cop breathing down her neck. "Wyatt, stop, you're scaring him," she said, walking quickly down the alley.

"He's not going anywhere until he tells me where the girls are."

"A woman took them away," Ben said, his eyes wide with fear.

"What woman?"

"My mom's friend."

"When was this?"

"A couple of weeks ago."

"Where did they go?"

"They didn't say," Ben said, struggling in Wyatt's grip.

"And you have no idea where they are now?"

"No."

"You better not be lying," Wyatt warned.

"I'm not. I swear."

"Wyatt, ease up," she said, moving closer to them. Wyatt shot her a dark look, as if he did not want her interference, but she didn't care. They were getting nowhere fast with his tactics. He stepped back, but he didn't let go of Ben's arm.

"Ben, where are you staying?" she asked, sending the boy a reassuring smile.

"Around," he said vaguely.

"Why don't you come home with me tonight? I can fix you something to eat, and you can tell us everything you know about the girls."

"I can't go home with you. You're a stranger."

"My name is Adrianna Cavello, and this is Wyatt Randall."

"So what?"

"So, we may be strangers, but we want to help you. Is someone waiting for you?" she asked.

"Yeah, sure. There are lots of people waiting for me."

"Well, then they can wait," she said, not believing him for a second. His face and hands were dirty and so were his clothes. She'd bet any amount of money that he'd been spending a lot of time on the street. "I just live a few blocks away," she added. "What do you say? It's cold out here, don't you think?"

"Is he going to be there?"

"Damn right I am," Wyatt said.

"Forget it," Ben retorted.

"You look like a smart kid, Ben, so I'll lay it out for you," Wyatt said. "We can either go to Adrianna's apartment or we can go to the police station."

"I knew you were a cop," Ben said sullenly.

"Then you should know better than to argue with me. It's your choice. What's it going to be?"

"We don't want to hurt you, Ben," Adrianna said reassuringly. "I promise you can trust me on that."

He didn't look like a kid who knew how to trust anyone, but he was caught between two bad choices, and he knew it.

"All right," he said. "I'll go with you, but I don't know anything."

"Don't even think of running," Wyatt said as he let go of Ben's arm. "Because the next time I catch you, you're going to jail."

She frowned at his rough tactics. "He's not going to run," she said firmly. "Come on, Ben, walk with me."

She was grateful that she didn't live far away, because she suspected that with every step Ben was concocting a plan to get away from them. But Wyatt was sticking to his other side, and she had no doubt that he would make good on his promise to chase Ben down if he was foolish enough to run.

She was relieved when they reached her building. Once they entered her apartment, she felt even better. Hopefully Ben would be able to tell them something that would help them find Stephanie.

"I'll make you some food," she said. "What do you like to eat?"

"Anything," he said, following her into the adjacent kitchen.

"How about scrambled eggs, pancakes and bacon," she suggested.

"That sounds okay," he said carelessly, but his eyes lit up at the thought.

"I love eating breakfast at night," she said. "It used to be a treat I shared with my mom."

"I like breakfast any time," he said.

Glancing past Ben, she saw the impatient frown on Wyatt's face. He wanted to get straight down to business, but she sent him a silent plea to go easy.

Wyatt took a seat at the counter. He pulled out the photo of his daughter and handed it to Ben. "Is this one of the girls you were with?"

"It kind of looks like her," he said.

"What's her name?"

"Emily," Ben said, apparently deciding that saying he didn't know wasn't going to work anymore.

"Emily what?"

Ben shrugged.

"She's not your sister, is she?"

"No, she's not."

Adrianna spun around at that answer. "So the other girl is your sister?"

"Sara is, yeah," he said. "Emily was just staying with us. Then her mom came and got her. She took Sara, too." Ben paused. "Can I have that banana?"

"Of course," Adrianna said, pushing the fruit bowl across to him.

"Where were you staying when this woman came to get Stephanie?" Wyatt asked.

"She said her name was Emily," Ben replied.

"Emily – whatever," Wyatt said impatiently.

"We were staying at a motel – the Fantasy Inn."

"Who was with you?"

"My mom and the girls and sometimes Rudy hung out there."

"Who's Rudy?" Wyatt asked.

"Some old dude who bangs my mom."

"Where is your mother now?" Wyatt asked.

"She's out somewhere."

As Ben continued to make short answers, Adrianna could sense Wyatt's anger beginning to burn. She paused from scrambling the eggs to say, "Here's the thing, Ben. We think Emily is in trouble and that the woman she was with might have kidnapped her."

Ben stared back at her. "She said she was Emily's mom," he repeated.

"She is her mother. She's also my ex-wife," Wyatt said, "And she stole Steph — Emily from me. She didn't have custody because she was a drug addict. She couldn't take care of our child, so the courts gave me custody. Her name was Jennifer."

Ben looked confused. "I don't know anything about that."

"What was the relationship between your mother and the woman who took Emily away?" Wyatt asked.

"They worked together at a club."

Wyatt sat up straighter. "What's the name of the club?"

"Ricky's. My mom said she was a waitress, but she's a stripper. She thinks I'm too stupid to figure that out." He paused. "Can I have cheese on my eggs?"

"Of course," Adrianna said, as she poured the eggs into a fry pan. She grabbed cheese out of the fridge and started grating while the bacon was in the microwave. It felt good to be cooking again, and it also felt good to be getting somewhere. Ben had finally given them information they could follow up on.

"Ricky's was closed down last month," Wyatt said. "What's your mother doing now?"

"I don't know."

"Why did your sister go with Emily?" Adrianna cut in. Something about the situation wasn't adding up. Why would Jennifer want to take another child with her?

"Because Emily was screaming she wouldn't go unless we went with her, but the woman said she couldn't take both of us, so she took Sara."

"And left you alone?" she asked, outraged at the thought.

Ben shrugged. "I'm old enough to be on my own."

"How old are you?" Wyatt asked.

Ben straightened on the stool. "Sixteen."

Wyatt shook his head. "Try again, kid."

"Fine, I'm fourteen."

"I'm betting you're closer to twelve."

"What does it matter to you?"

"You don't seem to have anyone looking after you."

"My mom's around. She's just out tonight."

"And the other nights when you went begging for food."

"She's had a hard time. She does the best she can," Ben said.

Adrianna inwardly sighed. Ben was protecting his mother, even though it was clear his mother wasn't interested in protecting him.

"I need to find the girls," Wyatt said. "Where should I look, Ben?"

"I tried to find them already," Ben replied. "They weren't in any of the usual places. The lady said she'd bring Sara back when my mom got home."

"And when is that supposed to be? Don't tell me you don't know."

"I don't know," Ben said with a sullen expression.

"Can you give me a list of the places you used to go?" Wyatt asked.

"I'm tired."

"You'll feel better after you eat something," Adrianna said, setting a plate of scrambled eggs and bacon in front of Ben and another full plate in front of Wyatt.

"I'm not hungry," Wyatt said, looking down at the food in bemusement.

"Eat what you want," she replied. "Pancakes are coming up."

Despite Wyatt's claim, he took one bite and then another and for a few minutes there was silence in the kitchen as both males cleaned their plates. They were fast eaters. By the time the first pancakes were done, they were holding out empty plates.

She flipped a stack of cakes on each plate and handed over her two favorite syrups, maple and blueberry.

It felt good watching them eat. She'd missed feeding people. It was what she was good at. What she needed to get back to doing.

"I have to go to the bathroom," Ben said a moment later as he slid off the stool.

"It's down the hall," she told him.

Wyatt stood up as Ben left the room. "You don't have a back door, do you?"

"No, but it doesn't matter, because he's not going to run."

"How do you know that?"

"It's cold outside, and it's warm in here," she said practically. "And because as much as he doesn't like you, he knows there are worse people in the world. I also don't think he has anywhere to go. You need to take it a little easier on him. You scared him back in the alley. You went into attack mode. It was the first time I saw you as a cop."

He frowned. "I wasn't acting like a cop but as a desperate father."

"You were acting like both," she said.

"Well, that's who I am. I didn't hurt him, Adrianna."

"Just remember that he's not the one who took Stephanie. In fact, he's probably been taking care of your daughter."

Wyatt stared back at her. "I didn't think of it like that."

"When he comes back, let me talk to him. We need to gain his trust. Or we'll never find out anything."

Ben returned to the kitchen with a wary glance. "Can I go now?"

"Why don't you stay for a while?" she suggested. "You could sleep here if you wanted. It doesn't sound like your mom is home tonight."

"She might have come back."

"Or maybe not," she said.

Ben debated for a long minute. "All right, I'll stay."

"Good. I have some sweats that would probably fit you. Let me show you what I have," she added. "Maybe we could throw your clothes in the wash, too. I have to run a load anyway."

Ben followed her into the bedroom. She opened a drawer and pulled out sweat pants and a t-shirt. "Will these work?"

He shrugged as if he didn't care.

"You can change in the bathroom. If you want to take a shower, feel free."

"I'm going to leave in the morning," he said firmly.

"Of course you are," she said.

Ben took the clothes and shuffled into her bathroom. She smiled as she heard the shower go on and then returned to the kitchen. She was surprised to find Wyatt doing the dishes.

"I can do that," she said.

"You cooked. I'll clean."

"Well, all right," she said, sitting down on the stool. "Ben's taking a shower."

"I heard the water go on. You have a way with him."

"I understand where he's coming from."

"Proving again how much I need you," he said, offering her a brief, somewhat pinched smile.

"I know you're frustrated, Wyatt, but Ben has already given us a few more clues to follow, like the club where his mom and possibly Jennifer were working."

"A club that was shut down," he said. "I guess I shouldn't be surprised that Jen was working as a stripper. How else would she make money?" He didn't wait for an answer. "I'm staying here tonight, Adrianna. I'll sleep in the chair or on the floor. I can't take a chance that I'll come back in the morning and Ben will be gone."

"I understand."

"Thanks."

While Wyatt finished cleaning up the kitchen, she got some extra blankets out of her hall closet and put them on the couch. Then she went into her bedroom to pull the comforter down. A few minutes later, a decidedly cleaner Ben walked in wearing her sweats.

She took the pile of dirty clothes out of his hand. "I'll run these downstairs to the laundry room."

"You don't have to," he said.

"It's not a problem. Why don't you sleep in here, Ben? Wyatt and I have things to talk about."

"I can't take your bed."

"Sure you can."

He stared back at her, as if weighing her motives. "I know you're just being nice to me so I'll help you."

"Actually, I'm being nice to you because I want to help *you*," she replied. "When I was fourteen, I lived on the street for two months. I remember what it was like not to have a bed or a home or clean clothes."

"My mom is coming back," he said, as if to convince himself as much as her.

"I believe you."

"What about the cop?" Ben asked, tipping his head toward the other room. "Is he staying?"

"Yes, and he's not here as a cop. He's a worried father. He wants to find his little girl. He's afraid she's in danger."

"Emily said her father was dead."

"Maybe she thinks he is." She paused, seeing the exhaustion in Ben's eyes, but she had his attention, and she needed to press it. "How long has it been since you've seen your mom?"

"A couple of weeks."

"You've been alone all that time?"

He nodded.

"Does your mother know that Sara isn't with you?"

He shook his head. "She wasn't around when Emily's mom came."

She frowned. "Do you have any idea where your mom is?"

"I never know where she is, but usually she comes back after a few days. I'm kind of worried about her."

"I'll bet you are."

"Why was Emily staying with you? Why wasn't she with her mother?"

"Her mom had to go somewhere for a while."

"And you don't know what Emily's mom's name is?"

"I don't remember." He stretched out on his side on the bed. "Did you really live on the street?"

"Yes. My mom died when I was eleven, and I was put in some foster homes that didn't work out. I ran away from one of them."

"I was in a group home. It sucked."

She met his gaze. "Living on the streets can be worse, Ben."

"My mom is coming back," he said again, but there was even less confidence in his voice now.

She patted his leg. "You're not alone anymore. I should have done more to help you when I first met you. I'm sorry about that."

"I looked for you at the restaurant, but you didn't come back after those guys broke in."

She shook her head. "No, I didn't. I was scared."

"How come you were there tonight?"

"I was hoping you and the girls would come by." She took a moment and then added, "You're worried about Sara and Emily, aren't you?"

"I shouldn't be. They're probably fine. Probably having a great time together," he said bitterly.

"You must miss them."

He shrugged. "Sometimes they get scared at night. I

don't know if Emily's mom will be around when that happens."

"Well, we're going to find them. And we're going to fix things."

"I don't know if you can," he said sleepily.

"What's your mom's name?" she asked.

"She wouldn't want me to tell you."

"Tell me anyway."

"Delilah Raymond," he said.

She let out a breath, feeling like she'd just cleared a hurdle. "Thank you."

"You can't turn me in," he told her, a plea in his eyes. "They'll put me in a home and last time I got beat up there."

"Let's take it one step at a time. I want to help you, Ben."

"Only until you find Emily," he said.

She looked into his jaded eyes and knew he'd been used before.

"And after, too," she said. "I told you I've been where you are. I'll do everything I can to help you."

"Can I go to sleep now?"

She nodded. "Yeah." She watched as he crawled under the covers, and then she walked to the door and turned out the light. As she closed the door behind her, she found Wyatt leaning against the wall outside the room.

He followed her into the living room.

She flopped down on the couch. "You heard everything?"

He sat on the chair across from her. "Yeah."

"It sounds like Ben's mother worked with Jennifer – if it's Jennifer and Steph that we're talking about. I wish we could be sure. But I guess we'll know when we find them. I think we'll get Ben's help," she said. "He wants to find his sister. He's worried about her. I don't get why Jen would take another kid with her."

"It doesn't make sense to me either, but I've never had

much luck figuring out why Jen does anything. Maybe it was to appease Stephanie. God, she must be so scared. I can't imagine what she thinks. It sounds like Jen dropped her with this other woman and these kids without even a thought."

"We don't know anything for sure," she said quietly. "But we have new leads."

"Yeah, I wish I could do something now."

"The morning will be here before you know it." She yawned as the full day began to catch up with her. "You should go home, Wyatt. Ben fell asleep before his head hit the pillow. He's not going anywhere."

"I know, but I'm going to stay."

"Really? You won't be comfortable."

He leaned back in the chair stretching out as the footrest came up. "This is perfect. I could sleep here."

His words brought up an old memory. "That's what Will used to say. He bought me that chair for my birthday, but I think it was really a present for him." She smiled to herself. "Will insisted that I needed a recliner to watch TV. Never mind that I'm hardly ever home to watch television, and when I am home, I'm usually in the kitchen trying new recipes."

"How long were you and Will together?"

"We were friends for four and a half years and then one night we went to a party, had a lot of champagne and ended up in bed together. I thought at first it was a mistake. I really cared about Will as a friend, and I didn't know what would happen to our relationship. But Will was really happy and it all worked out. We became boyfriend/girlfriend."

"By default?" Wyatt asked.

"It wasn't like that exactly. Will wanted us to be together for a long time, but I'm not good at commitment or giving my heart away. Growing up the way I did, love was something that hurt. So I never wanted to put myself out there." She drew in a breath. "The night that Will was shot, Lindsay and I found a ring box in his pocket. It just fell out when we moved his jacket. She wanted to look at it, but I wouldn't let her. I couldn't believe that he was thinking of asking me to marry him. It was too fast, too soon."

"But you knew each other for four years," he pointed out.

"Five years by then," she admitted, "but we never talked about marriage. Will used to joke about living together, but even that wasn't serious, at least not on my part. I just can't imagine what he was thinking to buy me a ring."

"Maybe he wanted to lock things down, seal the deal, take it to the bank."

She frowned. "That's a lot of clichés in one sentence."

He gave her a tired smile. "You know what I mean. He might have sensed you weren't as committed as he was, because you weren't."

"I wanted to be." She thought back to that night. "For the first few weeks after he died, I kicked myself for putting him off. He wanted to talk to me and I took pizza out to the kids. I kept thinking if I'd had that conversation …"

"Then what? Would you have said yes?"

She thought for a moment. "I don't think I could have said yes. And if he'd asked me to marry him, and I'd said no, he would have died knowing that I didn't want to marry him. I guess I'm glad that didn't happen. But it's all horrible, because Will is dead, and he had a lot to live for, whether we were going to end up together or not. The real tragedy was his, not mine. And I am talking way too much."

"It sounds like those words have been rolling around in your head for a while."

"I feel guilty about so many things. Will was distracted that night. Lindsay commented on it. I don't know if he was thinking about getting up his nerve to ask me, or if there was something else going on. He hadn't locked the front door of the restaurant, and he was in charge of that. Something else was on his mind."

"Did you tell Inspector Burton that?" Wyatt asked.

There was something in his tone that made her sit up straight. "Why would I?"

"The unlocked door. Is it possible that Will might have made a deal with someone to leave the door open?"

She stared at him in shock. "You're saying that Will was part of the robbery? He's dead." She was horrified by the accusation, and she jumped to her feet. "That is absolutely ridiculous. I can't believe you would say that."

His gaze was even and unapologetic. "I didn't know him. I'm just looking at the facts."

"He didn't lock the door, because he was thinking about something else. There was no ulterior motive."

"You don't know what he was thinking about," Wyatt pointed out. "Therefore, you don't know if there was an ulterior motive."

She really hated his logic. "I knew Will. I knew what kind of man he was. And besides, if he was involved, why would they shoot him?"

Wyatt tipped his head. "That probably means he wasn't involved."

"Exactly." She sent him an annoyed look as she sat down on the edge of the couch. "I can't believe you made me doubt him."

"I didn't make you doubt him. You had questions. You just never said them out loud until now."

Wyatt was right. She had thought about Will's odd behavior that night and wondered what had been behind his distraction. "Well, I'm never going to know the answers," she said. She leaned back against the cushions and added. "I asked Inspector Burton if they'd checked Will's phone, and he told me that the only calls he'd made or received had been to his parents."

"Would that have been unusual?"

"Yes. They were not close. All I can think is that he told them he was going to ask me to marry him, and perhaps they didn't have the reaction he hoped for." She had a feeling they would have told Will he was out of his mind to marry her.

"Or you're just imagining that because you don't think they liked you."

"I know they didn't like me. They wanted him with anyone but me."

"Oh, come on, you're not that bad," he said with a smile.

"Gee, thanks."

"Did you ask his parents about the calls?"

"I didn't want to upset them any further. They just lost their son. It didn't seem appropriate."

"It's been a few months. Maybe it's time to make that call now."

"For what purpose?"

"Closure?" he suggested.

"Maybe. Or would it just raise more questions in my mind?"

"I can't answer that, Adrianna."

"You're so honest and direct," she said. "You don't ever sugar coat things, do you?"

"I don't like sugar, except on my cereal."

She smiled. "I could turn you on to some really good granola, raisin, nut cereal that's really healthy."

He grinned back at her, a devilish light in his eyes. "You could turn me on, but it wouldn't be with cereal."

She picked up the throw pillow next to her and tossed it at him. "Don't start."

"Starting doesn't seem to be a problem …"

The teasing light faded from his eyes. "I don't want to talk about that."

"It's odd that you don't. I thought women loved to talk about stuff like that."

Maybe she would have wanted to talk about it if she hadn't felt so conflicted inside, if she hadn't enjoyed kissing him so much, if this was any other time but this time. "We both have a lot on our plate right now. We don't need to complicate things."

"I think we already did. But I'm good with not talking." He settled back more comfortably in the recliner. "I should get one of these for my house."

"You should," she agreed. Wyatt was only following her lead in changing the subject, but suddenly she wanted to change it back. Unfortunately, Wyatt now seemed to be more interested in her remote.

"Do you mind if I turn on the television?" he asked. "I'll mute it. I'm just too wired to go to sleep."

"Go right ahead, and you can play the sound. I can sleep through anything. To be honest, I like the noise and the company. It's been too quiet here the last few months." She was about to stretch out on the couch when she remembered something. "Damn I was supposed to start the laundry."

"You can do it tomorrow. It will give Ben a reason to stay here longer."

"That's true."

As Wyatt turned on the television, she rolled over on to her side, facing the back of the couch. She tried to relax, but her body had tensed up when Wyatt had teased her about turning him on. It was crazy to think of him in any other terms than friendship – if they were even friends. They were more like helpers or partners.

But he was remarkably easy to talk to and a good sounding board. He was smart and practical and didn't give her any bullshit, and she liked that about him. Sometimes, however, he was a little too honest. She thought about their conversation regarding Will and the unlocked door, and his suggestion that she contact Will's parents for answers. She had considered that, but would it really be worthwhile?

She knew Will hadn't had anything to do with the robbery. And she also knew that she would not have married him even if he'd asked her. So where did that leave her? What did she really need to know?

What she needed to do was let go of the past and move on, and maybe she could do that now. Hearing her doubts out loud had made them seem very unimportant.

As she listened to the sounds of late night comedy, she let her mind drift. She felt safe and warm and reassured by Wyatt's presence. For the first time in a long time, she actually felt like she might sleep.

Chapter Ten

Wyatt woke up just after seven, the television in Adrianna's living room still on mute. He'd meant to stay awake just in case Ben got it in his head to take off in the middle of the night, but exhaustion had overtaken him. He glanced across the room. Adrianna was curled up on the couch, fast asleep. Her cheeks were a rosy pink, her lips parted ever so slightly, her hair falling around her face and shoulders in soft, tumbling waves. His body hardened, and he was taken right back to the night before when he'd kissed those lips and ran his hand through that hair on two separate occasions. And neither one had been enough. He wanted more.

He drew in a deep breath, reminding himself that he couldn't have more. He couldn't possibly complicate his life with any kind of romantic entanglement. He just wished she wasn't so pretty, so smart and funny, that he didn't like her so much, that she didn't remind him that he wasn't just a father, he was also a man, and he'd been alone a long time.

Gazing over at her again, he thought about how great she'd been the day before, handling everything he'd thrown at her, his sister's rehearsal dinner, waiting in the alley behind Vincenzo's for the kids, bringing Ben back to her apartment and cooking them both a hearty meal in the middle of the night. She'd given up her bed for a kid. She was a very special person, and he was damn lucky his coin had collided with hers. He wouldn't be this far without her.

The way she'd grown up, she could have turned out to be a heartless and cold bitch, but instead she was warm and generous, and full of heart. She had had her life turned upside down not once but several times. Somehow she always found a way to land on her feet. He respected that. And in a strange way, she gave him hope that he'd also find a way to come out on top.

As he moved his chair upright, she stirred just a little. For a moment, he thought she might wake up, but after a stretch, she curled up with her hands pillowing her face and smiled as she fell into another dream.

He needed a shower – a cold shower.

On his way to the bathroom, he checked the bedroom. Ben was still sacked out on the bed.

He took a quick shower, focusing his thoughts on the day ahead. He had new leads to follow up on, and he was ready to get started.

After throwing his clothes on, he moved quietly through the living room and into the kitchen. As he started a pot of coffee, he heard the soft pad of footsteps.

"I can do that," Adrianna mumbled, her eyes still sleepy, the mark of the pillow cushion on her right cheek.

He smiled. "You're barely awake."

"I'm getting there. Is Ben –"

"Still asleep," he finished.

"How did you sleep?"

"Surprisingly well," he said.

"You already took a shower," she said, as her gaze began to sharpen.

"I hope you don't mind."

"Not at all. I think I'll do the same."

"I'll get the coffee ready."

As Adrianna left, he opened the fridge and studied the

contents. The shelves were very well stocked. It was obvious she'd been doing a lot of cooking the last few days. Since they'd had breakfast a few hours earlier, he opted to heat up some pizza from Vincenzo's. He had just popped a few pieces in the microwave when Ben entered the kitchen.

The kid gave him a wary look and said, "Where's Adrianna?"

"Taking a shower," he replied. "Are you hungry?" The microwave beeped and he opened the door, grabbing the plate of pizza. "Want a slice?"

"You made that?"

"No, I heated it up. It came from Vincenzo's."

"Okay, I'll take some," Ben said.

He handed him the plate and reached inside the fridge again for the pizza box. While he was heating up his slices, he poured Ben a glass of orange juice and passed it over to him.

"Thanks," Ben mumbled, his cheeks full of pizza.

"No problem. Take your time. The food isn't going anywhere."

Ben didn't slow down a bit, and Wyatt couldn't really blame him. It was clear the kid had gone hungry a lot in the past and when faced with food, his first instinct was to eat as quickly as possible.

"I think we should try and find your mother today," Wyatt added.

"I thought you were looking for Emily," Ben said.

"I'm hoping your mother might know where Emily and her mother are, and, of course, your sister, too." He hoped mentioning Ben's sister might keep him more involved in the search. "You must miss her."

"She's a pain most days," Ben said.

"Yeah, but what about the other days?"

"I don't think my mom knows where Sara is – or cares," he added bitterly. "When she gets drunk or high, she forgets she has kids."

"That's exactly the way my ex-wife was with Stephanie – Emily," he amended. "She just couldn't think about anything or anyone but herself and the way she felt at that moment."

"She seemed all right when she took Emily and Sara away."

Wyatt didn't quite know how to feel about that. He wanted Jennifer to be all right, but then again if she was sober and rational, she'd be better at hiding. "Speaking of that," he said, pulling out his wallet. "I should have shown you this last night. Is this the woman who took Emily?" He pulled out Jen's picture and handed it to Ben.

"Her hair is darker, but I think that's her," Ben said. "She wears sunglasses a lot."

His gut clenched as he took the photo back from Ben. He'd just received more confirmation that he was getting closer to Stephanie. Drawing in a breath, he warned himself not to skip ahead. One clue at a time. "So, you said your mom's name is Delilah Raymond?" he asked.

"Adrianna told you?"

"I overheard," he said, not wanting Ben to think he couldn't trust Adrianna. "I was eavesdropping."

"Figures."

"You also said you checked the usual places. I want you to show me those places today."

"I can't. I have things to do."

"Like what?" he challenged.

"Stuff."

"Well, maybe your stuff can wait a few hours."

"Why should I help you?"

"Because you want to see your sister again," he said. From what Adrianna had told him about Ben and the girls, he sensed the boy had a strong protective instinct.

Before Ben could answer, Adrianna walked into the kitchen wearing jeans and a peach-colored knit tank top. Her brown hair was still damp and pulled back in a ponytail and she didn't have a speck of make-up on her face, but she was still gorgeous.

Finding his breath caught in his throat once again, he turned away and grabbed his plate out of the microwave.

"You're eating pizza?" Adrianna asked in amazement. "For breakfast?"

"It's good in the morning," Wyatt said.

"I can cook something. I know we had eggs last night, but I could make some oatmeal or French toast or something."

"This is fine for me," Wyatt said. "And you should talk – you love to eat breakfast at night, why not dinner in the morning?"

"I suppose it kind of goes with the way my life has turned upside down," she replied. "What about you, Ben? Are you okay with pizza?"

The kid nodded, his mouth full.

Well, all right. You two are easy," she said.

"Want one of my slices?" he asked, holding out his plate.

"No, thanks. I don't usually eat much in the morning anyway."

Ben excused himself to go to the bathroom.

Adrianna sat down at the counter. "Did he say anything?"

"No more than he told you. We need to find his mother. I'm going to go down to the station and talk to Josh. He handled some cases that involved Ricky's nightclub. He might be able to hook me up with someone that worked there. That seems to be where Jen and Delilah met each other, although I wonder if that's her real name."

"It does sound like a stripper name," she agreed.

Ben returned from the bathroom. "Can I get my clothes?"

"I was just going to wash them," she said. "I'll throw them in right now."

"Ben," Wyatt said, drawing the kid's attention back to him as Adrianna left to do the laundry. "What's your mom's real name?"

"I told you."

"I don't think you did. Delilah was her stripper name. I'm betting she had another one."

Ben's gaze met his for a long moment. "Rebecca," he said.

The word jolted his memory. He thought back to what Mandy had told him the night before. "Rebecca Mooney?"

"That was her name before she got married. How did you know that?"

"Because I think she went to high school with my ex-wife. Where's your father?" he asked.

"He died when I was eight. My mom didn't have any money, so she had to take whatever job she could. She waitressed for a while, then she started stripping. A couple of months ago, she met someone and all of a sudden she started dressing up and going on dates, and we wouldn't see her for a couple of days. When she eventually came home, we would go out to dinner and to the movies. She used to promise that we'd move out of the motel and live in an apartment the way we used to. But she never seemed to make enough."

Wyatt felt compassion at the sadness in Ben's eyes. It was as if he had two different moms, the one who was good and spoiled him, and the other who was caught up in some other life that didn't include him.

"Can I watch TV?" Ben asked.

"Sure. Why don't you watch in the bedroom?" He wanted to keep Ben as far away from the front door as possible. While Ben had already given him some information, there could be more he could offer.

Adrianna returned to the apartment just as he was putting on his jacket.

"You're leaving?" she asked in surprise.

"Ben told me his mother's real name, Rebecca Mooney. That's the same name Mandy gave me yesterday. Rebecca and Jennifer were friends and apparently still are. I need to run her name through the computer. I also want to see what else I can find on any women that worked at Ricky's. Maybe there was another friend."

"We don't need more women, we need less," she said dryly.

"I get the feeling that Rebecca turned her stripping into something else," he said.

"Like working for an escort service?"

He met her gaze. "That was my thought. Ben said she started going on a lot of dates and disappearing for days at a time. When she came home, she had money." He paused. "Ben is watching TV in your room. Can you keep him here?"

"Well, he doesn't have his clothes yet, so I think I can hang on to him for awhile."

"I'll be back as soon as I can."

"Call me if you find out anything." She gave him a smile as he headed to the door. "Your eyes are sparkling, Wyatt."

He stopped next to her. "I feel like we're getting closer, Adrianna. All along there was a small doubt in my head that Emily might not be Stephanie, but if Ben's mother knew Jennifer in high school, then I'm sure it's her. I don't know where she is yet, but I feel a lot more hopeful than I have in a long time."

"I'm glad."

He impulsively gave her a hug. "Thank you." Her body molded so perfectly to his, her head reaching just under his chin. "I couldn't have done this without you," he added, feeling a strange reluctance to let her go.

"Don't thank me yet," she said, her cheeks flushed. "We still need to find your daughter."

"We will."

* * *

Adrianna watched Wyatt walk down the hall. His quick hug a moment earlier had reignited the desire she'd felt the night before. The more time she spent with him, the deeper her attraction grew, because now it wasn't just physical chemistry at play, there was an emotional connection as well. Fortunately, she'd managed to stop herself from giving him a good-bye kiss. Unfortunately, she was still going to have to talk about Wyatt spending the night at her apartment, because Lindsay was coming down the hall.

"Well, well," Lindsay said, a sharp gleam in her eye. "Guess who just let me into the building?"

"I don't have to guess. It was Wyatt."

"So, tell me everything," Lindsay said, as she entered the apartment.

Adrianna closed the door. "It's not what you think."

"You keep telling me that, but I'm starting to believe it is exactly what I think. Last night in the alley, you looked like you might have kissed him, and today he's leaving in the morning with wet hair and the same clothes he was wearing last night?"

"Okay, it looks bad," she admitted.

"You like him."

"I don't like him. We're working together."

"If that's what you want to call it."

"Look, we found one of the kids. Ben is in the bedroom watching TV."

Lindsay's eyes widened in surprised. "Seriously? Wow. I admit I did not think that."

"I told you so."

"So Ben is staying here now?"

"Temporarily." She paused. "Do you want some coffee? I really need some."

"Yeah, you don't look like you got much sleep last night."

"I slept on the couch," she said, heading into the kitchen.

Lindsay slid onto the stool by the counter. "And where did the hot cop sleep?"

"His name is Wyatt."

"Yeah, well, where did Wyatt sleep?"

"In the recliner."

"Really? And there wasn't any –"

"Lindsay, stop," she said quickly. "I told you it's not like that." She handed her friend a mug of coffee. "Do you want any cream or sugar?"

"No, black is fine."

Adrianna poured coffee for herself and took a long, hot sip, then leaned against the counter across from Lindsay. "We think that one of the girls who was with Ben a few months ago is Wyatt's missing daughter. He just left here to follow up on some leads on Ben's mother. It's a long story, but I think we're making progress."

"That's good."

Adrianna sighed at the doubt in Lindsay's voice. "Okay, what do you really want to say?"

Lindsay rested her forearms on the counter as she returned her gaze. "I've been worried about you the last two months. I was afraid you were never going to come out of the funk you sank into after Will's death. I know that Vincenzo's has been like a second home to you, and walking into that restaurant and seeing Will's blood on the ground changed the restaurant from being a safe harbor to being a dangerous, violent place. I wasn't sure that you could get past that."

"I wasn't sure either."

"But maybe you can," Lindsay said. "I admit I'm a little concerned that Wyatt is using you, and that you're going to get hurt –"

"He hasn't made me any promises, Lindsay. I know what's what."

"You are a smart girl in a lot of things, but not so much when it comes to love."

"This isn't love."

"But you like him. You like him like him," she teased.

"Maybe a little," she conceded.

"You've changed since you've met him. You're standing taller, and your voice is stronger, and you seem like you again."

"I still haven't made it inside the restaurant."

"I think that's coming."

"I think so, too," she said, smiling back at Lindsay. "Everything you said is true. I wasn't sure I could ever get over what happened, but now I feel like I might be able to move on. But it's not because I'm forgetting Will. I don't want you to think that."

"Of course you're not forgetting Will. But you don't have to justify feeling better and not being so sad, not to me anyway. Moving forward doesn't mean you forget your past."

"I don't want to disrespect Will."

"You couldn't possibly do that."

"Couldn't I? It's only been a few months. I'm in mourning. That's supposed to be at least a year, right? I shouldn't want another man."

Lindsay shook her head, giving her a sympathetic look. "There aren't any rules, Adrianna."

"Will didn't deserve to die."

"Of course he didn't deserve it. He was a great person. But you're alive. And I don't want you to be afraid to live, to be who you're meant to be. And that's a chef. Even if it's not at Vincenzo's, you need to be somewhere."

She nodded, moisture filling her eyes at Lindsay's thoughtful words. "You're a good friend, Lindsay. You're the closest thing I've ever had to a sister. And growing up without a family, it means so much to me to have you in my life."

"Oh, God, now you're going to make me cry," Lindsay said, her eyes watering. She took a sip of her coffee and cleared her throat. "Changing the subject..."

"As long as it's not to Wyatt," she said.

Lindsay gave her a pointed look. "Come on. If I'm like your sister, you can tell me the good stuff. Did anything go on last night?"

She hesitated for a long moment. "We had a kiss – two kisses actually, a few hours apart."

"Really?"

"It was a mistake – two mistakes," she amended, feeling a little foolish.

"Were the kisses good?"

"Yes," she said, finding it impossible to lie.

Lindsay nodded and grinned. "I knew I wasn't imagining the sparks between you two. I have a very keen sense when it comes to romance."

"It's not romance. It's ... I don't know what it is."

"Did you talk about it?"

"No. I didn't want to. He's searching for his daughter, and I'm getting over Will. It's the worst possible time."

"That's usually when love shows up," Lindsay said, taking another sip of her coffee.

"I didn't say anything about love," she said firmly.

"Well, you never do, so that's not surprising. Is Wyatt a good man?"

"Yes, I think so," Adrianna replied. "I wasn't sure I could trust him at first, because he's a police officer, and I had some run-ins with the law when I was a kid. But the way he talks about his daughter, and his love and determination to bring her back just amazes me. He's the kind of man who loves with his whole heart and soul. I've never really known anyone like that."

"That kind of ferocious intensity can be very attractive,

especially when it's turned on you."

"Well, it's not turned on me, not all the way anyway." She paused. "It's true that there's a chemistry between us. I feel it, and I know he feels it, too, but as I said it's the worst possible time, and we both have so much baggage."

"One thing I know about baggage, it's easier to carry it around when you have some help," Lindsay said, her eyes sparkling.

She grinned. "That's a good line."

"Can I ask you a question?"

"Can I stop you?"

"Is it the timing that's holding you back? Is it his daughter? Or is it Will?"

"It's all of the above," Adrianna answered.

"But you like him."

"Yes, I admit it," she said, surrendering to the inevitable. "Are you happy now?"

"Only because I think *you* might be happy," she said. "So what are you doing today?"

"I'm going to hang out with Ben and see what Wyatt finds out."

"Then I will leave you to it. I guess you won't be coming into the restaurant any time soon?"

"We'll see," she said. "I'm taking it one step at a time."

"Well, at least you're taking steps."

"Exactly."

Lindsay set down her coffee cup. "I'm going to spin class."

"I hope you can breathe after the cigarettes you've been sneaking," she said, following her to the door.

"It was only a few, and I'm getting a nicotine patch later today."

"Good."

Lindsay gave her a hug. "If the hot cop wants to kiss you again, don't say no."

"Linds –"

"And if you want to kiss him, don't wait to be asked. That's my advice."

"Did I ask for it?" she grumbled.

"No, but we're sisters, so you get unsolicited advice."

"I think I'm going to regret calling you my sister."

Lindsay laughed. "See you later, Adrianna."

"Bye," she said, shutting the door.

As she walked across the room, she realized she was still smiling. It had been a long time since she'd smiled for so long. And she knew it wasn't just because of Lindsay, it was also because of Wyatt.

She touched her fingers to her lips. His kisses hadn't been just good; they'd been great. And she really did want to kiss him again. But she wasn't going to take Lindsay's advice – not yet anyway. First, they needed to find Wyatt's daughter.

Chapter Eleven

Josh was at his desk when Wyatt arrived at the station Saturday morning.

"What are you doing here?" Wyatt asked. "Aren't you off today?"

"We made an arrest last night for the robbery/homicide at Vincenzo's."

He was more than a little surprised. "Really? I had no idea you were close to making an arrest. What happened?"

"A witness came forward late yesterday afternoon. She's the ex-girlfriend of one of the two teenage males involved. She said they didn't think anyone was inside the restaurant. When they were confronted, one of them got nervous and took a shot. They had no idea they had killed someone until they heard the news."

"Why did she wait so long to come forward?"

"She said she was afraid of her boyfriend, but that she's moving away, and she wanted to get this off her chest before she left."

"Is she credible? Or does she just want to bust her boyfriend?"

"Her story checks out, and she gave me the gun. It's in Forensics now. We found her boyfriend and his buddy at the bar where they work. Boyfriend tried to run when he saw us. The other one is willing to talk about how he didn't pull the trigger, but his friend did."

Wyatt nodded. "You've been up all night, haven't you?"

"Yeah, tell me why nothing ever breaks in the middle of the day, preferably a work day and not on the weekend?"

He smiled in sympathy. "At least you've solved the case."

"I didn't solve it. The answers were given to me. I just got lucky someone was willing to come forward."

"It doesn't matter how it happened. The victim gets justice. Two criminals are off the street. That's a good day in my book." He paused, as he remembered his conversation with Adrianna. "Was there any connection between the two men and the victim?"

"No, why do you ask?"

"The unlocked door."

"Apparently, just an oversight," Josh replied. "Victim's record clean as a whistle." He tilted his head. "Unless you know something I don't know?"

"I don't. Adrianna said her boyfriend was distracted that night. She didn't know why."

"She asked me about his cell phone, but the only calls he made or received were to his parents, and they had no connection with the shooter."

At least Adrianna would get some closure, he thought, but it would still be difficult for her to accept that two young men had taken the life of someone she loved with such casual disregard. "Well, I'm glad it's done."

"Everything but the paperwork." Josh rolled his head around on his shoulders and cleared his throat. "What are you doing down here?"

"I found one of the kids – the boy. His name is Ben. His mother's name is Rebecca Mooney. Mooney was her maiden name. Raymond is her married name. But the important thing is that she went to school with Jennifer."

Josh's eyes widened. "No shit! So the girl we saw on

the video is really Stephanie?"

"Yes," his nerves tingling at the thought of how close he was to finding his daughter. "And Ben identified the woman who took her as Jennifer. I need to find out everything I can about Rebecca, where she's been living, who she knows, how she pays her bills, everything. She's the connection to Jen. We find Rebecca, we have a good chance of finding Jennifer."

"The kid doesn't know where his mother is?"

"No, apparently she disappears every couple of weeks for a few days. I'm thinking she's involved in some type of escort service. Ben said his mom usually isn't gone very long, but this time she's been missing about two weeks. Not long after his mother left, a woman showed up saying she was Emily's mother – he thinks of Stephanie as Emily."

"Okay, go on."

"This other woman, whose name Ben doesn't recall, said she was taking Emily back, but Emily-Stephanie threw a fit. She didn't want to leave her friends. So the woman also took Sara, Ben's sister, with her. She said she would watch them until Ben's mother got back."

Josh held up a hand. "I'm confused. How many women are we talking about?"

"Just two – Jen and Rebecca."

"And three kids?"

"Yes, and one of them is Stephanie, but she was living under the name Emily."

"The other two are Ben and Sara."

"Right. Stephanie was apparently staying with Ben and Sara when Jen was somewhere else – God knows where."

Josh shook his head, his expression filled with disgust. "Jen steals your child and then just leaves her somewhere? I could kill her."

"Get in line," he said grimly.

"So where is Ben now?"

"He's with Adrianna."

"The chef from Vincenzo's?" Josh said.

"Yes, she's been helping me," he said, trying to ignore the new curiosity in Josh's eyes. "I used her as bait. I figured the kids might come out of the shadows if they saw her again in the alley behind the restaurant. And I was right."

"So, that's it? She's just – bait?" Josh asked.

He let out a sigh at the pointed look in Josh's eyes. "I don't have time for this right now."

"My questions? Or Adrianna? Because the two of you seem to be very close."

"Adrianna is helping me."

"Is that why you took her to the engagement party last night? I called Summer to tell her I was sorry I missed the party, and she filled me on you and some beautiful brunette that you couldn't take your eyes off of. She said you disappeared upstairs for over an hour."

"Summer talks too much."

"Summer also said she hadn't seen you smile that much in two years."

"I don't remember smiling," he grumbled. "And it's really no one's business. Adrianna felt guilty about not asking for help when she first met the kids, so she wants to make things right."

"That's very noble."

"She's a good person, remarkably good," he said. He saw the knowing gleam in Josh's eyes. "I don't have time for this. I need to get to work."

"All right," Josh said. "Give me about a half hour, and I'll help you."

"You're exhausted. You should go home."

"When you're so close to finding Stephanie – not a chance. What can I do?"

"Rebecca worked at that nightclub that got shut down several months ago – Ricky's. She stripped under the name Delilah Raymond. Jen may have worked there as well. I need to find anyone who worked at the club before it closed."

"I'll talk to the guys in vice. Maybe someone has a contact."

"Great, thanks."

"You know, Wyatt, it wouldn't be the worst thing in the world to have a woman in your life."

"I'm still trying to recover from the last woman," he said, as he headed to his desk.

* * *

An hour later, Wyatt had learned a lot about Rebecca Mooney. She'd married Henry Raymond when she was twenty years old and had two children, Ben and Sara, who were now twelve and nine respectively. Henry had died in a car accident when Ben was eight and Sara was five. Rebecca had gone to work as an administrative assistant at a computer company that went out of business a year later. For two years, she had a record of temporary employment jobs, and then she'd started working at Ricky's. Since Ricky's had shut down eight months earlier, there was no record of Rebecca working anywhere in San Francisco. She was obviously being paid in cash for whatever she was doing, which was going to make the trail more difficult to follow.

Frowning, he flipped through the computer looking for more information. Rebecca's last known address was for an apartment building in San Francisco, but Ben had told him that they'd been living at the motel for months, so that was no help.

"I think I've got something," Josh said, joining him at his desk, with a piece of paper in his hand. "Kim Brady was a stripper at Ricky's. Now she works at a flower shop on Union Street, and she's working there today. I told her I was looking for some advice on flowers for my wedding.

And I used your name. She's expecting you."

"That's great," he said jumping to his feet. "Thanks."

"No problem. I'll keep looking for other names just in case this doesn't pan out."

"I'll call you when I'm done."

On his way out of the station, Wyatt called Adrianna, relieved when she answered right away. "Is Ben still with you?" he asked.

"Yes, he's watching TV. I'm drying his clothes now. He doesn't seem to be in a rush to leave, and he's a little more relaxed since you left. What are you doing?"

"Looking for his mother. Josh found a woman who used to work at Ricky's. I'm on my way to talk to her now. I'll call you when I'm done."

"All right. I hope she can tell us something."

"So do I."

Wyatt jumped into his car and drove across town as quickly as possible. Union Street was a popular destination in San Francisco, offering upscale boutiques, restaurants and bars. It was only a few blocks from the marina and the bay, and as he parked his car and got out, he was assailed by the aroma of seafood and sourdough bread, two smells he always associated with this part of the city.

As he walked into the flower shop, he saw an attractive redhead arranging flowers at the front counter. "Kim Brady?" he asked.

"Can I help you?" she asked.

"I hope you can," he said, flashing her his badge. "Wyatt Randall."

"You called about wedding flowers?"

"Actually, I'm looking for information. Did you work at Ricky's?"

She frowned. "That was a long time ago."

"Try eight months ago."

"I've turned my life around. I don't want to be involved with anything that went down at Ricky's."

Ignoring her comment, he continued on. "Did you know Delilah Raymond aka Rebecca Mooney?"

"I knew Becky," she said shortly, not offering up any more information.

He pulled out Jen's picture and held it up. "What about this woman?"

"That's Carly."

He felt a rush of adrenaline pound through his veins. Finally, he had a name. "What was her last name?"

"I don't think I ever knew."

"When did you last see her?"

"Probably the day Ricky's closed."

"Do you know where Carly or Becky is now?"

"I never had Carly's number, and Becky's phone has been out of service for a while."

"What about an address for either one?"

"Becky was staying at a motel in North Beach. I don't remember the name. I don't know where Carly lived. Except for Becky, Carly kept to herself." Kim paused, as if debating whether or not to tell him more. "What's this about?"

"Carly kidnapped a child," he said. "I'm trying to find her."

Kim looked shocked. "Are you kidding me?"

"No, I'm not. It's very important that you cooperate."

"That little girl called her Mommy."

His heart jumped into his throat. "You saw the child?"

"A few times. They would wait in the dressing room until we were done."

He couldn't believe Jen had left Stephanie in the dressing room of a strip club.

"The boss didn't like it when she did that, but Carly and Becky had trouble with babysitters. They tried to cover for each other, but that didn't always work out."

"Where do you think they are now?"

Kim hesitated. "I've changed my life around. I don't

move in their circles anymore. It's been almost a year since I saw either one of them."

"Just think. I can't emphasize enough how critical your help could be."

She weighed his words for a long moment, then said. "One of the older strippers, Constance, started an escort service called Premiere Connections. She had met some high rollers during her days at Ricky's and other places, so she had a very exclusive clientele made up of celebrities, athletes, and wealthy businessmen who needed women to accompany them to events or on trips. Sometimes girls were needed to travel to foreign destinations. She made it sound like a dream job."

Kim opened a drawer below the counter and took out her purse. She fiddled through her wallet and removed a business card. "This is the contact number I had. I was tempted, but I never called it. I wanted to do something that didn't require me to take my clothes off. But I think Becky made the call. She was desperate for money. She had two kids to take care of, and she didn't feel like she had any options. I'm not sure about Carly."

"Is there anything else you can tell me? What about places you all used to hang out?"

"I can give you a list." She pulled out a piece of paper and a pen and started writing. "Joe's Diner was a popular hangout for an early dinner before the shows."

He started at the mention of the diner. Adrianna had suggested last night that they go down there. She certainly had good instincts.

"Elton's Bar had a great happy hour with free food Monday through Friday," Kim continued. "We could usually get some guys to buy us drinks, and then we'd eat for free."

As Kim rattled off locations in San Francisco, Wyatt felt a wave of sadness that Jen's life had sunk to such a low level and that she'd taken his daughter with her.

"The Graceland Apartments were a block away from the club," Kim said. "A lot of the girls lived there. I think Carly might have been there for a while." She jotted down the name. "The only other thing I remember about Carly is that she used to spend a lot of time with one of the customers. His name was Brad. He was a music promoter or something like that. Carly told me she wanted to be a singer."

He couldn't believe Jen was still chasing that dream. She had a nice voice, but nothing that special. "I really appreciate this."

"Just don't tell anyone where you got the information. I don't need any trouble. I worked really hard to get this job, to get out of that life. I don't want to go back."

He nodded. "I won't mention your name."

He walked out of the florist shop, pausing on the sidewalk to pull out his phone. His first call was to Josh. "Ever heard of Premiere Connections? Apparently, it's an escort service one of the strippers at Ricky's started. Kim Brady thinks that Rebecca Mooney otherwise known as Delilah Raymond went to work there."

"I can look into it," Josh said, "Anything else?"

"Quite a bit actually. Kim gave me a list of places to check. She identified Jen from her picture as someone named Carly. Carly spent time with a music promoter named Brad. Apparently, she still thought she could be a singer."

"Well, at least she was sober enough to have some goal," Josh replied.

"Kim said that Carly and Rebecca were friends, that Rebecca watched Carly's daughter. She also said that Carly had told everyone she was running away from an abusive husband." It still burned that Jen could lie about him so easily. He had never once laid a finger on her. She was the one who'd thrown a vase at his head and almost knocked him out.

"We're finally getting somewhere."

He sighed. "I should be happy, but I'm tired of chasing clues. I want to find my daughter already. It's been so damn long."

"You will, Wyatt. You're getting close. I can feel it."

"I hope so. I'll check back in later."

* * *

"Hey, Ben, what do you think about getting some lunch?" Adrianna stopped in the doorway of her bedroom, staring at the empty bed. The TV was still on, but there was no Ben. Shaking her head, she moved down the hall. She'd just come from the bathroom, and the door was still open, the room empty. The living room and kitchen were equally silent.

Ben was gone.

She opened the door to her apartment and stepped into the hall. Jogging down the stairs, she went all the way outside, looking both ways down the block. There was no sign of Ben.

Damn!

She'd only been in the bathroom a few minutes, but he'd obviously grabbed that opportunity to leave. She'd thought he was beginning to trust her, but he'd played her. He could be anywhere by now. She'd been in the bathroom at least twenty minutes.

Walking back into her building, she slowly climbed the stairs to her apartment. Wyatt was not going to be happy. All he'd asked her to do was watch Ben, and she'd screwed it up.

As if on cue, her phone rang, and Wyatt's number came up on the screen.

"Hello," she said.

"I got some new information," he said, his voice laced with excitement. "I'm on my way over to your place."

"Great," she said, wondering if she should tell him now or later that Ben had taken off.

"I'll see you in a few minutes," he said.

So, she'd tell him later, hoping that by some miracle Ben would reappear in the next several minutes. At least he hadn't left hungry, she thought, as she cleared the empty popcorn bowl from the coffee table.

She probably shouldn't have been surprised that he'd left. She might have done the same thing when she was his age. He'd had a meal. His clothes were clean, and there were two adults that could take away his freedom at any moment by calling in a social worker. That was the last thing Ben wanted. She just hoped he would be all right. She liked him, and she felt a kinship to his circumstances. His father had died. His mother had struggled. It wasn't his fault he'd been born into a life of need and loneliness. He deserved more than that.

While she waited for Wyatt, she cleaned up the kitchen and then checked her email. When her phone rang a moment later, she expected it to be Wyatt again, but it was Josh Burton.

"This is Adrianna," she said in reply to his query.

"It's Inspector Burton."

"Yes, I know. What can I do for you?" she asked, an uneasy feeling spreading through her body.

"I don't know if Wyatt had a chance to speak to you, but we arrested two males last night in connection to the homicide at your restaurant."

Her legs felt suddenly weak and she sank down on a stool by the kitchen counter. "Who – who was it?" she asked. "Did they have a reason? How did you find them?" The questions tumbled out of her.

"The men were in their late teens, eighteen and nineteen. They didn't expect anyone to be in the restaurant. When your friend appeared, one of them panicked and shot him. There doesn't appear to be any premeditation or any link between your friend and the two men."

"I never thought there was," she said, even though that wasn't completely true. "Are they definitely going to jail?"

"We have a very strong case. An ex-girlfriend of one of the guys turned him in."

"That was brave."

"Apparently, he cheated on her and anger fueled her courage."

"You don't think she's lying just to get back at him?"

"No, her story correlates to what we have. We have the right guys. You can rest easier now."

"Thanks, I appreciate the call." As she set down the phone, she let out a breath, waiting for a rush of relief, but it was not as big as she'd expected.

The police had the murderers in custody. They were going to jail. They were going to pay.

But Will was still dead.

At least he would have justice, she told herself. It was some measure of comfort, but not much. She wondered if his parents had been informed. She should have asked. But it wasn't her business to tell them. They'd made it clear to her that whatever relationship she'd had with Will had nothing to do with them. Still ... She thought about all those phone calls between Ben and his parents the night of the murder.

She opened the list of contacts on her phone. She'd put his parents' number in there so she could follow up with them about the funeral. She stared at their name for another minute and then impulsively hit the button to call.

Will's mother, Katherine, answered, "Hello?"

"It's Adrianna Cavello," she said. "Will's friend."

"Yes," Katherine said, in a discouraging voice.

"I don't know if you've heard, but they've caught the men who shot Will."

"I was informed. Is that all?"

"No, that's not all," she said quickly. "The night Will

died, he was distracted, and the police told me that he'd spoken to you and your husband several times that night. I was just wondering if you could tell me what was on his mind."

Silence followed her words.

Finally, Katherine said, "My husband offered Will a job in his law firm. It was time for Will to stop playing games with his life and settle into a real job."

She couldn't imagine Will in the law firm. "He didn't want to be an attorney," she said. "He liked working as a bartender."

"That's a kid's job," she said disdainfully. "We had bigger goals for him. If he had listened to us, he'd still be alive." Katherine's voice broke. "Please don't call here again."

"Wait –" She'd wanted to ask her about the ring, but Katherine had already hung up.

She set down the phone. At least she knew that Will's preoccupation had been due to his parents' job offer and nothing to do with her. She still wondered what he'd thought about the whole idea and whether or not Will had told his parents that he wanted to marry her. But it didn't matter anymore. She finally felt like she was ready to close that chapter in her life.

Her phone rang again, and she frowned. She hadn't been this popular in a long time.

"Stephan," she said, her gut tightening at the sound of her boss's voice.

"I'm waiting for your report on those dishes I sent home with you," he said. "Lindsay told me you had some ideas."

"I do. Uh…"

"Why don't you come in today, Adrianna? Between lunch and dinner. I'd like to talk to you. Come in around three-thirty. It will be quiet then."

She hesitated. They'd found the guys who had come

into the restaurant and shot Will. That should make it easier to go back in. So why didn't it feel easier?

"Adrianna?" he pressed.

"Yes," she said shortly, afraid if she said anything else, the *yes* would turn to *no*. "I'll see you then." She ended the call, hoping she hadn't made a terrible mistake. But she'd gone in the restaurant two days earlier. Now, she just had to make it into the kitchen.

Her doorbell rang, and she walked over to answer it. "It's me," Wyatt said.

"Come on up." She buzzed him in and then opened the front door. Maybe Wyatt would give her a reason to bail on the promise she'd just made. But that wouldn't be fair to Stephan. She had to make a decision – move forward, or say good-bye. Fortunately, she didn't have to decide right this second.

Wyatt bounded up the stairs and down the hall with energy in his step.

"You've learned something," she said, noting the decided change in his mood.

"A few things," he said with a nod.

She waved him into her apartment and then shut the door.

"Where's Ben?" he asked, looking around. "In the bedroom?"

She shook her head, knowing she was about to kill his mood. "He's gone, Wyatt. I was in the bathroom for a minute, and he took off. I'm so sorry. I really didn't think he'd run."

The smile in Wyatt's eyes quickly faded.

"I suspect he was afraid that eventually we'd turn him in, and he'd end up in a group home somewhere," she continued. "He told me that he got beat up in the last one he was in."

Wyatt sighed. "All right."

"That's it?" she asked, surprised by his less than angry

response.

"He wasn't wrong. I would have turned him over to Social Services, because he needs someone to watch out for him until we can find his mother. I know you wouldn't like that idea, but sometimes there isn't a choice."

"Well, it's not something we have to do anything about now," she said.

Wyatt cocked his head, giving her a speculative look. "Did you deliberately look the other way, Adrianna?"

"No. How can you ask me that?"

"Your aversion to social workers," he said.

"Oh, well, I do have an aversion, but I did not look the other way. I wasn't even thinking about that. I was focusing on finding Ben's mother."

"We may be a little closer. I found a woman who worked with Ben's mother and with Jen. Jen has apparently been calling herself Carly."

"Great, another alias."

"Yeah. This woman gave me a list of places that Carly and/or Jen might be. She also said Carly used to hang out with a music promoter named Brad. I still have to track him down." He stopped abruptly. "Oh, my God, Adrianna. I forgot to tell you something important."

His words made her nervous. "What's that?"

"Josh made two arrests last night –"

"I know," she interrupted. "He called me a few minutes ago and explained everything."

"I'm sorry. I should have told you earlier. I meant to. I just have tunnel vision when it comes to Stephanie."

"I understand. You have a lot on your mind. It's okay, Wyatt. The important thing is that the men are in custody and it looks like they'll go to jail."

"At least you don't have to worry that they're still out there somewhere. It should make it easier for you to return to work."

"You'd think so. Stephan wants me to come in later

this afternoon to talk to him about my plans. I told him I would. I'm still not sure I can do it."

"You can," he said, encouragement in his eyes. "You're stronger than you think."

"That's what people tell you when they want you to be strong – as if it will somehow make whatever is coming easier. Trust me, I speak from experience."

He gave her a soft smile. "I'm not just saying it. I believe it. I believe in you, Adrianna. You have an amazing spirit."

She was touched by the praise. "Well, thank you, Wyatt."

"You're welcome."

She swallowed hard as they exchanged a long look. There were a good three feet between them, and she needed to keep it that way. "So what's next?"

"We go down the list. At the top is your friend, Josephine. Apparently, she had a soft spot for strippers and girls that were down on their luck."

"I can attest to that – not the stripping part, but the other. I guess we should go," she said, feeling oddly reluctant. "It's going to be weird."

"Why?"

"I just haven't been back to the diner in a few years. I don't have a good reason. I actually feel guilty that I haven't seen Josephine." She wished she could explain her complicated emotions. "I really care about her, but I was always afraid that if I went back to the old neighborhood, I'd get sucked in, like dust into a vacuum cleaner. It's stupid."

"It's understandable. You worked hard to get away from that life. But I won't let you get sucked in to anything. You're safe with me, Adrianna."

"I know I am," she said, a little surprised at just how safe she felt. Who would have thought I could trust a cop?

His eyes warmed with her statement and his smile was

tender. "Who would have thought?" he echoed.

"So – Joe's Diner…"

"Yes, maybe it will be good for you to remember where you came from – to be reminded of just far you've gone since leaving the diner," he suggested. "That might give you the impetus to move forward, to meet with your boss, to get back to work."

"I guess there's only one way to find out."

Chapter Twelve

Joe's Diner was a small café near the strip clubs on Broadway. There were only fifteen tables and a long counter of barstools, but the diner had been doing a steady business for almost forty years. When Adrianna and Wyatt walked inside, she felt as if she had truly stepped back in time. It had been almost four years since she'd been in the diner, and as she'd told Wyatt, she felt a little guilty over her lengthy absence. Josephine had taken her in when she was a teenager. She'd saved her life in so many ways.

As usual, Josephine was working the counter. She was tall and thin with a square face that always wore a no-nonsense expression. Her stark white hair was pulled back in a bun, and she wore her usual attire, blue jeans and a long-sleeved bright orange Giants t-shirt. She supported all the local teams. In winter, she wore the jersey of the Golden State Warriors and during football season, it was 49'ers all the way. Josephine loved her sports, and she had many, many photos on the wall of the players who had stopped by for a meal.

It was lunchtime and the diner was crowded, but it didn't take long for Josephine to spot her by the door.

"Adrianna," she yelled in her boisterous voice. She

came around the counter and threw her arms about her. "I can't believe you're here. You finally missed my onion rings. I knew it would happen eventually."

"I miss more than your onion rings. I miss you," she said, smiling into the warm eyes of a woman who had been a second mother to her. "Sorry, it's been a while."

"Well, you have lots to do running that fancy restaurant."

"I don't run it. I'm just one of the chefs."

Josephine waved away her modest answer. "I know better than that. You're too good not to be in charge. I should know -- I trained you." She paused as the front door opened again. "Let's get you a table."

Before Adrianna could say they'd just come in to ask a few questions, they were being seated at a booth in the corner.

"I'm going to bring you all your favorites," Josephine said. Then she glanced at Wyatt. "Would you like a menu, or shall I bring the same?"

"I'm sure whatever Adrianna likes will be fine with me," Wyatt said.

"This is Wyatt Randall, Josephine Cooper," Adrianna said, introducing them both. "I told Wyatt that you're the reason I survived my childhood."

"Oh, I didn't do much," Josephine said with a vague wave of her hand. "You were almost grown by the time I got you. What can I get you to drink?"

"Iced tea for me," Adrianna said.

"Water is fine," Wyatt replied.

"I'll be right back with an appetizer."

"Sorry about that," Adrianna said when they were alone. "I know you just want to ask questions and move on."

"Actually, I'm kind of hungry, and it smells good in here."

"It does smell good," she said, feeling a sense of

nostalgia. "The first time I came in here I was freezing, wet, cold, and hungry. I must have looked like a drowned cat. I was just going to use the bathroom, but Josephine saw me, and she made me sit down and eat. Then we started talking, and the next thing I knew she was taking me to her apartment upstairs. I never left. She has the biggest heart of anyone I know."

"I'm glad you found her," he said.

"Me, too. It was here that I realized a restaurant was like a home. Josephine knows so many of her customers. They're like her family. She opens up on Thanksgiving and Christmas, too, giving away free holiday meals to anyone who wants one. I've been talking to Stephan about doing something similar at Vincenzo's. But I'm sure that won't happen if I don't go back to work."

"Another reason to go back."

As she looked around the diner, she thought about her early days as a budding cook. "Josephine taught me so much about cooking. She used to be in the kitchen and her husband, Joe, was out front, but after he died, she took over his place at the counter. She said she didn't like cooking as much when she wasn't cooking for him."

"Joe and Josephine – cute," Wyatt said.

She grinned. "Yeah. I never met him. He died about a year before I showed up. I think one of the reasons she took me in was because she was lonely." She paused, watching the cooks in the kitchen and suddenly realized something important. "This is the first time I've been in a restaurant since Will died."

Wyatt raised an eyebrow. "I didn't realize it was any restaurant. I thought you just had a fear of Vincenzo's."

"My fear has not been logical."

"Fear usually isn't," he said quietly. "How does it feel to be here?"

"Surprisingly great."

He met her gaze. "Sounds like you're getting better."

"The fog in my brain is lifting. It started when I ran into you at the fountain. Ever since then, I feel like you're this whirlwind tornado that I've gotten caught up in. Every day I get spun in a new direction. Look where I am today – back where I started."

"I feel like I'm caught up in the same tornado," he said. "Maybe that's why we feel the need to hang on to each other."

"Maybe that's why," she agreed.

As his gaze clung to hers, something deeper passed between them. It wasn't just circumstances that were keeping them together, she realized, it was emotion, feelings … desire. The thought shook her again, the memory of the kisses they'd shared making her lips tingle and sending a shiver down her spine.

Wyatt was remembering, too. She could see it in the sensual shadows that darkened his blue eyes.

"Adrianna," he began, only to be interrupted by Josephine's arrival.

She set down two salads and a stack of her famous onion rings with three kinds of dipping sauces.

"These smell wonderful," Adrianna said.

"They taste even better," Josephine replied.

"Can you sit for a minute?" Adrianna asked, sliding over on the seat.

"Let me clear a few orders, and I'll be right with you," Josephine replied.

"Okay."

"These are great," Wyatt said, dipping one of the onion rings into ranch dressing. "So far I like your favorites. What else is coming our way?"

"Probably cheeseburgers with grilled onions, mushrooms and pepper jack cheese," she said, grateful that their conversation had turned to food.

"I can live with that."

"I don't eat like that anymore, but I guess Josephine

still thinks of me like I'm a hungry sixteen-year-old."

"Well, I still eat like that, so I'm good."

As Wyatt dug into the onion rings, she said, "Speaking of teenagers, where do you think Ben went?"

"I have no idea."

"I'm surprised you're not more upset. You're handling it quite well."

He shrugged as he popped another onion ring into his mouth. "I think Ben told us everything he knew. He gave us the lead on his mom, which tied to Jen, which has led us here. We just have to keep following the trail."

While Wyatt took care of the onion rings, she dove into her salad, loving the freshness of the dressing. Josephine had never been one for bottled dressings. Even serving up food at a diner, she liked to use the best ingredients, organic and locally grown whenever possible.

"You're thinking about food, aren't you?" Wyatt asked.

She started. "How did you know?"

"I'm beginning to recognize the look on your face," he said with a grin. "You gaze at lettuce the same way I might look at a '79 Trans Am."

"Really? You're into cars?"

"Is that bad?" he asked, raising an eyebrow.

"No, just interesting. Actually, why would I be surprised? You drive pretty fast around the city."

"Because I've been in a hurry."

"I don't think that's the whole story."

"Well, I do like to drive," he admitted. "I took a road trip across county when I was eighteen with one of my friends. It was one of the best summers of my life. We would stop whenever we wanted. Total freedom, a ton of junk food –"

"A girl in every town," she finished.

He acknowledged her comment with a tip of the head. "Not quite that many, but we met a few along the way."

"It sounds like fun. I would love to do that some day.

I'd like to see the Rockies and the Grand Canyon, go to New Orleans for Mardi Gras, visit the Big Apple at Christmas, see the tree at Rockefeller Center."

"So what's stopping you?" he asked.

"Myself. I've been holding so tight to my dream of running my own restaurant that I refused to take one second to do anything else. I've been obsessed. That obsession has hurt most of my relationships, including the one with Will. He had to take a back seat, and even though he was supportive, I think it bothered him, too. I've probably been lucky that Lindsay hasn't given up on me. I just haven't had time to be the best friend or the best girlfriend. I need to do better in the future. I need to work at relationships." She paused, thinking of how much she'd learned about herself since Will's death. "The last two months, as I hid in my apartment, it became glaringly obvious to me how little I had in my life besides my work. It shook me up to realize how quickly life can change. I should have known that, because my childhood was certainly unpredictable, but I think I had forgotten that just when you think every thing is going great, something will usually go wrong."

"That doesn't always have to happen."

"It doesn't have to – but it seems to," she said. "I need to accept that and be ready for anything. I also need to expand my circle of friends."

"Am I in the circle now?"

She gave him a wry smile. "You're taking up a large part of it."

He rested his arms on the table as he leaned forward. "I think your friends understand your obsession, Adrianna. And from what you've told me about Will, he supported your career. He wanted the best for you."

"He did. He was good for me, too. He helped me take life less seriously. I'm not sure I helped him though. I called his mother earlier."

"Why?"

"My unanswered questions. She said that she and her husband had spoken to Will several times the night he was murdered. They wanted him to work at the law firm, reconsider law school. She thought it was time he had a grown-up job."

"It doesn't sound like they knew him very well," Wyatt commented.

"I don't think they knew him at all. Will didn't have a lot of ambition. He just wanted a job where he could have fun and make enough money to live on. He supported me, but I don't think he ever really understood my desire to have a big career. The irony is that now I'm being offered exactly what I always wanted, and I can't seem to take it."

"Because you're scared." He sat back in his seat, tilting his head, as his gaze settled on hers. "Maybe your fear of being in the kitchen has nothing to do with what happened that night."

"Of course it does," she said, surprised by his words. "What else would it be?"

"Maybe it has to do with the fear that you won't be able to do what you always thought you could do -- be the chef of your dreams."

"I'm a good chef," she defended. "I know that."

"But you don't have to prove it if you don't go back to work."

"I've already proven it. That's why Stephan is giving me the job."

"And that's why you should take it," he said. "Because you're good and you deserve it." He paused. "I think your mom would be very proud of you."

Her eyes blurred with unexpected tears. Very few people knew anything about her mom. She still couldn't quite believe she'd shared so much of her life story with Wyatt.

"She did the best she could for me. I don't blame her for not giving me some idyllic childhood. She was sick.

She gave me all she had."

"She gave you heart, drive, determination. I bet she was a fighter, wasn't she?"

"For a long time, and then she just got too tired. A couple of days before she died, she told me that she was sorry. She didn't have anything left, and I remember stroking her forehead and saying, it's okay, you can go. But inside, I was screaming, don't go." She took a breath and blew it out. "I didn't mean to go back there. Let's talk about you."

"I think you know way too much about me."

"No, I'm still learning. Today, I found out you like muscle cars. And that you're a really fast eater." She grabbed the last onion ring. "At least you saved me one."

"You snooze you lose."

"I wasn't snoozing. I was talking to you."

He laughed and the sound warmed her soul.

"You should do that more often," she told him.

At her words, he caught himself.

"Don't," she said quickly. "Don't stop. You deserve to laugh once in a while."

"I'll laugh my ass off when I get Steph back," he said.

"I can't wait to see her again," she said.

He frowned. "I forget that you've actually seen her, talked to her…"

"She didn't talk back. But she did look at me with your sharp, piercing blue eyes. She's a tough little girl, Wyatt. I suspect she takes after you, and I know she's going to come through this."

"I hope so. I can't believe I've missed so much of her life already."

"There's a lot more to come. She's only eight."

"That's what I keep telling myself." He paused as Josephine came over to their table.

"You'll still have to deal with her first date and getting her driver's license, falling in love, getting her heart broken

—"

Wyatt put up his hand. "Stop, that's way too much for me to think about. I'm still working on the easy things like learning how to make a French braid. Although, it's been so long, I've forgotten."

She smiled. "I can't quite picture you braiding your daughter's hair."

"It really was just me and Stephanie for a long time, even before Jen took off."

"Your burgers will be up shortly," Josephine interrupted, sliding into the booth next to Adrianna. "Now, let's talk. Why do I have the feeling this visit isn't purely social?"

"Because you could always see right through me," Adrianna said. "First, can I say that I feel badly that I haven't been back in a while?"

Josephine patted her hand. "Oh, don't give it another thought. I know why you stayed away."

"Because I'm inconsiderate and thoughtless?"

"Because you've made a life for yourself, and you don't want to look back. It's like when you're climbing a ladder, Adrianna. It's a good idea never to look down. You can freeze when you realize how high you are. It's better to just keep looking up, then you don't lose your momentum or get scared."

"That's remarkably right on the mark," she said, not sure why she was surprised. Josephine had always been able to read her so well. "But it was stupid to think that coming back here would derail me in any way. Seeing you isn't going to knock me off the ladder. It's only going to make me want to keep on going, make you proud of me."

"Oh, I already am." She glanced over at Wyatt. "What brings you here, Officer?"

"Actually, it's Inspector," he said. "But good guess."

She shot Adrianna a quick look. "I am surprised to find you hanging out with a police officer."

"I'm helping Wyatt look for his daughter. His ex-wife took her a couple of years ago, and his little girl needs to be rescued."

"Oh, dear, that doesn't sound good."

"We're hoping you can help," Adrianna continued. "His ex-wife was working at Ricky's as a stripper. She called herself Carly. One of her friends said she used to come in here."

"This is a photo of her and also my daughter from a few years ago," Wyatt said, pulling out two photographs and placing them on the table. "They've dyed their hair brown."

Josephine studied the pictures. "Sure, I've seen them, more than a few times."

"Did you talk to them?" Wyatt asked.

"I talk to everyone," Josephine said. "The little girl loved my tomato soup and grilled cheese sandwich."

At her words, Wyatt turned pale. "She ordered that?" he asked, his voice choked with emotion.

"Every single time," she said, her tone softening as she looked at him. "You used to make it for her, didn't you?"

He nodded, his lips tightening. "At least she hasn't forgotten everything I did for her."

"How long has it been since you've seen her?" Josephine asked Wyatt.

"Two years."

She shook her head, pursing her lips at the thought. "I knew there was something off with those two, but I couldn't get the woman to talk. She always sat facing the door as if she was used to looking over her shoulder. Now I know why."

"She told people that I hurt her, but that was a lie."

Josephine gave him a long hard look. "I believe you. Adrianna wouldn't be with you if she didn't trust you. She's a good judge of character, and she doesn't trust easily, so if she's invested in you, than you're all right in my book."

Adrianna was touched that Josephine had such faith in her.

"Do you have any idea where I could find my daughter?" Wyatt asked.

"I think she was living at the Graceland Apartments, a few blocks from here. I can't remember the last time I saw her, but I think it was a few weeks ago. She had Becky's daughter with her."

"So you knew Becky?" Adrianna asked.

"She was sweeter than Carly, a lot more trusting. That little boy of hers seemed to take care of her instead of the other way around. I think she got involved with some call girl service. I tried to help her, but when those girls get offered big money, it's hard for them to turn it down." She paused for breath. "I wish I could be of more help." She got to her feet. "I'll get your food, so you can be on your way."

"Thanks, Josephine," Adrianna said. "I promise to visit more often."

"I'm going to hold you to that."

When Josephine had left, Adrianna looked over at Wyatt, noting the tense expression in his eyes. "Are you all right?"

"It's weird that such a small thing like tomato soup ..." he couldn't finish the sentence. "Never mind."

"Do you want to skip the food and go to the apartment building now?"

"It looks like the burgers are on their way," he said, tipping his head to the waitress moving in their direction. Let's eat first."

"Okay. You're going to love these burgers. Trust me."

"I do trust you. And not just about the burgers."

His warm, caring gaze wrapped around her heart. "I'm glad," she said softly as the waitress set down their food.

* * *

Forty-five minutes later, they left the diner and walked three blocks to the Graceland Apartments, an aging apartment building of twenty-some units. "This looks like a dump," Wyatt muttered. "How could a rich girl like Jen want to live in a place like this?"

"I wonder why she didn't find a way to get money from her parents," Adrianna asked, as she stared up at the peeling paint and the metal sign dangling by one bolt.

He'd wondered about that, too. He'd always believed they'd found a way to help her. But maybe the money had run out. Or Jen had blown her parents' cash on drugs. "I've been watching their accounts for the last two years," he said to Adrianna. "It would have been difficult for them to move money without me being able to follow it."

As he finished speaking, it occurred to him that by keeping such a close eye on her parents, he might have forced Jen to live in places like this, not that he cared about her, but he'd put his daughter in the same position.

"It was probably because of my intense scrutiny that Jen and Stephanie had to live like this. I cut off the money supply."

"She had a choice. She could have surrendered. She could have put her child first. You didn't do any of this, Wyatt. It's all on Jennifer. But let's just see if she's here or has been here. If she's not, then we move on."

He liked Adrianna's take-charge attitude. He usually had an endless supply of energy when it came to searching for his daughter, but time was taking its toll, and some days it was more difficult to be optimistic than others.

Adrianna led the way into the office, a small room with a desk, some filing cabinets, and a TV hanging off the wall. It reminded him very much of the office at the Fantasy Inn. A skinny, pimply-faced male about twenty gave him a bored look.

"Yeah?" the kid asked.

"I'm looking for a woman named Carly," he said. "She

has two little girls with her." He flashed his badge and pulled out the photos.

"They don't look familiar," the kid said vaguely.

A blast of fury ran through him. He wanted to reach across the desk and squeeze some better answers out of this kid. He was so damn tired of being given the run around. Adrianna must have sensed his frustration, because her hand was suddenly on his arm, her fingers digging into his skin.

"Where's the manager?" she asked.

"Kyle will be back in an hour."

"Then we'll wait," Wyatt said. "Or you can look on your computer and give me a list of tenants."

"I can't do that. It's private."

"I can get a search warrant," he threatened.

"Then get one," the kid said, obviously not unfamiliar with cops wanting information about tenants. "You'll have to wait outside. I'm locking up for a while."

The kid got to his feet, and they had no choice but to leave. The door was locked behind them.

He paced back and forth on the sidewalk as he considered his options.

"Can you really get a search warrant?" Adrianna asked.

"Probably not," he admitted.

"Maybe the manager will give you more information when he gets back."

"Maybe, but doubtful," he said, wishing he could recapture the feeling of hope he'd had earlier. "Every time I turn around I hit a brick wall. I have no idea if Jen is here now, or if she's ever been here. I could waste another hour waiting for someone who's going to tell me nothing."

"That's the risk, but you still have other clues, too," she pointed out. "We're much further ahead than we were yesterday."

"Are we?" he asked, thrusting a hand through his hair. "Sometimes I feel like I'm just running around in circles."

"Eventually Jen will make a mistake."

"I've been telling myself that for two years. She was smarter than I gave her credit for. I underestimated her." He took a breath. "I have to admit that part of me doesn't want to find them here, because I don't want to think my daughter has been living in this shithole."

"Don't think about that. Just focus on the reunion you're going to have."

Adrianna glanced down at her watch, and he suddenly realized the time.

"You're supposed to be at Vincenzo's now, aren't you?" he asked.

"This is more important," she said. "That can wait."

"No, you need to go to your meeting."

"I can do it tomorrow."

"You need to do it today." As much as he liked having her by his side, he didn't want to be the reason she lost her opportunity at a great job. "Take my car. I can cab it back."

"I'll take the bus. It's a quick ride from here. And who knows where your next clue will lead you?"

He couldn't argue with that, but he still wasn't going to put her on the bus. "Hang on a second," he said, taking out his phone. "I'll get you a cab."

"That wasn't necessary," she said, when he ended the call.

"The bus takes forever. A cab will be here in a few minutes."

"All right." She shifted her feet somewhat nervously. "I hope I can actually do this. Go inside Vincenzo's."

"When you walk in the door, don't look away from the spot where you saw Will," he advised. "Fear is like a bully. When you run, it likes to chase. When you look it in the eye, it backs down."

"I'll try to remember that. But I'm not sure I can do it."

"You can. I have faith in you." A moment later a cab pulled up, and he opened the door for her. "Good luck."

"Thanks. I'll call you later."

He shut the door and watched her drive off, hoping she'd make it into the kitchen. He wished he could do more for her, but this was one battle she was going to have to fight by herself.

Chapter Thirteen

Adrianna felt like she had weights around her ankles as she got out of the cab and walked toward the front door of Vincenzo's. She kept reminding herself that she'd been inside the restaurant two days earlier, that she'd spent time in the office, and nothing bad had happened. But she hadn't looked at the floor. She'd been very careful not to do that. Did she have the courage to face her biggest fear today?

She hoped so. She felt stronger, more like herself again. Watching Wyatt search for his daughter, had given her new perspective. There was a whole world happening around her, and she needed to get back in it. She couldn't change the past. The men who had killed Will had already stolen enough from her; they weren't going to get the rest of her life.

Putting a firm hand on the handle, she opened the door and stepped across the threshold. It was that in between time where the restaurant emptied after lunch and the staff regrouped for dinner. The podium where the hostesses worked was empty. The bartender was at the far end of the bar, in discussion with one of the waitresses. There was no one around, no one to distract her from looking where she needed to look.

It was incredibly difficult to lower her gaze. Somehow

she managed to do it. The floor had been redone, the carpet ripped up, the wood beneath sanded to a fine sheen. But she could still see Will lying there, the blood pooling under his head and running through the strands of his blond hair. There had been so much blood.

Her stomach rolled over as Will's image flashed through her head. He'd been on his back, his eyes wide open and shocked.

She drew in a shaky breath, trying not to run away from the memory. She needed to confront it. She could feel her blood rushing through her veins, her heart thudding against her chest. A montage of images passed in front of her eyes.

"Will," she whispered, seeing his face again, but this time his eyes weren't lifeless. They were smiling at her. That's the way she wanted to remember him – not as that quiet, still, shocked figure but as the man who had made her laugh, who had forced her to take life less seriously, who had loved her ... even when she hadn't loved him back.

As she stared at the floor, Will's body faded away and all she saw was the wood – beautiful, shiny, dark wood. She'd chased away the bully.

When she lifted her gaze, she could finally see the rest of the room for what it was – a warm, welcoming dining room, where people came to share a meal, to converse, to enjoy themselves.

Her feet moved without conscious thought. She was vaguely aware of some of the servers saying hello, but her gaze was now fixed on the kitchen door.

She moved through the door, trying not to think about what she was doing. The quiet of the dining room was sharply contrasted with the bustling prep of dinner service. She saw Lindsay first, then Roberto, Cameron, and Jeannie. They were doing what they always did, chopping, slicing, broiling, sautéing ... One after the other looked up, until they were all staring at her, and a hush descended on the room.

Her gaze caught on a spill on the counter. She frowned. "That needs to be cleaned up," she said.

Jeannie, one of the salad chefs, rushed to do her bidding. "Sorry, Chef," she said.

The title resonated down deep. She'd worked long and hard to become a chef. She'd earned it. And she wasn't giving it up.

"Welcome back, Chef," Lindsay said with a broad smile and eyes that looked suspiciously moist.

The others followed suit with welcoming greetings. These people were her family, and this was her home. Why the hell had she ever been scared to come back to the place where she belonged?

"Adrianna?" Stephan said from behind her.

She whirled around to see the question and hope in his eyes. "I'd like to accept your job offer," she said.

Pleasure filled his gaze. "I am so happy to hear that. Are you starting now?"

She laughed. "No, I'll start Monday. I need to wrap up a few things. But I am coming back. I've missed this place."

"And we have missed you. Monday is good." He stepped forward to hug her. "I'm very happy with your decision. And our customers will be excited, too."

"I'm sorry I took so long, Stephan."

He grabbed hold of her hands and squeezed. "You suffered a loss. We all did. But together we move forward. We're family."

"Yes, we are family." She drew in a deep breath and then turned to the kitchen staff. "Before I leave, I have some ideas to share with you regarding the dishes I tasted the other night. So gather around."

Two hours later with new sauces underway and dinner prep almost finished, Adrianna said her goodbyes. Instead of leaving through the back door as many of the staff did, she made her way through the front of the restaurant one more time. The dining room was filling up now. There were families, and singles, and couples in love. Everyone was looking forward to a lovely dinner, an evening out, a break from their lives, and that's the way it was supposed to be.

Lindsay followed her out the door and onto the sidewalk. "I'm incredibly thrilled you're coming back to work. The food tonight is already going to be ten times better. I don't know how we got so far off track."

"I'm not sure Roberto will be happy that I'm taking over his position."

"Roberto was drowning in a job he wasn't qualified for. He might not admit it, but he knew it. We all did. So what changed your mind – or should I say who?"

"It was just time," Adrianna said.

"And the hot cop had nothing to do with it?"

"He did give me some good advice."

"Where is he anyway? You two have been attached at the hip the last few days."

"He's taking care of some business. I actually didn't realize I'd stayed so long," she said, realizing it was almost six. She pulled out her cell phone. There were no messages.

"Something wrong?" Lindsay asked.

"Just wondering why Wyatt hasn't called me. I thought he might have more news by now."

"Any more sightings of his daughter?"

"No, and Ben took off earlier, so I don't know where he is either."

"You're getting really involved with this guy and his problems."

"He needs my help."

"And what do you need?"

"To help him," she said, deliberately avoiding the question in Lindsay's eyes.

"Come on, Adrianna. Wyatt is a very attractive man,

and I can totally see why you're hot for him, but he seems to have a lot on the line with his daughter and his ex-wife, and I don't want you to get caught up in his problems. You've had enough darkness in your life, and you're just coming out of it. I don't want to see you dragged down. You should have some fun, so maybe a guy who isn't so intense is a better choice right now."

"Wyatt isn't dragging me down. In a strange way, he's lifted me up. I can't explain it, but he made me look at my life differently, and it was kind of an eye-opener. Besides that, we're not involved in the way you mean. We haven't slept together."

"I suspect that's coming."

"We're friends."

"Kissing friends."

"I'm leaving and you need to go back to work. And while I appreciate your warnings, I'm a big girl. I can take care of myself."

"You're a little naïve when it comes to love."

"We're not talking about love," she said, although her heart skipped a beat at the thought. Wyatt in love would be something to see. But after his experience with Jennifer, she doubted he'd be going down that road anytime soon. "I'll see you later, Lindsay."

"Call me if you need any more unsolicited advice," Lindsay said.

She smiled and said good-bye, then headed home.

* * *

Adrianna had hoped that Ben might be waiting at her apartment building, but there was no sign of him. No sign of Wyatt either, and he wasn't answering his phone. Once inside her apartment, she checked her mail and email, tidied up the bathroom, made a snack and then started to worry. Where was Wyatt? Why wasn't he calling her back?

By eight o'clock, she had the feeling something was very wrong. At nine, she hopped in her car and drove to Wyatt's condo. His car was out front, and there was a light on in the living room. Maybe something wasn't wrong. Maybe he'd found Stephanie and taken her home and was just too busy reuniting with his daughter to call her back.

Her hope faded a few moments later when Wyatt opened the door. He looked horrible. His button-down shirt was hanging out of his jeans, his eyes were bloodshot, his hair was standing on end, and his breath reeked of liquor...

"What happened?" she asked, preparing herself for the worst and praying it wouldn't be that bad. "Did you find them? Did you get into their apartment?"

Wyatt moved away from the door and headed over to the couch where a half empty bottle of vodka sat on the coffee table next to a dirty pink blanket.

Her heart turned over at the sight of that blanket. It had to be Stephanie's. "Wyatt, talk to me," she ordered.

He poured a shot of vodka and threw it down his throat. "Nothing to say," he finally got out, putting the glass down.

"Is this Stephanie's blanket?" She reached for it, but he grabbed her arm.

"Don't touch it," he bit out.

"You're scaring me. Is she all right?"

"How the hell would I know? This is all I have of hers." He drew in a ragged breath. "I found the blanket by the dumpster at the apartment building. Stephanie wouldn't have left it behind. She had this blanket since she was born."

"What else did you find?" she asked, worried about his answer.

"Nothing," he replied, pouring himself another shot.

"Wyatt, stop. Tell me what happened."

He ignored her plea and took another drink. Then he said, "I waited around for the manager. He finally showed up. He told me that the last time he saw Jen she was wasted, and some guy – some guy," he repeated, "was putting her and two little girls in the back of a cab. When he went up to the apartment, all their stuff was gone. Apparently, she skipped out on the rent. I checked the dumpsters to see if she'd thrown away any clues. That's when I found the blanket." He sank down on the couch, reaching for the bottle.

She snatched it away from him. "You don't need any more to drink."

"It's over, Adrianna. She's gone again, and I'll never find her. I can't keep looking. It's not getting me anywhere."

"No," she said firmly, sitting down next to him. "You don't quit. You told me that, and I believed you."

"Well, I lied."

"No, you didn't. You love your little girl. This is just a setback." She had to find a way to convince him. She couldn't stand seeing him so defeated.

"They could be anywhere, Adrianna. We're back to square one."

"We're not. They got in a cab. So call the cab company, find out where they went."

"I already did that. The cab took them to the airport. They're not in the city anymore."

She was beginning to understand the depth of his despair. "What airline?"

"United," he said dully, leaning back against the couch. "That's where the trail ends."

"Did they pay the cab with a credit card?"

"No that would be too easy."

"Did you talk to Josh? Does he have any ideas?"

"He's fresh out," Wyatt said. "And so am I. It's hopeless. It's done. Jen won. She beat me."

"She did not beat you," Adrianna said. "And I'm not done. I'm going to help you find her. I never should have left you alone earlier."

He gave her a weak smile. "You smell like garlic. You cooked today, didn't you?"

"Yes, but I don't want to talk about that right now."

"We might as well. It really is over, Adrianna. She left town."

"What about the passenger lists? Can you access those?" she asked.

"Josh couldn't find her name, but who knows what I.D. she is using now."

Adrianna got up and paced around the room, desperately wanting to help him. She had to think, because he was too exhausted and too sad to do it for himself.

"You said she was with a guy. Maybe it was that Brad guy – the music promoter."

"Brad Pennington. He moved out of his apartment two weeks ago, probably about the same time Jen did. I can't find any record of where he went."

"But someone knows him. He's a music promoter. He sounds like someone every club in town would know how to get a hold of." She sat down next to him. "We are not done fighting, Wyatt."

He leaned his head back against the couch. "You're amazing. Beautiful and strong and everything a woman should be."

"Thank you, although I suspect I owe that compliment to all the vodka you drank. I'm going to make you some coffee."

"Did you get the job?" he asked.

"Yes. I did what you said. I looked down. I faced the memories head on, and after a few minutes all I saw was the floor and not Will's body. And then I went into the kitchen and everyone was there, and I remembered why I love it so much. I helped with dinner prep and then I told Stephan I'd start work on Monday."

He gave her a nod. "That's good. You should get back

to work. You have too much talent to waste."

"Are you hungry? Did you eat anything?"

He shrugged. "I don't remember."

"Okay, I'll make coffee and something to eat from whatever I can find in your kitchen, and then we're going to come up with a plan of attack."

"I'm not hungry. Just thirsty," he said pointedly, as he tried to grab the bottle.

"That's why I'm making you coffee." She took the vodka bottle into the kitchen and drained what was left down the sink. She started coffee but didn't see much in the fridge to turn into a meal. She'd start with toast. At least it would soak up some of the alcohol. She was sorry that she'd waited so long to come over. She'd known something was wrong; she should have acted sooner.

When the coffee and toast were ready, she headed back into the living room, surprised to find Wyatt off the couch. She really hoped he hadn't left the apartment. Venturing down the hall, she found him lying on his bed, staring up at the ceiling. She sat next to him. "I made you toast. It's in the kitchen. Do you want me to bring it in here?"

"I'm tired," he told her.

"You should sleep."

"Can't. When I close my eyes, I see her face – Stephanie's sweet little face, her trusting blue eyes. I was supposed to protect her."

"Don't run from the memory," she said, "take your own advice. Close your eyes and let yourself see her."

"I love her so much, Adrianna."

"I know."

"When she was born, it was like this huge flood of feeling. It overwhelmed me. I wasn't even sure I wanted to be a father, but the second she was born, something clicked inside of me. Her tiny finger curled around mine, and I was lost. I'd never felt so much emotion. I wanted her life to be perfect. I did everything I could to make that happen. But her life wasn't perfect. Because I gave her a rotten mother." He paused, a bitter smile playing around his lips. "It used to drive Jen nuts that Stephanie would always run to me, instead of to her. But why would she run to a woman who wasn't there half the time or the other half of the time told her to go away?" He shook his head in confusion. "Stephanie and I had such a bond. We were in sync. I knew what she wanted before she did. Now…"

"The bond is still there," she said, wanting to reassure him.

"I don't know if I'll ever see her again."

"You will. This is just a temporary setback, Wyatt."

"You said that before."

"And I'll say it again until you believe it."

"You asked me how I could keep going –"

"And you told me it was by looking at Stephanie's picture." She pointed to one of the framed photographs on the dresser. "She's right there. Look at her."

"I can't," he said. "Every time I think I'm close, it turns out to be another dead end."

She needed to find a way to convince him that he would rebound. She wasn't surprised he was reeling from the latest piece of news. It certainly was going to be more difficult to start looking for Jennifer in a new city. But she couldn't think about that right now, and neither could he.

"You'll bounce back, Wyatt," she said firmly. "Because no matter how bad you're feeling right now, come morning, you will be on your game, on the attack. You'll have a new plan, a fresh point of view."

"Just because you say it doesn't make it true," he said cynically.

"Oh, come on, Wyatt," she said a little more harshly. "This isn't you. You stay positive. You keep moving forward. You don't quit."

"I quit on Jen," he said candidly. "I gave up on her long before the separation or the divorce, even before the first rehab. I don't know when it actually happened – when we stopped giving a damn about each other, but I think it was early on."

"Well, she wasn't worth fighting for."

"Maybe if I had fought for her, things would be different."

"Why? Because then she wouldn't have gotten depressed when she got pregnant? She wouldn't have abandoned her daughter when she needed her? She wouldn't have taken painkillers after a car accident? I know you want to control everything around you and that you think you have infinite power over people, but you don't. You can't make someone do the right thing. Trust me on that, I know," she added, thinking about all the people she had desperately wanted to change into someone better. Eventually, she'd had to face the fact that she could only change herself. "Why don't you eat something?" she said again. "If toast isn't good, I can go to the market or the nearest restaurant and pick you up something."

"I'm not hungry," he said. "And you don't need to take care of me."

But she wanted to take care of him, and she was shocked by how much she wanted to ease his pain. She'd closed her heart down a long time ago, and while she tried to help people, she also tried not to get personally involved in their lives. She had enough of her own issues. But she had gotten incredibly involved with Wyatt. She knew more about him than she knew about people she'd been friends with for years. She was heavily invested in his search, in his pain, in his need. It was a little scary. But it was too late to back out, to pretend she didn't know what she knew or felt what she felt.

"What about the television?" she said as the silence went on too long, as Wyatt's direct stare was beginning to rattle her. She looked around. "Where's the remote?"

"I don't want to watch TV."

"You can't just brood. You have to do something. What about a swim? You said it was your therapy. There must be a pool open around somewhere."

"On a Saturday night?" he asked with a small smile. "Most people have better things to do than swim." He let out a sigh and held out his hand to her.

After a moment, she took it. His fingers wrapped around hers in delicious warmth.

"I shouldn't be your problem, Adrianna."

"I want to help."

"I know you do, but you can't."

A slow minute ticked by.

"Maybe I should go," she suggested.

His grip tightened. "Or – you could stay."

The plea in his eyes was born of so many dark and swirling emotions that she was afraid to say yes and afraid to say no.

He reached out with his free hand and tucked a strand of her hair behind her ear. "You're so beautiful, Adrianna, so honest and courageous, full of heart. Why didn't I meet you first? Why didn't I find you before I got my heart ripped apart?"

How could she answer that question? "I don't know, Wyatt. Maybe we were meant to meet now. This is the right time."

"You said it was the wrong time, the wrong place, and that I was the wrong man," he reminded her.

She had said that. She'd been trying to convince herself that any kind of relationship with Wyatt was out of the question, but now she wasn't so sure.

"You were right," he continued. "I don't have anything to offer a woman."

"I think you have a lot to offer," she said. "You have an amazing amount of love inside your heart for your daughter, and I know that extends to everyone in your life, your family, your friends. Any woman would be lucky to be a part of your circle, to be the person that you care about."

He ran his finger down the side of her face, blazing a trail of heat that ignited all of her nerve endings. "Prove it," he said, his eyes glittering with desire.

"I don't have to prove anything."

"Then you should go," he said, but his hand still held tight to hers.

She wanted to get up, to break the connection, but his gaze, the lightness of his finger as it ran across her jaw, made it impossible for her to move. The attraction between them had been simmering since their first meeting. And now it was starting to burn.

She didn't play with fire. She was cautious in relationships. She protected herself.

So why did she suddenly want to jump off a cliff with Wyatt?

"You're not moving," he said.

"I'm trying to," she said with a helpless smile.

His fingers cupped her chin. "You have the prettiest mouth."

"I always look better after a couple of shots of vodka."

"Stop making this about that. You know I like you. You know I want you."

She caught her bottom lip between her teeth. Hearing the words said so boldly, so bluntly, sent a jolt of desire through her. She'd never had a man state himself so clearly. And she found it both heart-stopping and terrifying.

"You want me, too," he added, a knowing gleam in his eyes. "You don't want to, but you do."

"You think you know what's in my head?" she challenged.

He nodded, his eyes very serious. "Yes."

"Kind of cocky, aren't you?"

"I just know you, Adrianna. I've felt like that since the first minute we met, since our coins clashed, and you yelled at me for ruining your wish."

"I didn't yell, but your coin did knock mine out of the fountain."

"Your wish still came true. You got over your fear. You're going back to work, so I didn't ruin anything."

His hand threaded through her hair. "I like these curls. They're like you, messy, a little unpredictable, but gorgeous."

"You're quite the smooth talker after some drinks."

"I'm not drunk, Adrianna."

"Says you."

"I'm actually sober enough to tell you that you *should* go home."

"You just asked me to stay."

"I've thought better of that. I don't want to hurt you. You deserve someone…"

His words annoyed her. "Stop it, Wyatt. Stop trying to call all the shots and control everything."

"You mean like you try to do?"

"Okay, you're right. I like to have control and so do you. We've both had to fight for our lives and we've both been hurt in the past. But that doesn't mean we stop living, stop trying, stop putting our heart on the line." She took a breath and decided to act on what she'd just said. "I don't want to play it safe anymore. I don't want to hide in my apartment, or look the other way, or pretend that everything will be all right if I follow all the rules. Life is risky and short. I care about you, Wyatt. I don't know how it happened so fast, but it did."

"I don't want you to care about me," he said, his tone harsh and unyielding.

She touched his tensed jaw with her fingers. "It's not your choice. It's mine."

"Don't care about me, Adrianna," he said. A long pause followed, and then he added. "Just want me. Want me for tonight – the way I want you."

Her heart beat faster at his words, her nerves tingling from the look in his eyes, the need, the desire. All that intensity that she associated with Wyatt was fixed on her, and it was more than a little exciting.

It would have been easier if he'd reached for her, if he'd taken control, but she'd just told him she was making her own decisions, and he was giving her every opportunity to determine what happened next.

"You're killing me here," he muttered.

She smiled. "Impatient?"

"Hell, yes!"

She put her hands on his chest and pressed him back against the pillows, and then she lowered her head. His mouth was as hot as she remembered, and the way he slid his tongue along her lips, made her a little crazy. She opened her mouth, taking his tongue inside, wanting to be as close to him as possible.

Her breasts grazed his chest, her nipples suddenly on fire for the same attention from his mouth. She broke the kiss and sat back, then pulled her shirt up and over her head, shaking out her hair. She felt a little self-conscious as Wyatt gazed at her breasts, barely covered in a sheer black bra. She reached for the clasp but Wyatt stopped her.

"Wait."

"What? You don't like what you see?" she asked, not certain how to read the look in his eyes.

"Oh, God, no. You're gorgeous."

"Then what's the problem?"

"You should have wine, candles and flowers, lots and lots of flowers. You should have romance and soft music."

She put her fingers against his lips. "Stop it, that's not me, none of it. I've never had that kind of perfection."

"That's why you deserve it. You should have the fairytale."

She shook her head. "I don't believe in fairytales. But I believe in us. And I want this. I want tonight. I want you."

"You'll feel differently in the morning. You'll want promises that I can't give you."

"Let's let the morning take care of itself."

"Adrianna—"

"You said you wanted me – prove it," she said with a smile.

"You're going to be sorry you challenged me," he said with a wicked grin.

"I don't think so." She unbuttoned his shirt and slid her hands along his chest.

He groaned. "I want those hands all over me."

"Then you're going to have to take off some clothes," she said.

He stripped off his shirt before she finished talking. "Your turn."

She opened her bra and pulled it off. One long hungry look, and then his hands immediately covered her breasts, his heat burning her skin.

"So pretty," he murmured. And then he pulled her closer so she was straddling his legs and her breasts were at the same level of his mouth. He kissed one and then the other, light, teasing kisses that only built the anticipation. Finally, his lips closed around one nipple, his tongue licking it into a fine point of need that shot through her body. She ran her hands through his hair, holding him close, feeling his body hardening beneath hers.

Wyatt lifted his head and kissed her on the lips, then pushed her to the side as he shimmied out of his jeans.

She stared at him in delight. His body was honed from swim workouts and physical activity, and she couldn't wait to do what he asked, put her hands all over him.

He smiled and then reached for the button on her jeans. She fell on her back as he helped her off with her pants and tossed them on the floor. Then his body covered hers. Every point of contact was hot, from their mouths, to their breasts, to their hips and their groins. She loved the weight of him, the male scent, the power in his body.

He suddenly moved off of her and she was stunned to feel a sense of loss. But then his mouth found her breast again, then moved lower to her stomach and between her legs, tasting, touching, letting no part of her go unseen or unloved. She'd never had someone take such time, and the tension built to an incredible degree, finally bursting free. Still trembling when he made his way back up her body, she found new delight in touching him, running her hands up and down his back and buttocks, feeling his hard cock seeking her softness. She urged him closer, wanting to feel him inside of her, the ultimate connection. It was the bond she'd been seeking since they first met, and when he finally slid into her, she felt as if their connection was finally complete. And everything in her world was exactly right.

Chapter Fourteen

Holding Adrianna in his arms, listening to the soft sounds of her breath as she slept against his chest, sliding his hand down the curve of her back, feeling her move against him as she slept – it was so damn good. She'd responded to him with so much passion and heat it had taken his breath away. She was a mix of sexy and sweet, hard and soft, sharp and tender and he liked every little thing about her. It was a little shocking to realize just how much he cared. He'd had sex in the last two years, but this had been different, this had been mind-blowing. They'd made love slow, then fast, and then slow again, and he'd felt like they were completely in sync, as if they'd been made to be together, and that shook him up, too.

How had this woman gotten so far into his life, into his head, into his heart? He'd thought he'd closed himself off, locked up his emotions, but Adrianna had found her way in. She'd pushed past his defenses, and he had no idea what the hell they were going to do next.

Adrianna had told him she wasn't looking for promises, but that had been last night, and today was a new day. And she deserved promises. She deserved a man who was whole, whose heart was intact, and that wasn't him. He couldn't devote his life to her. Every last bit of focus had to go into finding Stephanie. He'd already disappointed friends and family with his lack of concern for their lives. Adrianna would be next. It was only a matter of time. He didn't want to hurt her. That was the last thing he wanted to do.

She stirred alongside him. "I can feel you tensing up, Wyatt," she murmured as she lifted her head from his chest.

She looked so goddamned beautiful, her lips soft, her eyes sleepy, her hair a soft cloud. She was like his personal angel and a very sexy angel at that.

"Are you feeling guilty?" she asked, meeting his gaze.

"For taking advantage of you – a little."

"You didn't take advantage. I gave you what I wanted to give. I thought we cleared that up last night."

"You gave me more than I deserved."

"I think we gave each other a lot. I don't want you to have regrets, Wyatt, because I don't. You said you couldn't make me any promises, and I'm not asking for any. It's not the right time. I know that."

"It might never be the right time," he said, the words coming out a little more harshly than he'd intended.

She caught her lip between her teeth. "Okay."

"Okay?" he echoed. "That's it?"

"Yes." She let out a breath. "I've spent so much time planning for the future that I haven't been enjoying the moment, and I want to enjoy this one. I like waking up in your arms."

"Yeah, it's not bad," he said, feeling a rush of warm tenderness toward her. "You're making things too easy for me."

"Well, if anyone took advantage last night, it was me. You were the one who'd been drinking. I was completely sober."

"I was sober enough. And I'm sorry about the vodka. That's the first time in two years I've touched alcohol. I always wanted to have my wits about me, be ready to act at any moment, but yesterday was a setback. Knowing that Jen had left town – it hit me hard."

"I know." She sat up, pulling the sheet up to her chest as she faced him.

"I've already seen everything," he told her.

"Yes, but that was different. Now we're talking," she replied with an endearing blush.

"I liked it better when we weren't talking."

She gave him a playful slap on the arm. "We have to get back to work. What's the plan? And don't tell me you don't have one."

"I don't have one." He felt guilty to admit that. "We'll have to start over, figure out where she might have gone, who she was with, how she paid for airline tickets." He felt overwhelmed by the thought of starting over again. They'd been so close, just a few steps behind. But wasn't that the story of his life the last two years?

Adrianna frowned, tucking her hair behind her ear as she thought for a moment. Then her expression suddenly changed. Her eyes filled with excitement.

"Oh, my God, Wyatt."

"What?" he asked warily.

"You're wrong. She's not gone. She hasn't left town."

"She went to the airport with a man. She got on a plane with my kid."

"She came back," Adrianna said confidently.

"You don't know that."

"I do know that. That flight was two weeks ago. I saw Stephanie three days ago by the fountain."

Her words took him by surprise. He'd forgotten that she'd seen Stephanie so recently. He'd been fixated on the times she'd seen Stephanie behind the restaurant that he'd forgotten about the fountain.

"They came back," Adrianna repeated. "Jennifer and Stephanie are in the city."

"Maybe you're right," he said, hope running through

his body, giving him energy again. "I didn't put the timeline together. I was so caught up in the fact Jen had gone to the airport, I couldn't think straight. I couldn't remember the dates." He jumped out of bed. "I'm taking a shower."

"So now we have a plan?" she asked.

"I'll think of one in the shower." He leaned over and kissed her. "Thank you."

"You're welcome," she said with a happy smile. "We're going to find her, Wyatt. I'm more convinced of that than ever."

* * *

As Wyatt took his beautifully rugged body into the bathroom, Adrianna threw on her clothes and walked into the living room. She put on some coffee and then pulled out her cell phone. She'd been running through the clues they had, and she had an idea.

"Hi Lindsay, it's me," she said when her friend answered.

"It's eight o'clock on a Sunday morning," Lindsay grumbled.

"Really? That late, then you should be up."

"What are you so happy about?" Lindsay asked suspiciously.

"I need a favor. You have a friend in a band, right?"

"You mean Danny, the drummer?"

"Yes. I need to find a San Francisco music promoter whose first name is Brad. He books acts into local clubs. Do you think Danny might know him?"

"I take it this has to do with your hot cop."

"Yes. Brad is linked to Wyatt's ex-wife."

"I'll call Danny. He may not be up yet," Lindsay warned.

"Get back to me as soon as you can. And call me on my cell phone."

"Because you're not at home?" Lindsay ventured.

She smiled to herself. "No, I'm at Wyatt's condo."

"Really?" Her friend's voice was filled with curiosity. "Did you spend the night there?"

"As a matter of fact, I did," she confessed.

"Oh, my God, Adrianna. You slept with him? Are you okay? Was it great? I hope it wasn't horrible. It couldn't have been horrible, or you wouldn't still be there."

She laughed as Lindsay rambled on. "It was amazing. That's all I have to say."

"There's no way that's all you have to say. I want details."

"Well, you're not getting any right now. Wyatt will be out of the shower any second."

"You left him in there alone?" Lindsay asked with disappointment. "You can have a lot of fun in a shower, Adrianna."

"I had a lot of fun last night – maybe a little too much," she said, feeling slightly guilty. She had pushed Will out of her mind the night before, but now he was back.

"No, don't do that," Lindsay said quickly. "Don't think about Will."

"It hasn't been very long since –"

"Since you were happy," Lindsay finished, cutting her off. "Will would want you to be happy. He was your best friend, Adrianna. Don't wreck this new relationship out of some misplaced sense of loyalty. You're not betraying Will."

"I'm trying to not think that way," she admitted. "It's just not fair that he's gone. He was so young. He had so much to live for. How can I be happy when he's dead?"

"Nothing about this situation is fair. But you're still alive, and you have to go on living. And that means you get to be happy, too."

"Well, this may turn out to be nothing more than a one-night stand. Wyatt's life is complicated right now. He has other priorities, and I'm okay with that."

"You say that now, but what about tomorrow or the next day? Do you really want to be in second place all the time?"

As she thought about Lindsay's question, her gaze caught on a hand-drawn picture hanging on the fridge, and the crayon markings took away any doubts. "Wyatt needs to find his daughter. That's all that matters now."

"And when he gets her back – where does that leave you? I'm just worried that he's using you."

"I don't know what will happen when he gets Stephanie back," she said, an uneasy feeling in the pit of her stomach at the idea of never seeing or being with Wyatt again. But she couldn't go there. She'd gone into the night with her eyes wide open, and she'd live with the consequences. "I'll be okay," she said. "Whatever happens."

"I hope so. But I know you, and you don't sleep with people you don't care about. Your heart is in this, whether you want to say so or not."

She couldn't argue with that. "Call me when you reach Danny."

"I will."

As she set down her phone, Adrianna got up and walked over to the refrigerator. Stephanie had drawn a picture of a house with trees and flowers nearby. There were also two stick figures of a man and a child. The word *Daddy* was printed along the bottom of the paper.

Adrianna felt a twinge of physical pain at the sight of that one word.

She had to help Wyatt get back together with Stephanie. She wouldn't be able to let go of him until that happened.

A little voice inside her wondered how she'd be able to let go *after* that happened, but she pushed that thought aside.

Wyatt walked into the kitchen, barefoot, wearing low

slung jeans, his chest bare, his hair still damp enough to leave drips of water along his shoulders.

Her breath caught in her throat. His gaze met hers. And the desire she'd thought they'd worked out the night before was back.

"Coffee," she sputtered, dragging her gaze away from his. "I made coffee."

"Thanks," he said.

She moved over to the coffee maker and poured him a cup. "I would make breakfast, but you don't have any food."

"I haven't been shopping in a while. I'll take you out to eat."

"You don't have to do that," she said.

They stared at each other for a long moment.

"Adrianna," he began, cut off by the ring of her phone.

"That's Lindsay," she said, grabbing the phone. "That was fast. Did you find out anything?"

"Yes. It turns out Danny knows Brad pretty well. His last name is Pennington by the way. Danny said Brad works out of his house and recently moved into a condo in Russian Hill – 1426 Hyde Street."

Her heart leapt into her throat. She had an actual address. "I owe you big time."

"I plan on collecting. Good luck!"

She ended the call and turned to Wyatt with excitement. "I found the music promoter --Brad."

"How?" he asked in shock.

"I remembered that Lindsay used to date a guy in a band. I took a chance that he might know Brad, and he did. Brad just moved into a condo in Russian Hill, not very far from North Beach or the fountain where I saw the girls."

Hope flashed in his eyes. "Let's go."

She ran into the bedroom, searching for her shoes, while Wyatt quickly threw on a shirt. Then they were in his car and headed across town. She prayed that this time their lead wouldn't turn into a dead end.

* * *

Brad Pennington lived on the first floor of a six unit building on a portion of Hyde Street where the cable cars ran. One was just clanging its way past his front door when Adrianna and Wyatt arrived.

"Security building," Wyatt said grimly, looking at the directory. "There's his name. He's not hiding."

"Why would he be?" she asked. "He may not have any idea what Jen is up to."

"Good point."

She glanced at her watch. "It's only eight-thirty. Do you think a music promoter is going to be up this early on a Sunday morning?"

"Let's wake him up," Wyatt said.

"Wait. If Jen is inside and you announce yourself as a cop, she might try to run."

He nodded, his expression grim. "Fine. You do it. Ring the bell, tell him something."

She thought for a moment. "I'll use Danny's name. I'll say I'm a friend." She pushed the doorbell.

No one answered.

Her nerves tightened.

She tried the buzzer again. She did not want this to end here on the street. Brad Pennington had to be home. It was too early for him to be anywhere else. And they needed a break – just one break.

She could feel Wyatt's tension as they waited. He had his hands on hips, his fingers clenched into fists. He was ready to fight.

She rang the bell a third time.

Finally, the speaker began to crackle. "Yeah?" a man answered.

"It's Adrianna. I'm Danny's friend. He said you could

help me."

"Never heard of you. Come back later."

"Wait. It will just take a second. I work at the Vinyl Room," she said, naming a well-known club down the street from her apartment. "You'll want to hear what I have to say. Trust me. I wouldn't be here otherwise. It could be a great deal for you. Five minutes, that's all I need," she added, trying to sound as persuasive as she possibly could.

"All right. You've got five minutes."

"We're in," she whispered to Wyatt as the front door buzzed.

His answering smile was tight, his eyes determined. "You did good. I'll take it from here." He led the way up the stairs. The door to 3B was partially open. They could hear the TV on ... and the sound of a child's voice.

Wyatt froze.

She put her hand on his back. "Go on," she said quietly.

She felt his body tense as he drew in a breath, and then he pushed the door open.

On the couch in the living room were two little girls eating cereal and watching cartoons.

A man came down the hall wearing sweat pants and a t-shirt. But Wyatt wasn't looking at him, he was staring at the girl whose blue gaze had swung to his.

"Stephanie," he breathed, surging forward.

Chapter Fifteen

"Daddy?" the little girl asked, shock on her face. Her spoon dropped into her cereal with a splatter.

"It's me," Wyatt said, moving across the room. Stephanie looked the same and yet different. Her blond hair was dark brown and longer than he remembered. He wanted to throw his arms around her, but someone stopped him. It took him a minute to realize that Brad had grabbed his arm.

"What the hell is going on?" the man demanded. "Who are you?"

"Wyatt Randall. You've got my daughter, and I'm taking her back," he said flatly.

"Hold on. She doesn't have a dad," Brad returned, refusing to let go. He turned his head and yelled, "Carly, get the hell out here."

"Yeah, get her out here," Wyatt said, feeling a rush of fury that gave him enough strength to shake out of Brad's grip.

As he turned back to Stephanie, he saw that she and the other little girl were cowering in the corner between the couch and the wall. They were clearly terrified.

It broke his heart that his daughter was looking at him with fear in her eyes. *Fear*! What had Jen told her about him?

"Carly," Brad yelled again. "Don't you move," he warned Wyatt. "Not one more step."

"He's a cop," Adrianna cut in. "He's an inspector with the SFPD and that little girl was kidnapped."

Stephanie's eyes grew wider at the word *kidnapped*.

"It's me, baby," he said, holding her gaze. "You don't have to be afraid. It's Daddy."

Stephanie's lips curled in confusion, her expression a mix of confusion and uncertainty.

"I don't know anything about a kidnapping," Brad said loudly. "This has to be a mistake."

"It's not a mistake," he said, not even bothering to look at Brad.

And then he heard her voice, the voice of his nightmares.

"Wyatt?" she said.

He turned around and there she was – the woman he'd spent two years searching for. Jen was super skinny, all long limbs and bony angles. Her hair had been dyed dark brown and was cut very short. She wore black knit pants and a tank top, and she looked like she'd just gotten out of bed. As she gazed back at him, her brown eyes filled with fear and what looked to be defeat.

"You finally found me," she said. "I knew coming back here was a mistake, but I didn't know where else to go."

"What is going on, Carly?" Brad demanded.

"Her name isn't Carly. It's Jennifer," Wyatt bit out.

Jen looked at Brad. "He's right. My name is Jennifer, and this is my ex-husband, Wyatt Randall."

Wyatt couldn't believe she was standing there making introductions as if they were at a party. "You stole my child. How could you do that?"

"Our child," she said passionately. "You were taking her away from me."

"I had a good reason," he said.

"There's no reason good enough to separate a mother

from her child."

"But there is to take that child away from her father?" he snapped. Anger burned through his veins. He wanted to hit her, shake her, scream at her, the years of frustration and fear and loneliness ripping him apart like a tidal wave hitting the beach.

But the sound of Stephanie's sob spun him around. She was clinging to the girl next to her, her eyes filling with tears. She obviously had no idea what was going on.

And suddenly he didn't care about Jen anymore.

He moved across the room and squatted down next to her so that she wouldn't be scared. "I missed you, Steph. Brown Bear missed you, too. He's still sitting on your bed waiting for you to come home."

Tears streamed down her face, and her lips trembled. "Mommy said you were dead."

"I'm not dead," he said, fighting the urge to turn back to Jen and rip her apart for the lie. "I've been looking for you for a very long time."

"Mommy said we had to hide. There were bad guys after us. She said people had to call me Emily. I don't like the name Emily."

"You can be Stephanie from now on," he said, fighting for calm. "The bad guys are all gone. How about a hug?" He opened up his arms and waited.

It was the longest minute of his life. Stephanie looked to her friend, to her mother, to Brad and Adrianna. And then she turned her serious blue eyes back on him.

He wanted to reach for her. He wanted to beg her to come to him. But something inside told him that he had to wait, that it had to be her decision. He just prayed that she would make that choice, and that she wouldn't turn to her mother.

Jen had been her anchor for two years, her only parent. She'd told Stephanie lie after lie. Who knew what was going on in his little girl's head? How much damage would he have to repair? But he would fix it, he told himself. However long it took, he would find a way to make it all better.

Emotion choked him the longer the silence went on. It would kill him if she ran away. He'd finally found her; he couldn't lose her now, not again – *not to her mother*.

His arms began to ache. Stephanie bit down on her lip, the way she'd always done when she was uncertain. He hated to have to put her in the position of choosing between her mother and her father, but that's all he could do.

Finally, she moved -- one step at a time -- until her little arms were around his neck and her face was pressed against his chest.

He held her small, trembling body as tightly as he could. "I love you, baby," he whispered. "I always have."

When she lifted her head, she was gazing at him in wonder and what looked like happiness. "I'm glad you're not dead," she said.

Tears filled his eyes. He'd never cried, in all the days that she'd been gone, but now the pent-up emotion was threatening to let loose. He had to hang on. He didn't want to scare her anymore.

She put her hands on his face. "You don't have any whiskers," she said.

He smiled at the familiar statement. She'd always loved to watch him shave. She used to sit on the counter and they'd talk while he got ready for work in the morning. How he had missed those days.

"Can we go home?" Stephanie asked.

"We can absolutely go home."

"Can Sara come with us?"

He looked over Stephanie's shoulder to see an extremely worried expression on the little girl's face. "Yes," he said, knowing that was the only answer he could give at that moment. He could not take Stephanie away from her best friend. They would have to sort everything out later.

Adrianna moved next to him. "Hi Stephanie, do you remember me?" she asked.

"You're the nice lady who gave us pizza."

"That's right. Why don't I help you get your things together? You, too, Sara," she added. "Ben is going to be so happy to see you both."

"Do you know where Ben is?" Sara asked.

"I know he's been looking for you," Adrianna said. "Where are your clothes?"

"In the bedroom," Stephanie answered.

"Why don't we go get them?" she said.

Stephanie looked to him for an answer, and he nodded. "Go with Adrianna," he said as he got to his feet. It was difficult to let Stephanie out of his sight for one minute, but he knew he could trust Adrianna to keep her safe. And he needed to speak to Jen alone.

When the girls had gone down the hall, he turned to his ex-wife.

"What happens now?" she asked, crossing her arms with a defiant gesture that told him she might be defeated, but she still didn't think she'd done anything wrong.

"You're going to jail," he said flatly. "You violated a custody order. That's kidnapping."

"You can't do that to me. Think of Stephanie. Think of how she'll feel if she sees you arrest me."

"You weren't concerned about Stephanie when you told her that I was dead. How could you do that, Jen?"

"I had to. She wouldn't stop crying. She kept saying, *I want to see Daddy*. It drove me nuts."

It drove him nuts to think that his daughter had been asking for him, and he hadn't been there.

He pulled out his phone and hit speed dial for Josh. "I've got Jen," he said shortly. "Send a car to 1426 Hyde Street." He could hear Josh swearing with excitement as he ended the call.

"Look, I don't know what's going on here," Brad

began, confusion on his face.

"You're harboring a fugitive," he replied.

"Well, I didn't know that. I was just giving her a place to stay for a few weeks. She's nobody to me. I'm not involved with her."

"But you love me," Jen said to Brad, as if she were shocked at his response. "You said you were going to take care of me."

"You didn't tell me you kidnapped your own daughter," he yelled back. "What kind of a lunatic are you?"

"You can't kidnap your daughter when you're her mother," she said hotly. She turned back to Wyatt. "I have as much right to Stephanie as you do."

"No, you forfeited your rights when you put your addiction before your child."

"I'm clean now. I have been for months. Tell him, Brad. Tell him I'm a good mother."

The other man shook his head. "I'm going to call my lawyer."

"Yes, call your lawyer," Jen said. "Ask him to help me."

"No," he told her coldly. "This is your problem, not mine." Brad walked down the hall.

And then it was just the two of them.

Wyatt faced the woman he'd once loved, the woman he'd vowed to stand by for all time. A montage of images flashed through his brain, their first meeting at college, their big production of a wedding, the night Stephanie was born, the day she'd been arrested for DUI, the pill bottles he'd found hidden away in his house, the nights he'd spent alone in his bed wondering where she was and when she would come home.

"It didn't have to be this way," he said.

"Of course it did. You weren't going to let me see Stephanie, because of one mistake."

"It wasn't one mistake; it was a hundred. And I did let you see her. That's when you took her." It was clear that Jen had no remorse for what she'd done.

"She loves me. I'm her mom. You can't keep us apart."

"You mean the way you did?"

For the first time her gaze softened. "I just love her so much."

"Do you? I don't believe you were thinking of her at all. I know you used to leave her with your friend, Becky. I know my daughter was begging on the street with some other kids. How could you let her live like that?"

"I was doing my best. I couldn't get any money from my parents. And the jobs I could get weren't paying enough. But she's fine. She's great. And she loves me."

She sniffed back a tear. He stared at her, completely unmoved.

"I'm clean now, Wyatt. I know I made some mistakes in the past."

"You drove while you were high. You could have gotten our daughter killed. And who knows how many times you did that before you actually got caught?"

"I had a problem, Wyatt, but instead of helping me, you had me arrested. You sent your buddies after me."

"I didn't. I wish I had, but I didn't know at the time how far gone you were." He paused. "But I was still willing to help you, to give you another chance, and you ran."

"Stephanie is fine. I have protected her and loved her for two years, and I am a good mother."

"Save your breath. You'll never convince me," he said harshly.

"I wish you could understand –"

"That will never happen. Now, tell me, why do you have Sara – where's her mother?"

"Becky is working for an escort service. She had to take a long trip with one of the clients. I said I'd watch Sara until she got back."

"What about Ben?"

"I couldn't take both of them. It was hard enough having an extra kid but Stephanie wouldn't go with me without Sara."

"Did Becky know you weren't taking Ben?"

Guilt flashed through Jen's eyes. "I don't know."

"Of course you know. You left a twelve-year-old kid to fend for himself. That's despicable."

She shrugged. "I gave him some money. I did the best I could."

"Which as usual sucks."

"You loved me once, Wyatt. Can't you just try to help me one more time?" Tears streamed down her face. "It was the drugs that made me act crazy. But I haven't taken anything for six months."

"Good for you. I hope it continues, but I don't care. You're going to pay for what you did."

"You think Stephanie will let you cut me out of her life?" she asked. "She'll hate you."

He didn't want to think about that part right now. He needed to talk to his daughter, spend hours, days, and weeks with her, discussing anything and everything. He wanted to know her again, to rebuild the trust and the love that they'd once had.

The doorbell rang, and he buzzed in his fellow officers.

"I have to say good-bye to Stephanie," she said somewhat desperately.

He wanted to tell her no, that she had given up all rights to say goodbye, but he didn't want to rip another parent out of his daughter's life.

"Wyatt?" Adrianna called his name from the hallway.

The girls were huddled behind her. Stephanie had a backpack around her shoulders and was holding a plastic bag that appeared to be filled with toys and stuffed animals. Sara had the same.

"You can come in," he said. He looked at his daughter.

"Your mom has to go away for a while. She wants to say goodbye."

Stephanie's bottom lip began to tremble. "I don't want Mommy to go."

His heart ripped again. "I'm sorry, baby, but she has to. Don't worry. I'm going to take you home, and you're going to see Grandma and Grandpa and everyone that loves you. It's going to be okay."

A knock came at the door. He walked over to open it.

Josh and two officers entered the room. "Are you ready for us?" Josh asked, his gaze perusing the room.

"Just about," he said. "Jen is going to say good-bye to Stephanie."

"Hey kid," Josh said to Stephanie. "Remember me?"

"Uncle Josh," she murmured, a small smile blooming on her lips.

"I missed you," he said.

"I missed you, too."

"You can talk more later," Wyatt said, eager to move things along. "Jen, it's now or never."

"Please, don't do this," she begged him.

"Now or never," he repeated.

She drew in a big breath and walked over to Stephanie. "I have to go now, but I'll see you again soon, honey."

"Why are you crying, Mommy?"

"Because I'm sad, and I'm going to miss you."

"Then why are you leaving?"

"I have to," she said.

"Where are you going?" Stephanie asked.

"I don't know yet," Jen replied. "But I'll talk to you soon, okay?"

"Okay, Mommy," Stephanie said, as Jen gave her a hug.

The hug went on and on. Finally, Jen let go and straightened. "Brad?" she called.

The other man reappeared, the phone next to his ear.

He saw the cops and his expression grew grim. "Yeah, they're taking her away now," he said into the phone. "I'll call you back."

"Can your lawyer help me?" Jen pleaded. "Please."

"I'm sure they'll get someone to defend you for whatever you did. You played me, Carly. I don't ever want to see you again."

Jen's face paled at his words, as if it were finally sinking in that no one would come to her rescue.

"Take her into the hall," Wyatt told the officers. He didn't want his daughter to see her mother cuffed and read her rights.

Jen gave Stephanie one last, yearning look and then the door closed behind her.

"Is Mommy going to jail?" Stephanie asked, looking to him for answers. "Am I going to see her again?"

He really didn't want to be the one who'd put her mother in jail, but he also didn't want to lie to her. He just had no idea what the right answer was. "We'll talk about everything," he promised. "Right now I want to take you home."

Chapter Sixteen

Adrianna couldn't believe they were walking up to the front door of Wyatt's condo with Stephanie and Sara. Wyatt had a hold of Stephanie's hand, and she doubted he'd be letting go any time soon. Sara had taken her hand when they'd gotten out of the car, obviously seeking reassurance. She couldn't blame her. The little girl was obviously very confused. She didn't know Wyatt. She didn't understand why Stephanie's dad had just shown up when he was supposed to be dead. She didn't know where her brother or her mother were. Poor thing. Adrianna's heart went out to her.

She was also still reeling from watching the reunion between Wyatt and his daughter. She'd been impressed with the way he'd managed to control his anger. He'd even had Jennifer handcuffed in the hallway so that Stephanie wouldn't be a witness to her mother's arrest. He'd been thinking of his daughter more than himself every step of the way. She was incredibly proud of him.

"Are you girls hungry?" she asked, falling back into her comfort zone as they entered the house. "I can make us some food. Maybe you can help me," she told Sara. The little girl needed something to do, and Wyatt and Stephanie needed a little privacy.

Sara gave Stephanie a long look, then nodded.

Stephanie gazed up at Wyatt. "Can I see my room?"
"Of course you can," he said. "It's just the way you left it."

Thank God, he'd never changed a thing, Adrianna thought. Stephanie would never know the torment her father had gone through without her, at least not right away. Instead, she'd be returning to the same bedroom she'd left.

As Wyatt and Stephanie went down the hall, she turned her attention on Sara. "I bet you're feeling pretty confused."

"I want my mom – and Ben," she said, speaking for the first time. "Do you know where they are?"

"I saw Ben the other day," she told her, not wanting to admit that she had no idea where he was at the moment. "He spent the night at my house.

"Where is he now?"

"I think he's looking for you, honey."

"Emily's mom wouldn't let him come with us. I wanted him to, but she said no."

Adrianna nodded. "I know you're worried about him, but he's okay."

"How come everyone is calling Emily Stephanie?" she asked, her tiny brows knitting into a frown.

"Because that's her real name. Emily was pretend name," she said.

"How come she was pretending?"

"She was having an adventure," Adrianna replied, deciding it was time to change the subject. "What kind of pancakes do you like? Plain or blueberry?" She frowned. "Actually, I forgot we don't have any food. We need to go shopping."

"Can we get Ben on the way? He's probably hungry too," Sara said.

"Where do you think Ben is?" she asked.

"He might be at the motel. If he's not there, he's probably at the park. He always said to go to the park if I got lost. Maybe he went there, too."

"Let's see if we can find him," she said, making an impulsive decision. "I'll just tell Wyatt and Stephanie that we'll be back in a few minutes."

Sara suddenly looked a little doubtful. "Maybe Emily should come with us, too."

"I think she's going to want to play in her room for a bit." She gave Sara a reassuring smile. "You can trust me, honey. I want to get you and Ben back together, and I want to find your mom, too. Okay?"

Sara slowly nodded. Adrianna didn't know if the little girl believed her or if she was just used to being told what to do by random adults.

They walked down the hall to Stephanie's room together.

Wyatt was sitting at the end of Stephanie's bed, watching her talk to her favorite bear. He had such an expression of love on his face that it made Adrianna's heart actually hurt. He'd been waiting for this moment for such a long time.

"Sara and I are going to the store to get some food to cook," she said.

Stephanie exchanged a look with Sara, and then glanced at her Dad. "Should I go with them?"

"Why don't you stay here with me?" he said. "I have some new toys for you to play with. I bought them for your last two birthdays. I was keeping them until you came home." His voice caught a little, and then he cleared his throat. "And we have to call Grandma and Grandpa, too."

"We won't be long," Adrianna promised, leading Sara out of the room.

* * *

After a momentary hesitation, Stephanie seemed to be fine with Sara's departure. She was obviously happy to be back in her room. He couldn't imagine all the beds she'd slept in the past two years. But he wasn't going to think about that time now. He just wanted to concentrate on her. In fact, he wasn't sure he could ever take his eyes off Stephanie. He kept noticing new things about her, the extra freckles across the bridge of her nose, the full set of teeth she now had, the pierced earring in her ear. He frowned at that, as she pushed her hair behind her ear.

It could be worse, he told himself. So far he hadn't seen any tattoos, no bruising or signs of injury, although he hadn't looked her completely over, but she seemed to be healthy. He should be grateful for that.

"Mommy is going to come back and see us," she told her bear, not looking in Wyatt's direction, although she had raised her voice, so he suspected she was talking for his benefit. "She's going to live here with us, and we're going to be a family again."

Her words broke his heart. They would never be a family again. It wasn't Stephanie's fault that she'd been born to two parents who had messed things up as badly as they had. And as much as he wanted to, he couldn't even blame Jen for everything. He'd missed some early signs. Maybe if he'd paid more attention in the beginning, things wouldn't have gotten so bad.

"Remember this book, Steph?" he asked, hoping to distract her.

He handed her the copy of *Goodnight Moon* that they had read so many times together.

"Will you read it to me tonight?" she asked.

"As many times as you want," he replied.

Her blue eyes gazed into his. "Where were you?" she asked. "Why didn't you come and get me? Mommy said you were dead. Did you come back from heaven?"

Her eight-year-old mind was completely confused, and he couldn't blame her.

"I didn't die, and I didn't come back from heaven," he said. "Mommy was wrong. I've been looking for you since the day you left -- me and Brown Bear – but we couldn't find you."

"Were you sad?" she asked.

"Incredibly so," he said, feeling a wave of intense emotion. "I missed you a lot."

"I missed you, too," she said. "Sometimes Mommy went away for a long time, and I didn't know where she was."

"She shouldn't have done that."

"Is that why she's going to jail?"

"Partly. She needs to get help, and I'm going to make sure that happens."

Stephanie's gaze filled with concern. "Can Ben and Sara live with us? Their mommy goes away a lot, too, and Ben takes care of me and Sara."

"I'm going to try to help them, too," he said, knowing that promise might be tougher to keep. "You don't need to worry. I'll take care of everything. Now, can I have another hug?"

This time she didn't take as long to decide. She scooted forward and threw her arms around him, and he held on to her for dear life, never wanting to let her go.

"Daddy," she said.

His heart swelled again. He'd never been sure he'd hear her say that word again.

"What baby?" he asked, looking down into her face.

"Can we go swimming later?"

He laughed at her practical question. "We can do anything you want." He paused as his doorbell rang. "Let me see who that is?"

"Do you think it's Grandma?"

"No, but we're going to call her as soon as I see who's here. Why don't you play with your toys? I'll be right back."

Josh was at the door, wearing a broad smile on his face and holding a present in his hand. "She's home," Josh said, slapping him on the shoulder.

"She's home," he repeated, exchanging a smile with one of his best friends. "I can't quite believe it."

"Well, believe it. You did it. You got her back."

"With a little help," he said. "How did it go with Jen?"

"She tried to cry on my shoulder. I wasn't moved." He shook his head. "She acts like the victim in all this."

"She always did," he said. "Did she call anyone?"

"Her parents. They're on their way. I'm sure they'll get her a good lawyer."

"It won't matter," he said, even though it made him sick to think he might still have a fight on his hands. But this time he'd be fighting with Stephanie by his side.

"How's Steph?" Josh asked.

"Playing in her room like she never left."

Josh nodded. "Good. Everyone in the department sends their good wishes. The captain said to tell you he's expecting you to take some leave, spend some time with your daughter."

"I can't think of anything I'd rather do."

"Have you called your family?"

"Not yet. I haven't been able to leave her alone." He looked down the hallway, happy to hear Stephanie talking to her bear. "I just don't want to lose her again."

"You won't." Josh paused. "So how did you find her anyway?"

"Adrianna's friend connected us to the music promoter, Brad Pennington."

"Lucky break."

"I've been lucky ever since I met Adrianna," he said.

"Where is she?"

"She went to buy some food, and she took Sara with her. I think they're going to try to find Ben."

"I wanted to talk to you about the other girl. I haven't called the social worker yet, but –"

"Can you hold off a day or two?"

"Well, it is Sunday," Josh said. "But tomorrow, I may need to make the call."

"Understood. I just don't want to tear Sara away from Stephanie without some kind of warning or explanation. There have been too many people ripped out of her life. Jen told me that Becky works for an escort service and she's away on a long job. I gave you that name yesterday, right?"

Josh nodded. "I'll follow up. Hopefully, we'll find her soon, and then we'll know what we're dealing with."

"Thanks."

"So, can I see my godchild now? I brought her a little something."

"After you." He followed Josh into Stephanie's room.

She was very happy to see her Uncle Josh and even happier when she saw the present he'd gotten for her. Wyatt watched from the doorway as she unwrapped a box filled with art supplies.

"I hope you still like to draw and paint," Josh said.

Stephanie gave an emphatic nod. "I love it." She gave Josh a quick hug. "Thank you, Uncle Josh. Maybe I'll draw Mommy a picture."

Josh nodded, then sent Wyatt a pained look.

He shrugged. He was not under the illusion that any of the next few days would be easy. But as long as he had Stephanie, he could face anything.

A short time later, he walked Josh to the door. As Josh stepped outside, he ran into Adrianna, Sara and Ben.

Wyatt was stunned to see them all together.

"I found Ben," Adrianna said with a big, happy smile.

"You're on a roll," he said, grinning back at her.

"I'm going to pretend I don't see anyone," Josh said. "I'll talk to you tomorrow, Wyatt."

"Sorry, I ran away," Ben told him. "I wanted to keep looking for Sara and my mom."

"I figured," he replied. "Stephanie is in her room. Why don't you guys join her while I help Adrianna with the groceries?" He took one of the shopping bags out of Adrianna's hands. "Looks like you bought out the store."

"We have three hungry children to feed," she said, as she moved into the kitchen and set the bag down on the counter.

"How did you find Ben?" he asked.

"Sara found him. Ben had always told Sara if she got lost to go to the park, and that's where Ben was. Sara burst into tears, and Ben pretended he had something in his eyes," she said with a soft watery smile of her own. She moved across the room and threw her arms around him. "I'm so happy, Wyatt. You have Stephanie back, and now Sara and Ben are reunited."

He hugged her tight and then said, "It's all good. Did I say thank you?"

"No thanks necessary. How's your reunion going with Stephanie?"

"It's all right so far. She's still talking about her mom, so I don't know what has sunk into her brain yet."

"You'll figure it out." She stepped out of his embrace. "What's going to happen with Ben and Sara?"

"We're going to try to find Becky. The escort service should be able to locate her."

"I was thinking that Ben and Sara could stay with me until you find her."

He frowned. "I don't know, Adrianna. Josh isn't going to call a social worker today, but tomorrow…"

"My apartment is as good as a foster home, and the kids already know me."

"It's not going to be up to me."

"You can make it happen."

He wanted to say yes to the plea in her eyes, but he couldn't lie. "I don't think I can."

Disappointment filled her expression. "Really?"

"Nothing is going to happen today. Let's see how fast we can find Becky, and then I'll do whatever I can to make sure the kids are in a safe place. I won't turn my back on them. You trust me, right?"

She looked into his eyes. "You know I do."

"In the meantime, we can all stay here tonight."

"You don't want to be alone with Stephanie?"

"Right now I think it's important for her to be with people who are familiar to her. It will make the transition easier."

"What will happen to Jennifer?" Adrianna asked.

"She's going to jail for a while. We'll see how long."

She gave him a thoughtful look. "How do you feel about that?"

"I'm glad she'll be out of the picture. It will be easier to reconnect with Stephanie without her around confusing things."

"Maybe easier for you. I'm not so sure about Stephanie."

"Me either," he admitted. "I'm just going to have to wing it, Adrianna. Just love Steph with everything that I have and hope that's enough."

She smiled. "It will be more than enough." She paused. "I better start cooking."

"One other thing," he said.

"What?"

He pulled her into his arms again. "Last night was amazing. I care about you. I want you to know that."

Her eyes blurred with tears. "You don't have to say anything else."

"I have to put Stephanie first."

"I know that," she said. She drew in a shaky breath. "It's going to be fine. We always knew this wasn't the right time for us to start anything."

"But we already started," he said, wishing he didn't have to hurt her, because despite her words, he knew that last night had meant something to her. It had meant something to him, too.

"So now we end it," she said. "I'll go home after breakfast."

"No, stay for today."

She thought for a moment and then said, "I can't stay all day. But I will make breakfast before I leave."

"I don't want you to go."

"But we both know I have to." She leaned in and pressed her lips against his. "Whatever happens. Last night was the best night of my life. Meeting you changed me in a really good way. So no regrets, okay?"

"No regrets," he murmured as he kissed her one last time.

Chapter Seventeen

December ...

Wyatt woke up to someone kneeing him in the rib cage. He groaned and opened his sleepy eyes to see his daughter's smiling face as she sat on the bed next to him.

"What are you doing up so early?" he asked.

"It's Christmas, Daddy," Stephanie said, delight in her blue eyes. "We have to see what Santa brought us."

"Haven't you gotten enough presents?" he asked. In the past four months, Stephanie had received all the gifts she'd missed for birthdays and Christmas from every member of the family and some of his friends. She had been showered with love and attention, and she'd deserved every moment of adoration. But he knew that at some point he was going to have to tone things down a little. He loved his daughter enough not to spoil her – at least not too much.

"Come on," she said, tugging on his shirt. "Let's look under the tree."

"You mean you haven't already?"

"You told me not to."

That was true. They'd spent Christmas Eve at his parents' house and after tucking Stephanie in to bed, he'd made her promise not to sneak out and take a peek.

"Hurry up, Daddy."

At Stephanie's insistence, he got out of bed and followed his little girl into the living room. She squealed with delight at the packages under the tree. Falling to her knees, she searched through the boxes, her smile fading just a little as she didn't come across what she wanted.

"Something wrong?" he asked.

"No," she said quickly. "Which one should I open first?"

He reached for a package on the bookshelf that she hadn't seen yet. "How about this one?" he said, handing it to her. "It's from your mother."

Her gaze met his. "Really?"

He saw the hope in her eyes and knew he'd made the right decision. "Yes," he said. "Why don't you open it?"

She took the box in her hands, but she didn't move to pull off the paper and ribbon. Instead she stared down at the tag for a long time.

"It's okay," he said quietly.

"You're not mad?" she asked.

He shook his head. They'd talked a lot about what had happened, the lies Jen had told. For an eight-year-old, Stephanie had shown great maturity. She'd cried a few times, especially when she'd learned that her mother was going to jail for a few years, but in recent weeks, those episodes had been fewer and less emotionally intense.

He'd taken Stephanie for counseling, and the doctor had told him that it was in Stephanie's best interests to have some sort of contact with her mother, so he'd supervised the exchange of letters, and when Jen's parents had sent the Christmas package a few days earlier, he had taken a look at the book of poems and the loving note from Jen and had agreed to give the present to Stephanie.

Some day, he would probably take Stephanie to see her mother, but that wouldn't be for a while, and he would never ever let them be alone again.

"What are you waiting for?" he asked, as Steph continued to stare at the present.

She looked up at him and then put the gift aside. "I want to open your present first, Daddy."

"Really?" he asked, his heart swelling with love.

She nodded. "Which one should I pick?" she asked, looking at the brightly colored packages. He'd stop spoiling her really soon, he told himself.

"I think there's one I forgot to put out here," he said. "It's in the kitchen. Why don't you go get it?"

She gave him a curious look and then ran into the other room. He followed her to the doorway, happy with her scream of delight. She opened the cage and let the small puppy cover her with happy kisses.

"I can't believe you got me a dog," she said, laughing as the golden retriever squirmed in her arms.

"You told me a million times you wanted one. What are you going to name him?"

"I don't know," she said. "Is he really mine?"

"All yours. And you're going to have to learn how to feed him and give him baths, and we'll walk him together."

She set the puppy down, and the animal went skidding around the tile floor in joyous exploration. Then she ran over to him. "I love you, Daddy."

"I love you, too," he said, as he wrapped her up in his arms. "Let's go open the rest of the presents. We have lots to do today."

* * *

Adrianna stared at the wild chaos of wrapping paper and ribbon spread across her apartment floor. She'd had so many quiet, somber, dark Christmases, that this one would stand out in her mind for a very long time.

"You gave them a really happy Christmas," Lindsay said as she joined her by the Christmas tree in her living room. "Ben and Sara got everything they wanted."

She smiled at the two kids who were sitting at the kitchen counter with their mother. "All they wanted was their mom."

"Becky is turning out to be a decent waitress," Lindsay said. "I wasn't sure when you first brought her into the restaurant that she would work out, but you're right. She just needed someone to give her a chance to be a good mother. And that someone was you."

"It's nice to put a family back together," she said. "I saw so many broken ones growing up, and I could never do anything about them. This time I could."

Lindsay put her arm around her shoulders. "You're a great person. I just wish you could be happy, too."

"I am happy," she said, not wanting to admit there was still a hole in her heart. She'd spoken to Wyatt only a few times in the past few months. He was busy rebuilding his family, and she couldn't blame him for that."

"You miss Wyatt."

She shrugged. "Today is not the day for being sad," she said firmly. "We need to get dressed and go to work."

"I can't believe you talked Stephan into opening the restaurant on Christmas day and into feeding the neighborhood for free."

"It was a tradition Josephine started, and one I always meant to continue if I ever ran my own restaurant, which I now do."

"And you're doing it quite well, I might add," Lindsay said.

"Thank you." Working at the restaurant had been great the past few months. She no longer had nightmares or panic attacks. She no longer saw Will on the floor by the bar. Instead she remembered the good times they'd shared.

She'd worked her ass off to make the restaurant as successful as possible, and business was booming. There was an hour wait on most weekend nights. She relished every moment of her job, and she had to admit that the work had given her less time to think about Wyatt. But days like today, he was on her mind. She wondered how he was enjoying Christmas with Stephanie.

"Hey, kids, Becky ... we gotta get a move on," Lindsay said. "Boss wants us to go to work."

Adrianna smiled. "It will be fun. I promise."

Fifteen minutes later they were walking through the streets of North Beach.

It was a beautiful California Christmas morning, blue skies, temperature in the mid sixties, and a cool, crisp breeze. As they headed up the hill toward Vincenzo's, she glanced at the sweeping view, the Golden Gate Bridge, Angel Island, and felt refreshed. This was her city, her life, and she was happy.

When they reached the square by Vincenzo's, she decided to make a small detour.

"I'll be inside in a minute," she told Lindsay. "I have to make a wish."

"Really?" Lindsay asked, with a curious smile.

"Yeah, this quarter has been burning a hole in my pocket for a long time."

She walked over to the fountain and pulled out the coin. Six months earlier, she'd wished for a way to get past her fear, to get her life back, and her coin had been knocked out of the fountain. But it hadn't mattered, because meeting Wyatt had made her wish come true.

Now, she had another wish.

As she was about to toss her coin, a man called her name.

Startled, she almost dropped her coin into the water, which would have been very anticlimactic. She managed to hang on to it, as she turned around.

"Wyatt," she said in surprise. "I can't believe you're here. Where's Stephanie?"

He tipped his head toward the front of Vincenzo's. She could see Stephanie laughing with Ben and Sara, Becky and Lindsay – and there was a puppy, too. She turned back to Wyatt. "You got a dog?"

"It was Stephanie's Christmas present," he said with a helpless shrug. "I'm a pushover."

"Yes, you are. Life has certainly changed for you."

"Yeah, my place is one noisy mess."

She saw the pure joy in his clear blue gaze and was truly happy for him. "You love it."

"I love you," he said, shocking her with the words.

She opened her mouth to speak, but nothing came out.

He grinned at her. "Speechless, huh?"

"We – we haven't seen each other in months."

"But I've thought about you every day," he said, his smile turning serious. He put his hands on her arms. "I wanted to call you a hundred times, but I had to take care of Stephanie first. And I had to figure out if I could give you what you deserve. My relationship with Jen was a mess. I wasn't a good husband."

"I don't believe that."

"It's true. I made mistakes. But I don't want to talk about Jen. I want to talk about you. You inspired me, Adrianna. You kept me going when I was ready to quit. You found my daughter for me."

"We did it together."

He squeezed her arms. "I love you, Adrianna. I didn't think I could ever say that again to a woman. I didn't think I could ever put my life into someone else's hands. But you changed my mind. You and your capacity to give without taking, your kindness, your spirit, your everything."

"You're making me blush," she said, feeling not only heat in her cheeks but moisture in her eyes. "I'm not perfect."

"You're perfect for me. I trust you, Adrianna. And that's big."

She was incredibly touched. "I trust you, too, Wyatt. I haven't been able to do that with everyone. But your courage made me face my own fears, not just about the restaurant and the robbery, but about myself, about not being good enough. I know now that I am."

"You are."

She drew in a big breath. "I was afraid when I didn't hear from you that our time was up."

"I didn't want to come to you until I knew what I had to offer."

"And what's what?" she asked, her heart starting to pound.

"A life of love," he said. "With me and my daughter … and our puppy. Crazy relatives," he added. "You'll have to take my family along with me. I know you don't like cops, but I don't think I'll be quitting any time soon. I don't know how to do anything else."

She put her fingers against his mouth. "Stop. I don't hate your job anymore, and all the rest sounds pretty good. But I have to say you're getting ahead of yourself. We haven't even been on a date yet."

He laughed. "You're right. What is wrong with me? How about Friday night?"

"I think I have to work."

"I'm not going to like Chef's hours, am I?"

"Probably not. I'm free on Sunday."

"So am I," he said, smiling into her eyes. "So what do you say?"

She wanted to say yes to the date, to the life, to everything, but some small part of her was still just a tiny bit afraid that she was so close to getting everything she'd ever wanted that something was bound to go wrong.

He tilted his head, his gaze narrowing. "Why the hesitation?"

"I'm worried this is too good to be true."

"It's not, Adrianna. We have both been through the fire, and we survived." He paused. "But I told you I wanted to be ready, and maybe you're not there yet. It hasn't been that long since Will died."

She cut him off with a shake of her head. "This isn't about Will."

"Are you sure? You were grieving when we first met."

"I love Will as a friend, but I was never in love with him. I wanted to be, but I wasn't. I've gotten past that."

"I'm glad. So go on a date with me."

She laughed. "Okay, I will go on a date with you." She pressed her fingers against his chest and kissed him.

He groaned against her lips. "Damn. You taste good, and it's been too long. You don't know how much I want to take you away right now."

She smiled. "Do you have someone who can watch Stephanie on Sunday?"

"My parents can't wait to have her spend the night with them, and it is Christmas vacation," he added, with a wicked smile.

A shiver shot down her spine, and she really wished that Sunday wasn't three days away.

Wyatt stole another kiss and said, "Were you about to make a wish?"

"Yes, I thought it was time to finally throw my coin into the fountain."

"That's the same quarter?"

She nodded. "I've been holding on to it for a long time, waiting to make just the right wish, but now I don't need to throw it in the fountain. Because I was going to wish for you, and here you are."

"And I'm not going anywhere."

"I'm so glad."

He kissed her again and then said. "Did Lindsay tell you she invited us to Christmas lunch at the restaurant?"

"That little matchmaker," she said with a smile. "I should have seen that coming."

"She told me I should get off my ass before you found someone else."

"There was never going to be anyone else." She wrapped her arms around his waist and looked up at him. "By the way -- I love you, too."

Epilogue

June ...

Adrianna pulled back the curtain covering the upstairs bedroom window at Wyatt's parents' house and glanced out the window. A dozen folding chairs had been placed on the grass in front of a gazebo, which was decorated with a multitude of colorful flowers. It was the perfect place for a wedding – her wedding.

Eleven months earlier, she'd met the man of her dreams, and now she was going to marry him. And she wasn't just getting a husband, but a little girl, an exuberant puppy, and a family who overwhelmed her with love. She'd come a very long way from her lonely teenage days where she'd had no one to count on but herself.

As she watched the crowd milling about below, she saw Stephanie in her pretty pink dress chasing the puppy around the yard with Sara and Ben. All the kids were doing well now. Becky continued to work at the restaurant and was making enough money to rent a small apartment. They'd become good friends over the past year. And Adrianna hoped it would stay that way. She'd come to realize that her past made her the perfect person to reach out to those in need. She'd been so busy trying to outrun the insecure, scared child she'd once been, that she hadn't seen the opportunity to use what she'd learned and help other people. Now, it was very clear. And a lot of that was due to Wyatt.

The man had quite simply become her everything -- her best friend and her lover -- and soon to be her husband.

She let the curtain drop as Lindsay entered the room with two glasses of champagne.

"Almost time," Lindsay said with a big smile. "Are you nervous?"

"Surprisingly, no," she said.

"That's because you're doing the right thing." She handed Adrianna a glass. "To you – and your happiness."

They clinked glasses, and she took a sip of the bubbly liquid.

"Hey, drink up," Lindsay said.

"I can't," she told her.

Confusion and then awareness flashed in Lindsay's eyes. "Oh, my God, are you?"

She nodded. "I am."

Lindsay grabbed her glass and set it down on the table alongside hers and gave Adrianna a hug. "Congratulations."

"Thanks, no one else knows."

"Not even Wyatt?"

She shook her head. "I'm going to tell him tonight."

"He may love you even more – if that's possible," she said dryly.

"I hope so," she said with a mischievous smile. He's very good at the love stuff."

"Now, you're going to tell me about your sex life? So I can be even more jealous of you?"

"Your time will come."

"I'm not worried. Unlike you, I'm still enjoying my single life."

As Lindsay finished speaking, the door opened again, and Summer entered with Stephanie. Summer wore a dark pink bridesmaid gown that coordinated well with Stephanie's pink flower-girl dress.

"Are you ready?" Adrianna asked Stephanie.

"Yes," Stephanie said, holding up her basket of petals. "Grandma showed me how to throw them."

"I'm sure you'll do a great job," she said.

"Adrianna," Stephanie said slowly.

She saw the nervousness in Steph's eyes and offered a smile. "Everything okay?"

"Do you want me to call you, *Mom*?"

Adrianna's breath caught in her chest. Jen was still in jail, but she and Stephanie continued to correspond with Wyatt's blessing. Jen had shown some remorse for what she'd done, but Adrianna doubted they would ever be able to completely trust her. But nothing would ever change the fact that she was Stephanie's mother and always would be.

"You can call me whatever you want," she said. "Adrianna is fine."

"Okay," she said with relief. "I'm glad you're marrying Daddy. He really likes you."

The other women laughed at Stephanie's innocent words.

"I like him, too," she told her.

"I think it's time for us to go," Summer said.

Lindsay handed her the bouquet, and they made their way down the stairs and out to the yard. When they reached the back deck, the music began to play, and Stephanie, Summer and finally Lindsay made their way down the short aisle.

Adrianna stood alone, feeling quite comfortable by herself. She had no one to give her away, but that was all right. Because she was giving herself away – to the man she loved.

As she started her walk, her gaze locked with Wyatt's, and she saw in his expression the promise of a life of love. She had never been more sure of the path she was taking.

When she reached his side, they joined hands. He looked down at her and said, "I love you."

"I love you, too," she said.

The minister interrupted them. "I didn't get to that part yet."

They looked at each other and laughed. Wyatt said, "Sorry, I couldn't wait."

"Me, either," Adrianna said.

"Shall I start now?" the minister asked.

"One second," Adrianna said.

For a split second, Wyatt looked nervous. "Everything okay?"

"I finally threw my coin into the fountain last month, and my wish came true. I'm pregnant, Wyatt. We're having a baby."

A wide grin spread across his lips. "Are you serious?"

"Are you happy?"

"Happier than I've ever been in my life. I'm never letting you go, Adrianna. I will fight for you and support you and love you every day of my life. I promise you that."

Her eyes blurred with tears. "And I'll do the same."

"I don't think you two need me at all," the minister joked.

"We just need each other," she said.

Wyatt sealed her words with a kiss.

THE END

Book List

The Wish Series
#1 A Secret Wish
#2 Just A Wish Away
#3 When Wishes Collide

Stand Alone Novels
Almost Home
All She Ever Wanted
Ask Mariah
Daniel's Gift
Don't Say A Word
Golden Lies
Just The Way You Are
Love Will Find A Way
One True Love
Ryan's Return
Some Kind of Wonderful
Summer Secrets
The Sweetest Thing

The Sanders Brothers
#1 Silent Run
#2 Silent Fall

The Deception Series
#1 Taken
#2 Played

Angel's Bay Series
#1 Suddenly One Summer
#2 On Shadow Beach
#3 In Shelter Cove
#4 At Hidden Falls
#5 Garden of Secrets

The Way Back Home – Angel's Bay Spinoff

About the Author

Barbara Freethy is a top selling author, having sold over 2.5 million ebooks since January 2011. She is also a #1 New York Times Bestselling Author, a distinction she received for her novel, SUMMER SECRETS. Her 30 novels range from contemporary romance to romantic suspense and women's fiction. Her books have won numerous awards - she is a five-time finalist for the RITA for best contemporary romance from Romance Writers of America and her book DANIEL'S GIFT won the honor and was also optioned for a television movie.

Known for her emotional and compelling stories of love, family, mystery and romance, Barbara enjoys writing about ordinary people caught up in extraordinary adventures. Her latest series, THE WISH SERIES, includes A SECRET WISH, JUST A WISH AWAY, and WHEN WISHES COLLIDE.

Barbara has lived all over the state of California and currently resides in Northern California where she draws much of her inspiration from the beautiful bay area. Barbara loves to hear from readers so please feel free to write her.

For a complete listing of books, as well as excerpts and contests, and to connect with Barbara, visit her website at www.barbarafreethy.com.

Made in the USA
Lexington, KY
26 December 2012